"Is m

S_____ _____ _____ _____ _____ _____ _____ of
th_____ _____ su_____ _____ _____ _____ _____ er
m_____ _____ _____ _____ _____ _____ _____
word of him, then for Thomas Henry himself, and
she couldn't bear to wait any longer.

"Is that why you've come here?"

Jack hesitated, then looked into her eyes again.
"Yes."

She made a small sound and looked away,
clutching at her skirts in the great effort it took to
stay upright and in control.

"I'm sorry, ma'am," he said again. "To bring
you such bad news. I see this isn't the time for
us to talk, ma'am—you aren't well enough yet.
I shouldn't have said anything. I will take my
leave. When you're stronger—"

"I want to hear what you've come to say. I want
to hear all of it, Mr. Murphy."

CHERYL REAVIS

The RITA® Award-winning author and romance novelist describes herself as a "late bloomer" who played in her first piano recital at the tender age of thirty. "We had to line up by height—I was the third smallest kid," she says. "After that, there was no stopping me. I immediately gave myself permission to attempt my *other* heart's desire—to write." Her books *A Crime of the Heart* and *Patrick Gallagher's Widow* won a Romance Writers of America's coveted RITA® Award for Best Contemporary Series Romance the year each was published. *One of Our Own* received a Career Achievement Award for Best Innovative Series Romance from *RT Book Reviews*. A former public health nurse, Cheryl makes her home in North Carolina with her husband.

The
Soldier's
Wife

CHERYL REAVIS

Love Inspired

Recycling programs for this product may not exist in your area.

™ LOVE INSPIRED BOOKS

ISBN-13: 978-0-373-82928-6

THE SOLDIER'S WIFE

www.LoveInspiredBooks.com

Printed in U.S.A.

For he shall give his angels charge over thee,
to keep thee in all thy ways.
—*Psalms* 91:11

In memory of Joanne and Dot,
two of the finest nurses I've ever known.
Thank you for teaching me. Thank you
for helping me. Thank you for making me laugh.

I miss you rascals.

Chapter One

Jack Murphy hadn't intended to go looking for the wounded man. He couldn't hear him now, and it was likely that he had finally died, but for which heartfelt cause, Jack couldn't say. The soldier they all heard calling from the battlefield could be one of their own or one of the Rebels—or it could be a ruse engineered by either side to draw some gullible soldier into the open.

He stopped crawling and listened intently. It wasn't gullibility that had brought him out here, and it had nothing to do with the Golden Rule Father Bartholomew and the Sisters at the orphan asylum had done their best to teach him. His hands were still shaking badly, and he simply hadn't wanted the others to see him like this. He was Jeremiah "Jack" Murphy, and Jack Murphy's hands never shook.

The sweet, dank smell of scarred earth rose up from the ground beneath him, land that should have been plowed for spring planting by now, not fought over and bled on. He could hear his comrades in the distance, the quiet murmur of their voices. Every now and then, one of them laughed despite their recent ordeal. Little

Ike was finally reading his letter from home, sharing it with the others. Jack envied him that letter. It had been a long time since he himself had gotten one from the only person who ever wrote to him, Elrissa Suzanne Barden, the girl who had promised to marry him when the war was over. The irony was that he hadn't wanted to go to war at all. He'd enlisted because so many of the boys he'd grown up with in the orphanage had already joined. He'd always looked out for them; most of them had been culled from the dirty backstreets of Lexington as he had. They looked up to him. He couldn't let them deliberately go into harm's way without his overseeing the effort. He gave a quiet sigh. So many of them dead now, despite his determination to keep them all safe and together, their faces coming to him whenever he was on the verge of sleep, faces of the boys who had too quickly become men and then were gone. A line of clouds moved across the moon. He lifted his head, trying to see in the darkness. He couldn't detect any movement, couldn't hear any sound. Most certainly the wounded man had died.

His hands were steadier now, the tremors fading as they always eventually did. There was no reason for him to stay out here. He'd made what must at least seem like a humane gesture, and now he could go back. He could eat some hardtack and wish he had coffee to soften it. He could make Little Ike reread his letter. He could think about Miss Elrissa Barden standing in lantern light on a dark and windy railroad platform and try to remember her pretty face.

"Wait," a voice said distinctly when he began to move to what he hoped was a less conspicuous place.

The voice was close by, and he turned sharply in that direction.

"Will you…wait?" the man asked.

Jack made no reply. He was still trying to get his bearings. Where—and how close—was he? And how close was his musket?

"Please," the voice said, feebler now. "I don't…"

The moon appeared from behind the clouds, and Jack could just make him out in the semidarkness. Surprisingly, he was sitting upright, leaning against the wheel of a broken caisson. And he was farther out into the open field than Jack was willing to go.

"Wait!" the man said sharply when Jack was about to move away again. "I'm shot. Don't leave me…out here. Please…"

Jack hesitated, his head bowed. This man was nothing to him. Nothing. For all he knew, he was the one who had shot him.

The soldier was weeping now, his sobs carrying eerily into the night. Jack waited, knowing if he waited long enough, he wouldn't have to make the choice.

"Have…mercy…" the man said, the words suddenly lost in a near animal-like moan.

Jack clenched his fists. How many times had he been in this kind of situation no matter where he found himself? The orphanage. Mr. Barden's dry goods store. The army. Always when he least expected it, a sudden choice between right and wrong would be staring him right in the face. It was as if his life were some kind of classroom, one where he was supposed to learn the principles of moral rectitude—and he was always getting called on.

Here's another one, Jack, old boy. Let's see what you do with this one.

And this one could get him killed.

The man grew quiet, but he was still alive. Jack had no doubt about that, just as he knew what Father Bartholomew would say:

It's not that we don't know what is right, Jeremiah. We always know. It's that we don't want to do it.

Jack exhaled sharply. *All right, then.*

He began to crawl again, making a wide circle to get to the wounded soldier without being seen from the far side of the open field. Whatever happened, however it turned out, Father Bartholomew and the Sisters, at least, would be happy. The Golden Rule and the parable of the Good Samaritan all rolled into one.

But he wasn't about to take any chances. He made his way slowly. The closer he got, the more he could tell about the uniform—or what was left of it.

"Here, Reb," Jack said when he had moved to where he thought—hoped—he'd be out of sight and could sit up. He pulled the cork from his canteen despite the color of the uniform, and he tried to get the man to drink from it. Most of the water ran down his neck. The smell of death rose from his body.

"Much…obliged," Jack thought the man said. He couldn't be sure because the soldier had suddenly hunched forward in agony.

"What…are you doing…out here, Yank?" he said when he could, his voice barely audible.

"Came to see what all the fuss was about," Jack said, and the man actually laughed, a pain-racked laugh that immediately died away.

"Just to…keep me company, I…guess."

"Or rob your pockets."

"You're out of…luck…there, Yank. I'm…going to ask you…to do…something for me."

"I doubt I'll do it."

"I'm going to ask…anyway. You…got a…wife?"

"No."

"Sweetheart?"

"Yes," Jack said, despite the dearth of letters from Elrissa.

"You should have…married her before you…left… lest you end up…like me. My wife…she's not going to know…what happened to me…if you don't…tell her."

"I can't do that, Reb."

"Take my…blanket roll," the soldier said in spite of Jack's refusal. "My letters…I couldn't mail them. Take them—take everything. Her name is…Sayer Garth. She's in…Ashe County…North Carolina side of…the Tennessee border. Anybody can tell you… where the Garth place is. Get them to her…tell her… Thomas Henry gave them…to you. Say I know how… hard she's…prayed for me. I know…she wanted me… to be…ready if I fell. Say her prayers were answered… and I wasn't afraid to die. Tell her…I don't want her…to grieve. My little sisters…they'll cry when they know… I'm not coming home, but…you tell them…I don't want that. I don't want any…sad faces. You say I went…easy. Don't…don't tell them about…the pain."

The soldier was quiet for a time. Jack could see the rise and fall of his chest, but he couldn't tell if he was conscious.

"I can't save…her," the man said abruptly. "Marrying her won't be enough…if I'm dead." He gave a heavy sigh. "I'm afraid…for her. I don't know…what…to do. I swear…I don't. I don't know if it…was the right thing. I don't know what to do!" He threw back his head suddenly and began to moan, overwhelmed by the agony of his wounds. "End…this…" he whispered.

"No," Jack said. He knew exactly what the man meant.

"You were…ready enough…to take my life…this morning…"

"I'll leave you my canteen—"

"It's your revolver…I need."

The man gave a long shuddering sigh. His head dropped forward for a moment, but then he lifted it and looked in Jack's direction.

"First time…I saw her I was…eight years old," the man said. "She was six…living…with her daddy's kin. Rich people, they were. They came…to the mountains every summer. Came all the…way from…I can't…no. No…I remember. Town on the Yadkin River. It was… bad there in the…in summer. They…always stayed in the…high country till…first…frost. Her people didn't want her. Why didn't they…want her? I never did… know. She tried so hard not to…vex them. Big scared eyes…she had. All the time. I told my…mama…when I got…grown…I was going to marry that…sweet girl… take her away from those people…that didn't want her. *I*…wanted her. But I had to leave her…with those big… scared…eyes of hers come back again. She's so pretty… so…pretty. Sayer…Sayer…if I could just see you…one last time…" His voice trailed away. Then, "I think I'll have…some more of that…water now…if I might," he said politely, as if they were in some situation where politeness mattered.

Jack lifted him upward and held the canteen to his lips. It was the only thing he could do for the man. If he still prayed, he might offer the Reb a prayer, but he was too weary and his emotions too raw. Even such a simple gesture as that was beyond him.

This time the Reb managed a swallow or two before he fell back against the caisson wheel. There was a breeze suddenly, carrying with it the sounds of the soft spring night. A whip-poor-will in a tall pine at the edge of the field, crickets in the grass, frogs in a ditch somewhere nearby. Not the sounds of war and dying at all.

"Graham?" the man said suddenly. "You listening to me, Graham!" He was looking directly at Jack, but Jack had no sense that he was actually seeing him. He grabbed on to the front of Jack's uniform, his grip surprisingly strong. "Promise me! Promise you'll help Sayer!" He made a great effort and lunged forward, his other hand clasping Jack's shoulder. "Promise me!"

"All right," Jack said, trying to keep him from falling on his face. "All right. Let go—"

"Give me…your word," the man insisted. "Say it… Promise…me…"

"I promise," Jack said to placate him, pulling the man's fingers free from his jacket. The Reb began a quiet, but urgent mumbling.

"…teacheth my hands to war and my…fingers to… fight. Is Graham dead?" he suddenly asked as his mind shifted to another time and place. "I don't… I can't— Hey!" he cried, his attention taken by something only he could see. "All right, now! Get ready! Get ready!

Sun's in their…eyes." He abruptly raised his hand as if he were about to give a signal, and Jack struggled to keep him from falling.

"Let's go! Let's go! Come on! We got 'em, boys. We got 'em!" the Reb said, his voice stronger now. He suddenly threw back his head and cried out. The terrible sound he made rose upward in a blood-chilling yell Jack had heard a thousand times in battle. He knew it had nothing to do with the pain. The Rebel soldier was shouting his defiance one last time, and it echoed over the battlefield and into the soft spring night.

But then the cry ended, suddenly cut short, and the still-raised hand fell onto the dirt.

Sayer Garth started as a pair of mourning doves suddenly took flight from a nearby rhododendron thicket. She couldn't see any reason for it, no one coming along the narrow pathway leading down the mountainside to the old buffalo trace that passed for a wagon road. A cold wind blew off the mountain, and her hair swirled about her face. She pulled her shawl tighter around her and listened intently, but she couldn't hear or see anything that might have caused the birds' alarm. Even so, her heart pounded with fear.

"Please," she whispered, and it occurred to her that all her prayers since Thomas Henry went off to war had come down to that one word. She felt it with every bit of strength she had whenever she thought of him, or the girls, or herself.

Please.

She took a quiet breath and waited. She was so tired

of jumping at every little sound and shadow, of being hungry, of being on a mountain ridge alone.

"Thy will," she whispered. "*Thy* will, not mine."

For nearly four years she'd lived in the Garth family cabin with Thomas Henry's two younger sisters. His mother, a kindly but frail woman, had died less than a year after he'd left. He had been gone so long! Sayer wondered if she would even recognize him when she saw him again. And how strange it was. Of late, in her mind's eye, he always looked the way he'd looked when he was a boy. She could barely remember the dashing young soldier she had so hurriedly wed. The truth was she'd been too ill at the time to remember much of anything. She knew that he had suddenly appeared at her bedside early one bright Sunday morning and had informed her uncle, John Preston, and his wife, Cecelia, that he would be bringing a preacher that very afternoon, and ill or not, he intended to marry one Sayer Preston before he marched off to war. He wouldn't be put off and he wouldn't take no for an answer.

Sayer gave a quiet sigh because the truth was she didn't really know if she remembered the incident or if she only knew about it because people who claimed to have been there had told her. She could recall the illness easily enough, the fever, the way her body had ached and sunlight had hurt her eyes and made her head pound so. She knew that she had said yes to Thomas Henry's proposal and that she had worn a freshly starched and ironed—and far too big—nightdress borrowed from her aunt. It was much more elaborate than anything she'd ever owned. There were tucks all over the bodice and around the sleeves at the wrists. And so much lace—

lace on the nightdress and the intricately tatted lace of the Spanish shawl she'd been covered in for decency. She remembered the beautiful butterfly-and-iris pattern of the shawl and the cedar-and-lavender smell of it—but not much else. She must have said the right words when the preacher asked, because their names—and the preacher's—were written in the Garth family Bible, along with the names of two church-member witnesses. She thought that Thomas Henry's mother had attended the ceremony, and the cook and the two hired girls had been allowed to come—which was only fitting since Sayer had spent so much of her time in their company.

But what she remembered so clearly had nothing to do with the wedding at all. What she remembered was a long-ago wagon ride from the railhead to the mountain house, and the way a boy named Thomas Henry Garth had stared at her the first day they met, stared and stared until she'd wanted to cry. She was used to living in her uncle's house all but unnoticed—unless someone—her aunt Cecelia—decided she had done something wrong—and she hadn't known how to withstand the scrutiny of this fair-haired boy with the gentle brown eyes. She remembered, too, the first thing he ever said to her.

I won't bite you.

After a moment of forcing herself to return his steady gaze, she had been certain somehow that he was telling her the truth. He would never hurt her, and that belief was reinforced every summer because of the way his face always lit up when the train bringing her uncle and her aunt—and her—finally arrived at the railhead.

Thomas Henry was the one person in this world

she knew she made glad, not because of anything she did or didn't do, but simply because she existed. All through her childhood he had never missed waiting for the train, and he'd always brought a secret gift for her— some dried apples and cherries or pieces of honeycomb wrapped in brown paper, and once, when they were both nearly grown, a pencil—just in case she might like to write him a letter once in a while.

The pencil had alarmed her at first, but he had immediately understood.

"You just write to me if you feel like it," he said. "Tell me what it's like living in a town. I've never even been to a big town with a railroad through it. I won't write back," he hastened to reassure her. "It might cause…" He hadn't finished the sentence, but she had known what he meant. Her aunt would never allow it. She knew that, but she had already begun arranging in her mind all the things he might like to know about the place where she lived—the ferry that crossed the river and the trains. He'd especially want to know about the trains, what kind and how many. She could count the whistles she heard in the daytime and at night and give a good estimation of that.

Remembering her forbidden enthusiasm for the plan suddenly made her smile. She had been pleased with all his gifts, but she had truly cherished that cedar pencil. What little was left of it she now used to write to him while he was away fighting in the war, because it made her feel some kind of connection to him, and she sorely needed that.

She sighed. Why couldn't she remember his face? Not long after he'd left, he'd written that he had had a daguerreotype made and had sent it to her. The daguerreotype had never arrived, and it seemed to her now that she very much needed it.

She stood watching the path a little longer, until she was certain that no human had disturbed the mourning doves. A sudden snippet of memory came to her after all. Thomas Henry, leaving her almost immediately after the wedding ceremony, taking her hands and pressing a kiss on the back of each one, despite the onlookers. And then he'd winked, the way he often did when no one was looking, and pulled the blue ribbon from her hair, the closest thing she'd had to a bridal veil. He'd stuffed the ribbon into an inside pocket in his uniform. "Now, don't go and forget me," he whispered in that teasing way he had. It had made her want to laugh and cry all at the same time. And then she'd given him the only cherished possession she had—a small Bible that had belonged to her mother.

"I can't take this," he said, clearly moved that she wanted him to have it.

"It's so you'll know," she whispered.

"Know what?"

"Know I won't go and forget you."

No, she thought now. She would never forget him. It was only his face she had trouble remembering. She knew in her heart that she might not have survived her illness if not for God's grace in the form of the gift Thomas Henry Garth had offered her. Marriage to him had given her a sincere hope for a better life. It was true that so far that life had been hard, but she thanked God every day for it. Thomas Henry had left for a seemingly unending war, and she had remained in the mountains, never regretting for a moment that she hadn't returned to Salisbury with Uncle John and Aunt Cecelia on the train. She looked toward the cabin. Both of Thomas Henry's sisters were dancing around trying to stay warm while they poured limewater into the pans of shelled corn to make hominy. Hopefully, some of it would actually hit the corn.

Amity was eight, and Beatrice was ten, and they both had the Garth brown eyes and curling honey-blond hair. Since Thomas Henry's mother had died, they had been both a great responsibility and a great help. Sayer went out of her way to make sure they were aware only of the latter. She didn't want them to ever feel the way she had felt in her uncle's house. Her real worry was that she was neither brave enough nor strong enough to keep them safe. She believed she might have long since given up trying to hang on to Thomas Henry's land if not for them. They were the true Garth family legacy until Thomas Henry came home again, and she hoped desperately that she wouldn't fail them.

The winters had been particularly hard, and she had no doubt that they would have starved if it hadn't been for old Rorie Conley, who lived atop the ridge on the other side of Deep Hollow. It was a short distance to Rorie's cabin as the crow flies, but a hard trek down into the hollow and back up again to the other side on foot. The big sack of shelled corn she'd brought them on the back of a mule would last them for a while, and Sayer had taken great pains to make sure both girls understood that they were not to tell anyone—*anyone*—where the corn had come from, lest Rorie begin to suffer the same mishaps and accidents Sayer had: crops decimated by deer and other wild animals because of mysteriously downed fences; chickens and pigs stolen, supposedly by deserters from both armies hiding in the mountains; her one milk cow inexplicably shot.

The only clue Sayer had as to the cause of these troubles was Halbert Garth's overconfident smile. Thomas Henry's uncle constantly urged her—in the face of all her "bad luck" and her ignorance of farming—to write to Thomas Henry about the supposedly generous offer he had made to buy the Garth land. Surely, he kept telling her, Thomas Henry would want her and the girls to go live "somewhere safe," though the Lord only knew where that might be. He had already written to Thomas Henry himself, of course, but he thought that it would be better for him to hear the truth from her. Halbert Garth didn't realize how much of the "truth" Sayer was actually privy to. She knew that he had expected to inherit all the Garth land when his father died and that he considered the acreage Sayer and the girls were living on *his* birthright, to claim and to dispose of as he pleased, despite the fact that old Mr. Garth had made it plain in his unbreakable will that he intended the land to be a family legacy for all the Garths who followed after him and not the ante in some high-stakes Louisville poker game.

"Sayer! Sayer!" the girls suddenly called to her, and she began walking in their direction.

"Will you read to us after supper?" Beatrice wanted to know, twirling again around and around the pan of corn. Sayer suddenly imagined her all grown-up and dressed in a white gown with gardenias in her hair, dancing the evening away at the Harvest Moon Ball in Salisbury, the event Sayer had heard so much about when she still lived in her uncle's house, the one she had known even then that she'd never be allowed to attend.

Poor Cinderella, Sayer thought a little sadly, thinking of them both. *No white dresses and gardenias for us.*

"What shall I read to you?" she abruptly asked, putting her fanciful notions about the social events in Salisbury aside. She smiled, because she already knew their answer. She had diligently tried to make sure that neither of them forgot their brother, despite the lost daguerreotype and the years that had passed, especially Amity, who had been only four when he left.

"Read us a letter from Thomas Henry!" they both cried.

Chapter Two

"What's wrong?" Jack asked. There were too many of his comrades still awake. All of them should have been lying exhausted on the ground save the two on watch, but it looked as if the entire group was alert and waiting—for him, apparently.

"Nothing," Little Ike said after a silence that went on too long.

Jack sat down on the ground close to his blanket and haversack. He was emotionally and physically spent. He'd managed to get the dead Rebel wrapped in his blanket and more or less buried. Jack impulsively kept the man's letters and personal belongings and stuck them inside his jacket. He took them out now and began looking at them. Not a single man asked him what he had or what he was planning to do with whatever it was.

He glanced in Little Ike's direction. "You get your letter read?"

"Oh! Well—" Ike said. "I— It was—" He stopped. He took his battered cap off and twirled it in his hands. Then, as if suddenly wondering how it had gotten there, popped it back on his head again.

"You know," Jack said after a long moment, "I didn't think the question was all that hard."

"We got the canteens filled," Ike said, clearly hoping to move Jack along to some other topic of interest.

"Did you get the letter read?" Jack asked again. He looked at the soldiers closest to him—Boone. Donoho. Weatherly. James. All of them looked elsewhere.

"Are we the Orphans' Guild or not?" he asked. It was the name that had been given to them the first day the company mustered, one they'd taken for their own with a fierce kind of pride. They looked out for each other and they didn't keep secrets, especially not from him.

"Tell him, Ike," Boone said finally.

But Little Ike was fiddling with his hat again.

"Tell him!"

"It was in the letter," Ike said in a rush. Most of the words went down his jacket front.

Jack waited, but that seemed to be the only information Ike was willing to impart. He didn't suggest that he continue, however. Jack had learned early on, from his days in the orphanage, that the quickest way to a revelation was not to demand it. He went back to looking through the dead Reb's personal effects: a Bible, a clay pipe bowl, an empty leather tobacco pouch, a daguerreotype he couldn't see in the erratic moonlight, a packet of letters tied up with a ribbon, the color of which he also couldn't determine. He could feel the watchful attention of every man around him, but he didn't look up. He pulled one of the letters free and tried to decipher the address. He could only make out part of the handwriting: Co. G Highland Guards. He had heard of the Highland Guards, but that was after what was left of the Orphans' Guild had been shifted from the Army of the Ohio into an equally decimated company in the Army of the Potomac. Jack had been half convinced that the Guild soldiers had been the ante in some kind of high-stakes poker game. A general from the Army of the Ohio folded, and off the orphans went. Even so, he and the rest of them still thought of themselves as soldiers of the Kentucky regiment they'd volunteered for, regardless of what the generals said.

He turned the letter over in his hands, but he made no attempt to read it. The Highland Guards had been at Sharpsburg and at Malvern Hill, just as he and the newly reassigned Orphans' Guild survivors had.

Sharpsburg.

Malvern Hill.

One thing he had learned in this war. Nothing qualified for cannon fodder more than a company with a true majority of bona fide orphans.

"Jack?"

He looked up.

"She went and got married, Jack," Ike said.

"Are you going to tell me who 'she' is or do I have to guess?"

"Miss Elrissa Barden," Ike said, his voice full of misery. "My cousin…she says he's rich," he added helpfully.

Jack reached for his haversack, rearranging the contents so that he could add the dead Rebel's belongings. He might find a way to mail the letters, and then again, he might not. "His name?" he asked.

"It's…Vance."

Jack looked at him. "Farrell Vance?" he said, surprised by his response to the information. He should have been intensely disturbed, at the very least, but he wasn't. After a short moment, it seemed…only logical. Farrell Vance had money—a lot of money—more money than good old Jeremiah "Jack" Murphy would ever have, even if a marriage to a wealthy store owner's daughter had happened. Vance was a store owner, as well—among other things—but his real money came from the war, from army contracts. There was plenty of profit to be made there, especially if a supplier was willing to cut corners. He had no doubt that Farrell Vance fell into that camp.

"That's him," Ike said. "My cousin, she wrote it was a really big wedding. Nobody ever seen anything like it in Lexington before, I can tell you that. Her wedding dress come all the way from Paris somehow or other. Must have been hard, what with the war and everything. It had all these…rosettes or some such thing. What do you reckon a rosette is— Ow!" he said, his report interrupted by his nearest comrade's elbow. "What did you do that for, Boone!"

"I did it hoping you might start using that head of yours for something besides parking your hat!"

"Well, you said to tell him!"

The argument, peppered with insults, continued, but Jack was no longer listening. *Elrissa Suzanne Barden… Vance.*

Jack had never formally asked her father for her hand. She had wanted him to wait until he came home again, and he had agreed, thinking that Mr. Barden would be more apt to remember how important Jack had been to his business if he was standing right in front of him. He hadn't really considered that Mr. Barden would say no. The man had set the precedent that his beloved Elrissa could have whatever she wanted a long time before Jack Murphy came along.

But clearly Elrissa had changed her mind. It occurred to Jack that no one in her circle likely knew anything about his marriage proposal much less that she'd accepted him. And when this greater matrimonial opportunity arose, she must have realized she could marry Farrell Vance without consequence. With any luck at all, Jack Murphy would end up like all too many of his fellow orphans and wouldn't be coming back from the war at all. Or if he did survive, he wouldn't likely go around telling people he'd been taken for a fool. It occurred to him, too, that it must require many months to put together a wedding that included a dress from Paris with "rosettes," and Elrissa must have continued writing to him until she was absolutely sure the better marriage was a certainty.

"That's that, then," he said, realizing too late that he'd said it out loud.

"That's right, Jack," Ike said. "Ain't no use worrying about it."

"Whose turn is it to take watch?" Jack asked, ignoring Ike's comment.

"Fred's," somebody volunteered. "And Jacob's…" The sentence faded away into a different kind of silence.

"Mine, then," Ike said after a moment. "And Boone's."

"Well, don't the two of you be squabbling like a couple of old women," Jack said despite the fact that two more of the Orphans' Guild were dead and gone. He was glad it was Ike's turn. Ike couldn't tell when he was putting a foot wrong and stumbling all over something socially, but he had finely honed senses when it came to anticipating danger, probably because of the years he'd spent hiding from his violent drunkard of a father.

"No, Jack," Ike said earnestly. "We won't. I ain't letting them Rebs sneak up on us."

"That's good to know, our situation being what it is," Jack said. "What's that?" he asked because of a sound in the distance he couldn't identify.

"Sounds like singing," Boone said.

And so it was, but Jack couldn't make out the song. It was something wistful; he could tell that much. A farewell for a fallen comrade, he decided, as more voices joined in, perhaps for the man whose letters he still held. He felt a burning in his eyes suddenly, an ache in his throat. He stuffed the letters into his haversack. His hands were beginning to tremble again. This time he wrapped himself in his blanket to hide them and turned his back to the others. He lay down on the ground and closed his eyes, but he had little hope of sleep. His body ached with fatigue, but his thoughts swirled around and around in his head so fast he couldn't dwell on any of them. He tried to find some sound to concentrate on—the whip-poor-will, the singing, anything—so that he could shut out everything else, but it didn't help. The more he struggled, the more his mind raced. Eventually, though, as it had more than once, the sound he so needed turned out to be one inside his own head. After a moment, it rose out of the chaos: Father Bartholomew reading aloud to them on the cool upstairs porch on Saturday afternoons after their chores and their Saturday baths were finally done. *The Rime of the Ancient Mari-*

ner. It had been a favorite of the younger boys and, he thought, of Father Bartholomew. The ancient mariner. The man who could not pray.

Jack concentrated on the poem, word by word, line by line, not caring if they were out of sequence or not. After a time he began to whisper random phrases to himself. "'The praise be given…the gentle sleep from heaven…slid into my soul….'"

But there was no chance of that happening this night.

"Jack," Boone said, shaking him hard.

"What!" he snapped because he hadn't been asleep.

"They're not singing now, Jack. Maybe you better come listen."

He sat up and struggled to his feet, wishing for the second time tonight that he associated with men who could speak in specifics. He looked toward the battle-field, keeping his fists clenched because the second episode of shaking hadn't yet subsided. The soldiers he couldn't see had stopped singing, just as Boone said, but what they were doing instead, Jack couldn't tell.

"You see anything, Ike?" Jack called.

"Nothing!" Ike called from some distance away. "Whatever it is, it's coming this way."

"Us or them?"

"Don't know!"

"At the ready!" Jack shouted, and they all scrambled to grab up their gear. Then they waited, muskets resting on whatever prop they could find, all of them straining to see in the darkness. Every now and then Jack could hear the whip-poor-will in the tall pine at the edge of the field.

"Jack!" Ike suddenly cried. "Did you hear that! Lee surrendered!"

"Stay down!" Jack said sharply, before the rest of his charges forgot where they were in the excitement of Ike's announcement. He'd been at this too long to trust a voice shouting in the night. And if it was true, he had enough sense to know that the war would be over for the Rebs, not for them.

The shouting grew louder as the news came down the line. He could hear the men clearly now, again and again. "Lee surrendered!"

So.

Just like that. This morning they were at war and now they weren't. *How could it be over?* he thought. And they had won. After all this time and all this killing and dying, they had *won*. But what exactly was the prize, he wondered, and at what cost?

Unable to contain their joy any longer, the men around him sent up a rousing cheer. He tried to feel their elation, but he was too worn down by the events of the day to feel anything.

"Where are the tin cups?" he asked abruptly, not really addressing anyone in particular.

"What tin cups, Jack?"

"Fred's! Jacob's! Where are they!" He needed them. Whenever an orphan fell, he sent their army-issue tin cup to Father Bartholomew. He scratched their names and when and where they died on them. He didn't know what Father Bartholomew did with them. All he knew was that he, Jack Murphy, needed to send them.

"It's all right, Jack," Boone said, grasping him by the arm. "Ike took care of it. He wrapped them up good and tagged them to go to the orphanage. The hospital wagon was picking up the wounded, so he sent them back on it. Somebody will see they get there."

"The names— Did he—"

"He scratched the names. He did all of it. You don't have to worry."

"Good," Jack said. "That's good."

He could feel Boone staring at him. He pulled his arm free and sat down on the ground again. He had to pull himself together.

Elrissa's marriage, he thought, wiping the sweat from his brow with a shaking hand. Her betrayal had laid him lower than he had been willing to admit.

Lee surrendered.

Lee surrendered…

And that was the thing that bothered him so, he suddenly realized. General Robert E. Lee had surrendered.

Too late for Frederick and Jacob and the rest of Father Bartholomew's dead orphans. Too late for Thomas Henry Garth and for a young woman called Sayer.

Chapter Three

It took the Orphans' Guild nearly three months to get back to Lexington, though to Jack it seemed hardly any time at all. He'd long ago lost the need to mark the passage of time when it had so little bearing on what he did. Not meals. Not sleep. Nothing. For four years, he had been dedicated only to going where he was told to go and doing what he was told to do—and staying alive while he did it. He'd learned early on to let the passing of the minutes and hours and days take care of themselves. They had nothing to do with him, at least until he returned to Lexington. It was only then that clocks and calendars became important again, because he needed to decide on what day and at what time he might be able to see the new Mrs.Vance face-to-face, and he had no one he wanted to ask for guidance in the matter. He already had too many unsolicited opinions regarding his situation with Elrissa.

His best guess was early afternoon. Elrissa should be at home then and Farrell Vance should not. And with that simple conclusion, he took pains to shave and to wear a freshly starched and ironed white store-clerk shirt and the best suit a sizable chunk of his army pay could buy. It was a long walk from the orphanage, where he was staying in the visitors' quarters, to Farrell Vance's impressive new stone residence. The walk itself was pleasant enough, given his recent history of ambulating from battlefield to battlefield over more of this country than he cared to think about. It eventually took him to a cool, shaded street lined with several newly built houses—or new to him at any rate. It rather surprised him that Vance hadn't acquired a place near Mary Todd Lincoln's house, and it was just Jack's luck that his destination turned out to be the biggest house of them all.

Jack recognized the Vances' new maid the moment she opened the front door, despite the cap covering most of her wild red hair. The freckles were still visible, however, as was the ever-present wariness in the clear blue eyes. She had learned before she could walk not to trust people, and she wasn't about to let go of the lesson just for Jack Murphy.

"Hello, Mary," he said easily. "I'm here to see Mrs. Vance—if she's at home to visitors."

"Jack, are you crazy!" Mary stepped out onto the huge porch and pulled the door to behind her, her heavily starched, pink-and-white uniform rustling in the process. Clearly, even the maids in Farrell Vance's house dressed better than the girls at the orphanage ever would. "You can't come to the front door like this!"

"I can't? Why not?"

"You're the hired help. You work for Mr. Barden."

"I haven't worked for Mr. Barden for four years," Jack reminded her. "Nice house," he added, looking around the front porch at the potted ferns and assorted flowers.

"Mr. Vance won't like this," Mary said.

"I'm not here to see Mr. Vance. I'm here to see Elrissa."

"Why?"

"I want to thank her for her…kindness while I was away—in person, if you don't mind. All you have to do is ask her if she'll see me. You can't be blamed for what happens after that."

"You'd be surprised what a body can be blamed for in this house. Besides that, you are such a liar. She's *married* now. You've got no good reason to see her and plenty reasons not to."

"That's a matter of opinion, Mary."

Mary looked at him for a long moment—while Jack struggled to hold on to his impatience. He'd come a long way to stand on Elrissa's front porch—or was it a veranda?—and he'd done it against the advice of practically every orphan he knew. Only Little Ike had opined that Elrissa needed to own up to her poor treatment of one Jack Murphy. And, in this rare instance, Jack heartily agreed. Now all he needed was to get past Mary.

"I heard she didn't even send you a letter to tell you she was marrying somebody else," Mary said, reminding Jack that while the mail wagon for the Army of the Potomac might not have come as often as he and the rest of the Orphans' Guild would have liked, it did run in both directions. He didn't need reminding that what one orphan knew, they all knew.

"And *that* is none of your business," he said anyway. "I want to see her. The whole rebel army couldn't stop me from getting what I want, Mary, so I'm not really worried about *you*."

She exhaled sharply. "Jack, if you do something to make me lose this job—"

He smiled his best smile, rusty though it might be, and that was all it took.

"Oh, all right, then," Mary said. "And stop smiling at me. Kissing the girls and making them cry—that's all you're good for."

His smile broadened. "They don't always cry, Mary. *You* know that."

She shook her head at his blatant teasing. "I'll…go ask her. You stay right here. *Right here.* And I mean it." She reached behind her and opened the door. "I mean it!"

"Yes, Mary," he said dutifully. "I'll stay right here."

"See that you do," she said, determined to have the last word. She backed into the house and made a point of closing the door as firmly as was possible. He waited, listening to the sparrows chirping from their nests under the eaves, looking around the wide front porch again, wondering idly if Elrissa had decorated the stone pillars with red, white and blue bunting for the anniversary of national independence. He thought she might have, even though he'd never known her to care much about the Fourth of July celebration. Her husband would, of course. It would be bad for his business, given the country's recent victory, if he didn't participate as noticeably as possible.

A large yellow cat wandered up from somewhere behind the spirea bushes and made several passes against his legs. He reached down and scratched its ear for a moment and wondered what was taking Mary so long. The cat walked away and there was nothing to do but inspect the porch again. There was a swing and two comfortable-looking chairs a few feet away, and he was tempted to go sit in one of them. He had always wanted a porch like this, a place where he could bide his time and drink lemonade and read the newspaper on a quiet Sunday afternoon. He had never been able to see Elrissa sitting in a rocking chair beside him when he imagined this idyllic setting, however.

The front door opened, and Mary stuck her head out. "Well, come on, then," she said. "She says she'll see you. I still say you're crazy, and I'm beginning to think she is, too."

"You may be right about that, Mary. Lead the way."

He followed her into the dark coolness of the wide center hallway. He could immediately feel the strong draft created by the opening and closing of certain windows and transoms. It was a tribute to how well the house was built that, even on a hot summer day like this one, there was a steady breeze blowing on the inside.

The inner breeze carried the scent of lemon and beeswax Mary had likely spent hours applying to every wood surface in the place. He had no doubt that she would have learned the ins and outs of furniture polishing at the orphanage, and to such a degree that she could make her living doing it. He couldn't smell any food cooking. It was likely that there was a big summer kitchen detached from the main house somewhere out back.

"Don't you stay long," Mary whispered before she

let him into the room where Elrissa must be. "*He'll* be home to check on her in a little while."

"Check on her? For what?" It occurred to him even as he said it that Elrissa must already be having a child.

"None of your business. Just do as I say."

He smiled at her again, giving her a wink. She swatted the air in exasperation, then opened the door.

"Mr. Murphy, ma'am," she said, standing back so he could enter.

Elrissa waited on the far side of the room, and she was even more stunning than he remembered. Her pale blond hair had been twisted into ringlets and intricate rolls and braiding. Her hands were clasped at her waist as if she needed to hide their trembling. He might feel a small pang of sympathy if that was so, though trembling hands wouldn't be in keeping with Elrissa's head-strong personality at all. She was much more likely to cause the affliction rather than suffer it.

"Mrs. Vance," he said with a quiet calmness he must have learned on the battlefield. His voice didn't reflect his inner turmoil in the least, and he was glad of that.

She stood looking back at him, leaving him nowhere to go and nothing to say. He knew very little about women's clothes, but even he could see that when it came to afternoon dresses and maids' uniforms, Mary's was not the only wardrobe that had been significantly enhanced.

"It's good to see you, Jack. It's taken you a long time to get home," Elrissa said, smiling.

"Not that long. We were lucky. Some companies aren't being discharged at all. The ones that came to the party late or didn't see much fighting. It's only fair, in my opinion."

"Oh. Well. It seems a long time to me. I've been wondering if you'd even come back to Lexington at all. No one seemed to know."

"You asked about my return?"

"Well, about the regiments," she said. "We're all very proud of the Kentuckians. Papa and Farrell and I traveled down to Washington in May for the Grand Review. It was…thrilling. *Two days* for the army to pass. I looked for you in the parades, but I didn't see you. Were you there?"

"Yes. All the orphans were there—what's left of us."

She was looking at him so intently, as if she expected him to make some comment about her having witnessed the Grand Review. He had no idea what she expected him to say—that he'd looked for her among the throng of spectators? He hadn't. The truth was that it never occurred to him that she might be there.

"Why are you here, Jack?" she asked abruptly.

He looked at her in surprise. "Why? Well, I thought we'd start with an explanation—yours. I think I deserve that much—and then we could conclude with an apology—also yours."

"Apology? My goodness." Clearly such a thing had never occurred to her.

"You said you'd marry me, Elrissa."

"Yes, well, that was never really…official, now, was it?"

"It was official to me. Why did you do that? Say you'd marry me if you had no intention of doing so?"

She waved one hand in the air. "I was very young,

Jack. To tell you the truth, I just didn't think. You were leaving. The train was coming—I had no *time* to think. Later I realized my father would never have agreed. You're not…"

"Not what?" he asked when she didn't continue.

"Oh, you know what I mean," she said airily, moving to the sofa—carved rosewood likely from Massachusetts, he noted, because he'd been a very able clerk in a dry goods store that could special-order coffins *or* fine furniture, and it had been his business to know such things—before it was his business to kill men wearing the wrong uniform.

She sat down carefully so as not to rumple the dark green silk of her dress. It was a becoming color for her, he decided. He had never seen her wear anything like it before, and he supposed that such colors must be a privilege that came with marriage.

"You're looking very well, Elrissa," he said after a moment, and she gave him a brief but stricken look.

"What's wrong?" he asked immediately, moving closer to get a better look at her face.

"You look very well, too, Jack," she said instead of answering. She kept picking at a fold in her skirt. "Now, what were we talking about?"

"You decided not to marry me because I'm not good enough for you. No connections. No money to speak of." He didn't point out that his management had likely kept Barden's Dry Goods from going bankrupt.

"I didn't say that."

"I don't believe you needed to. Your recent behavior has been eloquent enough. It would have been a kindness to have received a letter telling me of your new plans, Elrissa—instead of hearing about them after the fact and secondhand."

"It didn't seem important," she said, and she actually smiled.

"No. I don't suppose it was. To you."

"Oh, Jack, I haven't broken your heart, have I?"

"My heart, no. My pride has taken quite a beating, I will admit. I suppose your father never knew about the marriage proposal. Mine, that is."

"No," she said, but *Of course not* was what he heard.

"I *am* sorry, Jeremiah. Truly."

"About what exactly?"

"Well, that you…misunderstood."

"I certainly did do that—*misunderstand*. I'm not sure why. I know that yes and no can mean anything other than what they're designed to mean. Orphans find that out very early. But in this instance, my…admiration and respect for you led me to forget my early lessons. I suppose I should thank you. I won't ever make the mistake of trusting someone so far above my station again, especially that she actually means what she says."

"Don't be cruel, Jack. There's really no need—"

"I don't think I'm the cruel one here. I'm only stating the truth. According to Father Bartholomew and the Sisters, I'm supposed to learn at least a little something from every situation, good or bad. And truly, I have."

"He came to see me, you know," Elrissa said, glancing at him and then away. "Your Father Bartholomew. When the engagement—Farrell's and mine—was announced in the newspapers. He was really quite cross with me. I couldn't imagine what you must have told him."

"I told him if I was killed, I wanted him to give you what money I had put by. It wouldn't have been a lot by your standards—especially now. But it was all I had in this world, and I thought you might buy yourself a little something with it—a keepsake. Or you might have wanted to give it to charity as a memorial gift. Knowing Father Bartholomew, it's likely he would have suggested it go to the orphanage."

"Well, luckily, you can use the money for yourself."

"Yes. Luckily."

"What are your plans now that the war is over, Jack?" she asked, actually looking at him directly now and not at other, more interesting aspects of the room.

"Well, coming back to work for your father isn't very likely. Do you think Farrell has any job vacancies?"

"No, seriously," she said, smiling slightly when she realized the grim humor in his comment. He had always been able to do that at least—make her smile.

"I thought maybe I'd...go out West," he said, as if the notion to migrate beyond the Mississippi River weren't something he'd just made up on the spot. Still, it seemed as good a plan as any.

"Go back into the army, you mean?"

He gave a short laugh. "No. I've had enough of armies."

She started to say something, then didn't, lapsing into a quiet sigh instead. "Don't stare at me so, Jack," she said after a moment.

"I don't mean to. It's just that I'd...forgotten."

"Forgotten what?"

"How very pretty you are. I used to think about that—on the march or when our situation was...bad."

"You mustn't say things like that. My husband won't like it."

"Won't he?"

"Farrell is very…protective of me. He will be home soon," she said, glancing at the quietly ticking clock on the mantel. "You must leave before then. Now, actually."

He made no move toward the door.

"Please," she said. "I want you to leave now—and go out the back way. Mary will show you. You should never have come to the front door."

"My mistake," he said. "It won't happen again. Goodbye, Elrissa. I hope you'll be happy."

"Jack," she said, as he was about to open the door.

He looked back at her.

"When will you go? Out West, I mean."

"I…haven't decided."

She got up from the rosewood sofa and came toward him, guiding her dress around a table in the effort to get to him.

"Jack, you were right. Something is wrong—terribly wrong. It's been so— He—Farrell—he isn't at all obliging like Papa. Truly he isn't. I— It's so difficult. I don't know that I can abide it much longer, this…penchant he has to tame me. No, I'm certain I can't abide it. I want you to take me with you when you go."

"What?" Jack said, despite the fact that he'd heard her clearly. She was very close now and once again he was struck by her prettiness. He was also struck by her familiar expression, one he'd seen many times when he worked in her father's dry goods store, one that meant she wanted something unsuitable and she intended to have it—or else.

"I'll meet you someplace. We can leave here together—whenever you say—the sooner the better."

"No, we cannot," he said, trying to remove her hand from his arm.

But she kept reaching for him, trying to hang on to him. "Yes! Yes! You and I—we can go where nobody knows us. We'd be happy, Jack. Truly, we would—"

"Elrissa, stop this!" he said sharply, and she suddenly put her face in her hands.

"You're upset. Let me find Mary," he said, because it was the only thing he could think of.

"No! I don't need Mary! I need you to say you'll help me!"

"I can't help you."

"But you *have* to. Who else can I turn to?" she said.

"Your father. He won't see you unhappy."

"You don't understand!" she cried, but Jack was very much afraid that he did. Marriage proposals weren't the only things Elrissa Barden refused to take seriously. She clearly thought she could ignore her marriage vows, as well.

"I'm going now," he said firmly, still holding her at bay. "Everything will be all right—"

Someone knocked urgently on the door behind him.

"Jack!" Mary said on the other side. "Come on, come on—you have to get out of here!"

Elrissa finally let go of him and stepped away. He gave her a moment to compose herself, then opened the door.

"Goodbye," she said, her voice cold and controlled now, as if they hadn't just been in an inexplicable tussle by the door. He started to say something more to her, then didn't. He turned and followed Mary down the wide hallway toward the back of the house.

"*He's* coming up the walk," Mary said over her shoulder. "Hurry!"

"I'm not afraid of him, Mary."

"Well, I'm afraid enough for the both of us. I can't lose this job, Jack. He'll put something about so nobody else will hire me. Hurry!"

He let Mary lead him through a breakfast room and out a side door, checking first to make sure no one would see him when he stepped into the manicured garden.

"The gate is over there—down that path," she said, pointing the way.

"Next time maybe I'll listen to you," he said, making her give a small laugh despite her worry.

"You're well rid of that one. You know that, don't you?" She suddenly reached up and touched his cheek. "What happened to you? Your face is the same, but you've got the eyes of an old man, Jack."

He didn't say anything.

"Go!" she said, giving him a push. "And take care of yourself. And don't you be coming back here!"

For the second time that day she closed the door firmly and left him standing.

"Jack! What are you doing here!" Little Ike cried as Jack came through the back hedge at the orphanage.

"Delivering fish," he said, holding up the large string of catfish he intended for the orphanage kitchen. "See? Good fishing down at the creek today. I thought the sun was too high, but the catfish didn't. What are *you* doing here?" he countered because he'd always enjoyed teasing Ike when he was overly excited about something and because Ike actually had a distant cousin who was letting him stay in a converted storage room at her house—now that he was grown and useful—the same cousin who had given him such a detailed account of Elrissa's wedding.

"You've been *fishing?*" Ike said incredulously, his voice giving a little squeak they way it always did whenever he was really excited.

"You can see I have, Ike."

"Father Bartholomew said you didn't stay here last night."

"I didn't."

"Well, where were you!" Ike cried, and Jack gave him a look to let him know he was dangerously close to crossing the line.

"You shouldn't be here, Jack. You should be long gone—"

"Why?"

"*Why?* The watchmen! They're looking for you!"

Jack was still not alarmed. "I've got to deliver these fish," he said, trying to get past him so he could take his catch to the kitchen door.

"Forget the fish! They're going to arrest you, Jack. Elrissa told her husband you were at the house. Her husband wants you arrested and charged."

"What are you talking about? Charged for what?"

"She says…you put your hands on her. You tried to hurt her."

"That's crazy. Mary was there. I don't have anything to worry about."

"You've got a lot to worry about! They've already been here once looking for you. Father Bartholomew sent me to see if I could find you—we didn't think you'd be coming back *here*. Farrell Vance aims to have your head, and he'll get it, too. You've got to get away!"

"I'm not running when I didn't do anything—"

"And how are you going to prove that? If Elrissa says you did—that's all it'll take. You don't have any money. You don't have any connections. There's nobody to vouch for what really happened."

"I told you Mary was there."

"Who's going to believe her, even if you could get her to tell the truth—which I doubt would happen if they came after her. She's going to be too scared to go against whatever Elrissa claims you did. And even if she does, Jack, Vance's lawyers will say us orphans always stick together—"

"Well, we do."

"Jack! Listen to me. I think if Vance gets half a chance, he'll kill you. It'll be like when General Sickles killed his wife's lover. He'll get off, just like Dan Sickles did, and you'll be in a pine box. Ain't that many of us left, Jack! You got to go! You got to live for the ones we had to bury down South. You got to live for all of us! You hear me!"

"Jeremiah," a quiet voice said behind them.

"Father Bartholomew," Jack said. "It's not—"

"Come inside," the priest said. "Ike, you take those fish to the kitchen. Don't say anything about Jeremiah being here."

"Yes, Father," Ike said, taking the string of fish out of Jack's hand.

Jack followed Father Bartholomew inside the building through a side door and down the quiet hallway to his office. They had to pass several classrooms along the way, and he thought idly that he could have identified where he was blindfolded because of the smell of chalk and India ink. One of the classes was singing today—"The Battle Hymn of the Republic." Another group struggled with multiplication table rotes.

"Nine-times-one-is-nine!"

"Nine-times-two-is-eight-teen!"

Father Bartholomew looked inside the office before he allowed Jack to enter.

"Close the door, Jeremiah," he said when they were inside. He indicated that he wanted Jack to sit in the one chair—the "scamp seat," as Jack and the rest of the boys at the orphanage had called it—the one directly in front of the desk, where it was impossible to escape Father Bartholomew's all-seeing gaze. Father Bartholomew took his usual place on the other side. It was a scene reminiscent of many Jack had experienced in this room, times when the young Jeremiah Murphy had let his foolhardy nature get the better of him and he'd had to be taken to task for it. The desk had seemed much bigger then, and so had Father Bartholomew.

Jack waited for the priest to say something—because that was the way it had always been done. Father Bartholomew sat quietly for a moment, tapping his fingertips together, perhaps praying. Jack couldn't tell for sure. Motes of dust floated in the shaft of sunlight that came in through the high windows. He could hear the distant sounds of orphan life going on around them, and he felt such a sudden pang of homesickness and longing that it made him catch his breath.

Father Bartholomew looked up at him. "I believe Ike is correct in his assessment of this situation," he said.

"Father, I—"

The priest held up his hand. "You have been in difficult circumstances before, ones which must have led you to rely on the Scriptures you were taught—"

"No, Father, I didn't rely on them," Jack said. He expected the priest to react, but Father Bartholomew merely let him twist in the wind after his remark and waited for him to continue.

"The Rime of the Ancient Mariner," Jack said finally. "I would think about...being on the upstairs porch after the Saturday chores were done. I would think about it so hard, I could hear your voice reading the poem. It... helped."

"A story of sin and redemption. God's messages appear in many places. And I know for certain that when we need Him, He often chooses to speak to us in a way that we will accept and understand, and we have only to pay attention.

"I have known you since you were a small boy starving on the streets of Lexington, Jeremiah. Since then, you and I have had to address a number of sins and punishments—but I do not believe you are guilty of this accusation. I want you to stay in here out of sight until dark. I don't believe the watchmen will be back looking for you until then. In the meantime, I have some arrangements to make. Will you do that? Stay here until I get back?"

"I'd rather talk to the police."

"No," Father Bartholomew said firmly. "I'm told that the watchmen looking for you are also in Farrell Vance's employ, and they will prevent you from doing that."

"Prevent—why?"

"Farrell Vance is a vain and arrogant man. He also has considerable authority regarding the enforcement of the law in this city. I believe he takes unnatural pleasure in perceiving insult where there is none so that he can inflict his own retribution. Your seeking out his wife without his knowledge is no small matter in his eyes. I don't believe he will allow you to challenge the veracity of her accusations in court or anywhere else—whether he believes them or not. In his mind, you have crossed a line, and the man now wants you dead. You've come through a hard time, Jeremiah. You've lost many of your orphanage family and you've survived the horrors of war by the grace of God and…by your own ingenuity." He paused, perhaps giving Jack the time to understand that he was referring to his unorthodox use for a poem about an ancient mariner.

"But all that hasn't made you immune to the harm this man intends to do you. This is not a situation you can handle alone. You must trust in God and in the people who care about you. You must wait here."

But Jack was unwilling to do that. He abruptly stood.

"This isn't right, Father."

"No, Jeremiah, it isn't. But it's not you or I who are the wrongdoers."

"I don't want to hide here, and I don't want to run away."

"You haven't been home in a long time. The war has changed things here and not for the better. Farrell Vance was—is—a profiteer. You don't understand how far this man's influence can reach. It is absolutely necessary for you to leave Lexington. I don't think you can stay alive otherwise. It's either be murdered by his henchmen or be hanged for defending yourself," the priest said, slowly getting to his feet, as well.

They stared at each other, and Father Bartholomew gave a quiet sigh. "I don't want to lose another one of my boys, Jeremiah."

"I'm not a boy, Father."

"No. But you still need to trust my judgment. I will return as soon as I can. Don't let any of the others see you. We want them to be telling the truth if they have to say they haven't seen you and don't know where you are." He walked to the door and opened it, and Jack realized that the old man was trying not to limp. The past four years hadn't been kind to him.

"There are apples in the cupboard there," Father Bartholomew said. "Eat one if you're hungry. Put the rest in your pockets. And move over there—into that corner. If anyone opens the door looking for me, I don't want them to see you."

"Father, I don't understand why you're doing this—"

"I told you. I don't want to lose another one of my boys, especially if there is something I can do to prevent it. You are innocent and you belong to all of us here," he said. "That is enough for me."

"Are you that sure I'm not guilty of what Elrissa accuses me of?"

The old priest gave a slight smile. "Guilty men don't risk being caught in order to bring a fine catch of catfish to an orphanage kitchen, Jeremiah. At least not in my experience. Rest now while you can. I fear you will need it."

Jack stood for a long moment after Father Bartholomew had gone. Then, despite the fact that he was no longer one of the elderly priest's charges, he did as he was told. He ate an apple. He filled his pockets with some of the ones left in the basket. He sat on the floor behind the door so that no one who opened it would see him. He was so tired suddenly, and there was nothing to do but wait. He kept trying to sort out what must have happened after he left Elrissa, and he couldn't. Despite her earlier comments and his struggle to keep her at bay, Elrissa didn't in any way seem distraught when Mary saw her—and couldn't Mary say that?

No. Ike was right. No one would take Mary's word, not when she would be contradicting the wife of Farrell Vance. Whether he'd been here these past four years or not, he knew enough about the power of wealth to know that. He'd seen it every day in the dry goods store.

It was nearly dark when Father Bartholomew returned. He came in carrying a large basket, and he had Ike in tow. He immediately sent Ike to keep watch along the hallway and outside the building while he apprised Jack of the escape plan.

"The money you left in my keeping," Father Bartholomew said, giving him a leather pouch. "I wouldn't carry all of it in that, though. Times are hard and I imagine the roads are full of desperate and misguided souls who will try to take it from you."

The priest had brought the haversack Jack had carried for the duration of the war, and he handed it to him. Jack had left it and the rest of what remained of his army equipment in the storage room in the visitors' quarters at the back of the orphanage until he had need of it again. He hadn't expected to require it quite so soon.

"The knapsack will be too conspicuous," Father Bartholomew said as he took boiled eggs from the basket and handed them to him. And there was hardtack and beef jerky among the numerous small wrapped packets. The boiled eggs must have come from the orphanage kitchen, but Jack had no idea how the priest would have come by the army rations.

"One last thing," Father Bartholomew said. "I seem to remember you had a great fondness for these." Incredibly, he handed Jack several sticks of peppermint candy. "You do still like them?" he asked with the barest of smiles.

"I...don't know," Jack said truthfully. "It's been a long time."

"All the more enjoyable, then," the priest said.

Jack shook his head. He was just short of being amused that Father Bartholomew would think peppermint sticks could make him feel better. Even so, he put the candy into his pocket.

"I don't think you should head west," Father Bartholomew said. "I believe Vance's assassins will be expecting you to try for Louisville. Going south into Tennessee will be a better choice. Get to Knoxville and then head east into the mountains. It will be easier for you to get lost there and it is not a likely route since you've so soon come from the war. Farrell Vance is not going to think you would want to go back into that troubled land. Then, later, after he tires of looking for you, you might head farther south and by some circuitous route eventually make your way to St. Louis."

"Father—"

"It would be better if we didn't argue about this, Jeremiah. You haven't the time."

"I was only wondering," Jack said. "You seem well versed in how to make a man disappear."

"You aren't my first fugitive, Jeremiah, and I sincerely doubt you'll be my last. Now. I want to give you this, but don't open it," he said, handing Jack an envelope. "I've written down some things I want you to know, but this…wisdom, if you will, won't be helpful to you now. You are still too raw. From the war. From your association with Elrissa Vance. I want you to wait before you read it. Wait until you are…content."

"Content?" Jack said, thinking he hadn't heard right.

"Contentment is one of life's finer accomplishments, Jeremiah. You won't understand what I've said unless you have it. Now. Ike is going to go with you to the edge of town. He's hidden a horse for you in the cemetery. If you're stopped, Ike will seem very drunk, and you will react to his inebriation accordingly."

"Little Ike has never had a drop of liquor in his life," Jack said.

"But he's wearing a good dose of it on his clothing and he's very good at mimicking its effects. I'm sorry to say it was something he saw in his own home far too often when he was a small boy. Once you're out of the town, travel mostly at night and stay to yourself. And don't look like you're on the run. People are going to remember a horseman riding fast no matter what time of day it is. Now, you must hurry. I expect the watchmen to come and search the premises again tonight and I expect they will prevail upon the smaller children to tell what they know. I need to be on hand to calm them."

Jack looked at him. Elrissa's lie was more far-reaching than he had realized. "I'm sorry for all this, Father."

"We must concern ourselves with what is, Jeremiah, and not become entangled in regrets, especially those over which we have no control. And we must keep a firm grasp on our hopes. My hope for you is a good, new life, one that begins this very minute."

Father Bartholomew opened the door quietly and looked in both directions before he stepped out into the dark hallway. They moved quietly through the building toward the side door, cutting through the main dining hall as they went. Several votive candles in red holders burned on the mantelpiece, and Jack could see a long row of tin cups behind them. Thirty-seven of them; he knew how many without counting.

Thirty-seven.

"It was a great kindness to send us those, Jeremiah," Father Bartholomew said when Jack stopped to look at them. "We keep them in a place of honor, and I believe our boys know we are remembering them."

Did they? Jack thought. He had no idea. At the moment he had other things to worry about. If he were caught, his attempt to escape would only underline his already-presumed guilt.

He would just have to see to it that he wasn't caught.

Ike waited by the side door, reeking of the O Be Joyful just as Father Bartholomew had said. Thunder rumbled in the distance, a sound they both mistook for cannonading for a brief moment. The wind was picking up and the trees on the grounds of the orphanage began to sway.

"A good storm will give you cover," Father Bartholomew said. "Be watchful and Godspeed to you both."

"Thank you, Father," Jack said, offering the old man his hand. "This is twice now you've given me my life."

"I believe it to be worth the effort," Father Bartholomew said. "You're a good man, Jeremiah. Sometimes in spite of yourself. Now go! Hurry!"

The rain came only moments after they'd left the grounds. Ike led the way, alert as he always was whenever the Orphans' Guild—or one of its members—was in danger. He zigzagged through back lots and alleys Jack had never even seen before or didn't recognize. It was taking twice the time it ordinarily would have to reach the old cemetery where the horse was supposed to be. As the thunder grew louder, Jack began to lose hope that it would still be there. Tied securely or not, horses didn't wait well in a thunderstorm without a human in attendance, and even then it could be difficult.

"Wait," Ike whispered when they were about to cross a street. His warning was well-timed. Two of the city's watchmen were coming out of the narrow lane they intended to travel. They waited in the shadows until the men had passed.

"Now!" Ike whispered, and they began to run, the noise of their passing hidden in the sound of the rain and wind. "Not much farther—"

It took only minutes to reach the iron gates. Ike pulled one of them ajar. It creaked loudly, and they hurriedly took refuge behind an ornate but eroded angel-covered tombstone until they could be certain that no one had heard the sound.

"That way," Ike said after a moment, and Jack followed him as best he could in the dark, stumbling several times over footstones along the way.

"I don't see the horse," Jack said.

"Over there—"

Jack still didn't see it—and then he realized that Ike meant inside a nearby mausoleum, one he immediately recognized.

Ike laughed and slapped him on the back. "I knew you'd be thinking that horse was long gone. Ain't, though, is it?"

"I'll tell you after we actually find it," Jack said, making Ike laugh harder.

But the horse was where Ike had left it. Dry and out of sight inside an ostentatious marble structure dedicated to the erstwhile Horne-Windham family. Jack remembered playing in the mausoleum when he was a boy. It was a good place to hide—except that Father Bartholomew always found him.

"Don't reckon the Horne-Windhams ever expected a horse to be in here," Ike said as he lit a candle stub he had in his pocket. He let some hot wax drip onto a narrow ledge and planted the candle firmly into it. The rain was barely audible inside the thick marble structure and the candle flickered in the draft from the entrance.

"They're not the only ones," Jack said, wiping the rain from his face and attempting to calm the horse because it had become unsettled by their sudden appearance.

Despite the animal, there was still enough room to get around. He looked at the many bronze plaques placed one above the other on the opposite marble wall and appearing to reach well above his head. "It's a good thing there were so many of them."

"Biggest marble box in the place. Here," Ike said, bringing a small bundle out from under his coat.

"What is—?" Jack began, but then he recognized the weight and the feel of it.

"Things must be bad if Father Bartholomew is giving me a sidearm." He turned the bundle over in his hands.

"He ain't," Ike said. "I am. It's loaded so don't go throwing it around and shoot the horse or something. Now all we got to do is get you out of here."

Ike moved to the entranceway, alert and watchful as Jack led the horse forward.

"Ike," Jack said. "I...don't know how to thank you. I can't ever repay you—"

"There ain't but one way, Jack," Ike said without looking at him. "Die in your own bed when you're ninety—and don't you ever come back here."

"Ike, if—"

"Shh!" Ike said sharply. "Watchmen—I think it's the same two."

The horse, alarmed by the sudden tension in both men, began to toss its head and shift about.

"Easy," Jack whispered, hanging on to the bridle. "Whoa! Easy!"

"Out the candle. I'm going to draw them away," Ike said, slipping outside before Jack could stop him. Incredibly, as his footsteps faded into the darkness, Ike began to sing, a rousing song about a little chicken that wouldn't lay an egg, the one he used to sing on the march to make the Orphans' Guild perk up and laugh.

"O, I had a little chicky and he wouldn't lay an egg…"

Jack waited, listening hard, but the storm was nearly overhead and the walls too thick for him to hear whatever it was Ike had heard. All he could do was stay put and try to keep the horse from bolting. His hands were beginning to shake, but he didn't let go of the bridle. He leaned his head close to the animal's nose and breathed evenly, quietly, until he could loosen his grip. Then he reached into his pocket and gave it a piece of the peppermint candy.

"All right," he said to the horse after what seemed a long time. "In for a penny, in for whatever's in that leather pouch."

He moved to the doorway and stood for a moment, then led the horse outside. It was still raining, but the worst of the storm had passed. He couldn't see or hear any activity in the cemetery.

He made sure his haversack was secure, then he mounted the horse and let it find its own way among the tombstones until he reached the road leading out of town. He knew better than to take it. He cut through more back lots and alleyways instead, hoping the watchmen would be more interested in staying dry than in obeying Farrell Vance. Eventually he found a part of the town he could still recognize even in a downpour. He cut across a field, careful to stay between the rows of corn and not leave an irate farmer in his wake. Heading into the mountains was a better plan than Father Bartholomew had realized. Jack had impulsively told

Elrissa that he was heading out West, and it seemed likely that she would have told her husband.

In a very short time and through any number of plowed and planted fields, Jack had ridden beyond the Lexington town limits, but he stayed off the main road until he was certain he was beyond any watchmen assigned to monitor the comings and goings of nighttime travelers. It was still raining, and he stopped for a moment and listened to get his bearings. Then he crossed into yet another field and ultimately came out onto the road again. He headed for London, and he didn't look back.

Chapter Four

❧

"Who are you?" The voice was muffled behind the closed cabin door, but Jack could understand her. He had managed to get this far—from Lexington to Knoxville and over the Tennessee border to Asheville, and then the final long hard trek toward Jefferson—without ever having to fully answer that question. At one point he'd even ridden rear guard on the stage heading through bushwhacker country on the so-called buffalo road, apparently the only way to get through the mountains, still without identifying himself by name. He had no intention of breaking that precedent now.

He wasn't here by accident. Somewhere on the way to London, he had checked his haversack, and he had realized that he had a true destination after all. He just hadn't expected how hard it would be to get this far.

He had some serious misgivings about his decision at the moment—since it was becoming increasingly clear that this endeavor could be as dangerous as facing Farrell Vance's men. The best plan he could devise under these circumstances was simply to wait for the woman inside to give him the information he wanted and to hope she had a bad aim.

"I'm looking for someone," he called after a moment. He couldn't see the musket trained on him, but even without Ike's skills, he could feel it.

"I don't know you," she said, and it was clearly a serious accusation. "Leave your hands where I can see them!" she shouted when Jack would have reached for his haversack.

"I was asked to deliver some letters and personal—"

"Letters for who!"

"Mrs. Garth."

"And what Mrs. Garth would that be?"

"Mrs. Thomas Henry Garth," he said. "Sayer."

"Sayer?"

"Yes."

"They come from Thomas Henry? Is he dead?"

"Where can I find her?" Jack asked instead of answering.

"Is he dead?"

Jack didn't say anything, and after a moment the door cracked open and a woman stepped outside. The musket was still trained on him, and he had no doubt that she would kill him if she thought it the least bit necessary.

"Is he *dead?*" she asked again.

"Yes," he said, and the woman let the musket fall.

"Oh, no! Oh, no," she said, lifting the musket slightly and then letting the barrel swing downward again. "That poor girl."

"Can you tell me where to find her?"

"She ain't here," she said, wiping at her eyes with the back of her hand. "You're on the wrong ridge."

"I've come a long way," he said. "I just want to give her the letters and then I'll be gone."

"I'll take them to her—if she's alive."

"What do you mean?"

"They got sickness at the Garth cabin. The two little girls—I don't know about Sayer. She didn't holler this morning."

"Holler?" Jack asked blankly.

"It's how we know one another's all right. Give a loud holler so whoever lives closest can hear you. You send it back to them and if there's anybody else can hear you, you pass it on. She didn't holler. Ain't no smoke coming out the chimney, neither."

"You can see the place from here?" he asked, looking around for a clearing in the trees.

The woman stared at him warily without answering.

"I don't mean her any harm. I just want to give her the letters and tell her what happened."

"You was with him at the end?"

"Yes."

"He die easy?"

"No," Jack said truthfully, mostly because she had lifted the musket again and because he thought that this old woman would spot the lie before he got it out.

"You ain't going to tell *her* that."

"No. I'm going to tell her what he—Thomas Henry—wanted me to say."

"Who are you?" she asked, studying him hard, and they were back to that again.

But he still didn't answer the question.

"You soldier with him?"

The horse was growing restless, giving him the opportunity to ignore that question, as well.

"You the one what killed him?" she asked bluntly, her voice louder now.

He stared back at her and drew a quiet breath. "I... don't know."

"Well, at least you ain't a liar," she said after a moment. "These here hills is full of liars and I can't abide any of them."

"Where's the Garth cabin?" he asked, still hoping to get some information out of her.

"You going to help or hurt?"

"I told you. I don't mean Thomas Henry's wife or his little sisters any harm."

She continued to stare at him and the minutes dragged on. "You wait for me," she said abruptly, as if she'd suddenly made up her mind about something. "I'm going to get my sunbonnet. Make that there horse come up here by the porch."

He considered it an encouraging sign that she left the musket leaning against the door frame, and he walked the horse forward. She returned shortly, wearing the blue-flowered cotton bonnet she'd gone to fetch and carrying a basket. The bonnet was faded but clean, and her withered face had disappeared into the deep brim. He thought she would have a horse of her own someplace to get her to wherever they were about to go, but she had other plans.

"Hold that," she said, shoving the basket into his hand. "Well, let me grab your arm. How do you think I'm going to get up there?"

He shifted the basket and the reins to his other hand

while she awkwardly caught him by the forearm and swung up behind him. She was much stronger than she looked. He expected to have to help her a lot more than he did.

"*My* name's Rorie Conley," she said when she was situated and he'd handed the basket back. "And yes, I already know—you ain't got one. That's *Rorie* Conley. Try to remember that. I'm a old widder woman and I don't suffer fools gladly. That's something else you need to remember. That way," she added with a broad gesture that could have meant anything, and poking him in the ribs for emphasis.

He set the horse off in the direction she'd more or less indicated.

"That basket's heavy. You got a revolver in it?" he asked after they'd gone a short way.

"Wouldn't you like to know?" she countered.

"I would," he said.

"I ain't telling you."

He waited for a time, but apparently she meant it.

"Well, they say ignorance is bliss. I'm not feeling particularly blissful, though."

"Life's like that, ain't it?"

He smiled to himself and urged the horse back onto what may or may not be the path.

"You ain't the first one," she said as the way grew more wooded and more precariously downhill.

"The first what?" he asked, glancing over his shoulder.

"Soldier without a name. No-name soldiers been coming to these hills ever since George Washington had an army. Some men just don't like armies, I reckon."

"Not much to like," he said.

"Don't reckon there is," she said agreeably.

"How far are we going?"

"Why? You got a train to catch?"

He couldn't keep from smiling. "No, ma'am. No train."

"This trip ought to work out real well, then. I ain't catching no train, either."

They rode for a while in silence. He could feel the air growing cooler as they descended farther and farther down into the wooded hollow. He could hear water flowing somewhere, and every now and then a bird flew up or something scampered off among the bushes and undergrowth. There was nothing to do but follow the path he could barely see, in lieu of more specific directions.

"Jeremiah," he said when they finally reached the bottom and crossed a small but bold stream and started up the other side. "My name's Jeremiah."

"Oh, I see," she said. "You got yourself *half* a name. Well, I'm proud to know it. Half of something's better than all of nothing, ain't it, Jeremiah?"

"Yes, ma'am," he said. "That it is."

"Did you up and run off from somewhere?" she asked, verifying what he already suspected regarding her penchant for bluntness.

"War's over," he said, assuming she was asking if he was a deserter.

"More things to run from than a war, Jeremiah. Must be one of them other things, then."

He wasn't about to ask what she meant, but she continued as if he had.

"You don't look like you got no money, so I ain't thinking you up and robbed a bank. Don't look like no gambler what can't pay his loses, neither. Must be something to do with a woman," she said. "You running from somebody's mad husband?"

He didn't say anything, and she chuckled softly. "Didn't take you for one of *them,* Jeremiah. Still, men ain't the smartest creatures God put on this earth. They get themselves in all kind of messes and don't never know for a gnat's second how they got there. That's how we ended up brother-fighting-brother these here last four years, to my way of thinking—and poor Thomas Henry Garth dead."

That remark seemed to have ended the conversation. For a while.

"I'm worried, Jeremiah," she said, but he had lost sight of the path and wasn't really listening.

"That way," she said, pointing over his shoulder. "I'm worried and that's why I'm running on so. Well, I like to talk anyway, and I don't get much chance except when I get down the mountain to church. So when I'm all vexed like this—well, it just comes out and I'm a sight. I'm right fond of all of them Garth girls—Beatrice and Amity and Sayer. If the Lord takes them, it's going to break my heart—and I told Him that, too. Don't know that He sets much store by what's going to happen to my old heart if He does one thing or another, but I figured it won't hurt for Him to know for sure I *ain't* going to be happy. I been real good about not asking for things for myself for a long time now—didn't even mention how bad my knees is been paining me. But then it come to me—right out of the blue—right when I was of half a mind to shoot you for a bushwhacker. I thought, 'Quit your yammering, Rorie Conley. Get that boy with the horse and go see about 'em.' So here we are."

"Yes, ma'am," he said, because she had stopped talking and seemed to be expecting him to make some kind of response.

"Sayer, now, she's a outsider," Rorie continued when he'd obliged her by using the small space she'd given him. "She ain't from these here mountains, but she tries. Thomas Henry's mama showed her how to cook. And me, I showed her a couple of things about making soap and hominy and such as that. But there's a lot of things she don't know. There's a lot to be said for trying, though. I didn't reckon she'd last half as long as she has. Life's hard enough around here when you got your man. When you ain't, well…" She gave a heavy sigh. "Thomas Henry's uncle—Halbert, his name is—he's been plaguing her to death. If Thomas Henry knowed what that sorry uncle of his is been doing to Sayer and his little sisters, he'd kill him first thing he was home—blood kin or not. I know that for sure—but he's dead, so what good is he?" She suddenly squeezed his shoulder. "I'm scared, Jeremiah. I'm scared we're going to go in there and find them girls as dead as Thomas Henry."

He didn't say anything to that. He could hear her sniffing from time to time.

"No use worrying till we know," he said, and he could feel the bonnet nod against his shoulder.

"You better hang on to that horse now," she said.

"Why?"

"I smell a bear."

"Maybe we ought to hurry, then."

"Well, my stars, Jeremiah. You ain't nearly as simpleheaded as you look."

With that, she gave the horse's flank a dig with both her heels, not knowing that this particular piece of horseflesh would take such a gesture completely to heart and bolt to the top of the ridge, path or no path, whether they wanted it to or not. Unfortunately, the mount Ike had found for him was a seasoned warhorse whose war still continued at every turn—something Jack had discovered the hard way.

Rorie Conley was hanging on for dear life, but he didn't try to slow the animal down. He already knew how useless that would be. A charge was a charge to this horse, at least until it ran out of room. They finally broke into the clearing around the Garth cabin, and he had to work hard to rein it in. "Next time, you let me give this animal his instructions," he said as he helped her swing down.

He dismounted and looked toward the cabin. Someone had put a lot of work into building it. It was tall enough to have a good-size loft if the small window near the eaves was any indication. There were two more windows off the front porch—double-hung three-overtwos, the kind he would have thought would be too expensive and complex to build for a mountain farmer. Two straight chairs sat on the porch, and a glass jar with some kind of fading wildflowers in it had been placed in the middle of one of the windowsills. Apparently Sayer Garth liked the little touches.

Rorie was still trying to get her breath. Her bonnet had fallen off her head and was hanging down her back, but she still had a good grip on the basket.

"Did you hear what I said?" he asked.

"Yes, Jeremiah, I reckon I did. And I'll remember it. Another ride like that one and I'll be simple-headed, too."

She untied her bonnet and put it on top of whatever she had in the basket, then stood for a moment, listening.

"You hear anything?" she asked, turning her head side to side.

"Nothing but the wind in the trees," he said.

"Well, I reckon I got to go see."

"I'll go," he said.

"No, you won't. How many times a day do you want to come that close to getting yourself shot?"

"Used to be a pretty regular thing," he said. "Of course, 'wanting' didn't have anything to do with it."

"Well, now it does. Sayer might be in there with a musket sighted on the door. She's got those girls with her, and you'll scare her so bad she'll shoot first and then worry about what you was wanting."

She began walking toward the cabin, and he came with her. "Used to be she had a dog," she said. "Good old dog. Wouldn't let nobody come up on the cabin unless Sayer called him off. Something happened to him."

"Thomas Henry's uncle, you mean?"

She flashed him a look of what could have been appreciation for his powers of deduction or one that indicated she didn't find him quite as "simple-headed" as she'd first thought.

"You hear that?" Rorie said suddenly. "I hear crying." She moved forward quickly. "Sayer! It's me! I'm coming in!" She stepped up on the porch. "You stay out here," she said over her shoulder.

He watched as she disappeared inside. He could hear the crying clearly now, but he couldn't be certain if there was one person in distress or two.

He kept looking around for anything that might be amiss outside the cabin. He'd heard enough now about Thomas Henry's uncle to think that the dead Reb had been right to worry about his wife's safety.

The horse began to prance nervously, something Jack took as a sign that this situation might not be safe for ex-soldiers. The crying coming from inside the cabin seemed to be tapering off, in any event. He pulled the horse's reins forward and dropped them on the ground, because he had learned from an ex-cavalryman riding the stage to Jefferson that it would stay put as if it were tethered. Jack's not knowing about the animal's war training had seemed to satisfy the man's mind regarding Jack himself and the all-too-obvious U.S. brand on the horse's left shoulder. A man who hadn't been a Union cavalryman and who had bought a warhorse cheap wasn't going to know the fine points. The imaginary tethering and the fact that it would come whenever he whistled—unless it thought it was in the middle of another charge—thus far had proved at least somewhat useful.

"She ain't in here and she ain't in the privy," Rorie called after a moment. "The girls don't know where she got to. That path yonder leads down to the spring. You walk down that way, Jeremiah. See if you can see her. I'll tend to these young-uns. They're still fevering and they're both scared might near to death. I'm going to

leave the back door open. You holler if you find anything—you can holler, can't you?"

She didn't wait for him to say whether he could or
not. "Watch out for snakes! We got some big rattlers
and copperheads around here!" she yelled as she went
back inside.

Jack stood for a moment. He had thought Mary was
accomplished at having the last word, but Rorie Conley was a true artist.

He began walking through the tall and probably
snake-filled grass to the path that led...somewhere.
He kept looking for livestock. He would have expected
chickens, at the very least, but what he took for a hen-
house and a chicken lot were clearly unoccupied as was
the pigpen and the barn. He could see a smokehouse and
tobacco barn, and there was a planted field on a slope
some distance away—hay that needed cutting and dry-
ing. There was another field lying fallow with the rot-
ting stubble of a corn crop beyond that one.

But what was most apparent was that Sayer Garth
had no animals to feed of any kind. Uncle Halbert didn't
seem to favor one species over the other. Chickens, cows
or child's pet, they were all the same to him.

The path grew very steep suddenly, and it was difficult to keep his balance because there was nothing but
tall grass to grab on to along the way. It occurred to
him that if the path led to anything of importance, the
grass needed to be scythed. If he was going to run into
any snakes, this would be a good place for it. The path
needed to be terraced and braced with thick planks,
something he supposed Thomas Henry might have done
if he'd lived.

Once again he could hear water flowing, not the rushing of a stream in a rocky bed like the one they had crossed at the bottom of the hollow on the way here, but a steady, quiet sound of water hitting water.

The path made a sharp bend, and as he came around it, he saw a woman lying on the ground next to an overturned bucket a few yards ahead.

"Rorie!" he yelled, moving as quickly as he could down to where the woman on the ground lay, still trying not to lose his balance. He could immediately see a gash in her forehead that ran into her hair.

He couldn't hear Rorie coming, and he yelled again. "Rorie!"

"Oh, no, what is it!" she cried from somewhere behind him.

"I found her!"

He knelt down by the woman.

"Is she—?" Rorie called. She came down the path as far as she could make it without falling.

"No," he said. "No, she's breathing. Looks like she might have hit her head on one of these rocks. I don't think she's been out here too long. The place is still bleeding a little."

"Get her up from there, Jeremiah. Don't let her lie on the hard ground like that. Oh, no, I hope she ain't snakebit. I'm going to get the other bed ready. You carry her in," she said, and she was running—hobbling— away again.

He grabbed the bucket Sayer Garth must have intended to carry back to the house and filled it in the small pool that collected the water running in a steady stream from a split in the rocks. She was very pale—

and thin—unnaturally so. Hers was the kind of thinness he'd seen far more times than he'd ever want to count. It was the kind that came from starving.

He took off his neckerchief and wet it, then began wiping the dried blood from her face. She stirred after a moment and caught his hand. Her eyes opened.

"Thomas Henry... Oh, Tommy," she whispered as her eyes closed again.

He picked her up as carefully as he could and began the long climb back up to the cabin, going down on his knees once when his feet slipped. He didn't drop her, but the jarring made her rouse again. She reached up her hand and grabbed on to his shirtfront, gripping it tightly, not because she was afraid of falling, he thought, but because she still believed he was Thomas Henry. He could smell her soft woman smell—soap and rose-water—and he realized suddenly that she was crying.

"It's all right," he said quietly as he struggled to carry her upward to flatter ground. "I've got you."

"You're home," she murmured, pressing her face against his chest. "You're home..."

"Yes," he said, knowing he shouldn't.

Home.

"Where is he?"

"You rest easy, honey—"

"Where is he!"

"It weren't him, Sayer."

"No! I saw him! I saw him!" Sayer said, trying to get up. The room swam and she fell back on the pillow. "I saw him," she said again, hating that she sounded so pitiful. Tears began to slide down her cheeks.

"Rest now," Rorie said. "You got yourself a big knot on your head, but you'll be all right. Amity and Beatrice, I think they'll be all right, too. Their fevers' done broke. They're both right over there in the other bed, sleeping away like they need to be. They been washed up and the bed's changed. I got the sheets boiling in the wash pot. Next time you wake up, I'm going to have some good healing broth ready for all three of you. Just let go, honey. We're going to take care of things for you. Let go now. Sleep."

Sayer wanted so much to do that—let go. But how could she? She had seen Thomas Henry. But her eyes closed in spite of all she could do.

We? she suddenly thought. She wanted to ask about that, but she couldn't manage, somehow.

Sleep...

And perhaps she did sleep, but there seemed to be a noisy argument nearby. Rorie and...someone with a man's voice. She tried to lift her head enough to see.

"Now see what you gone and did? You woke her up!"

"I told you. She ought not sleep for very long. I know a little something about head wounds!"

"Well, all right! I'm willing to allow as how maybe you seen more than I have. What do you want to do about it?"

"You need to talk to her for a little bit. Then she can sleep again—for a while."

"Who are you?" Sayer asked, and they both looked around in surprise. She realized that a good deal of time must have passed, because Rorie looked much more tired now than she had earlier.

"Talk to her," the man said, and he left the cabin.

"Wait! Who is that?" Sayer insisted.

"I…ain't for sure," Rorie said. "I reckon I just up and took him over. I needed to get over here to see what was happening with you and the girls. My knees— You know how my knees get. That old mule of mine, he ain't about to let nothing ride him that's heavier than a sack of corn. I knowed good and well I couldn't walk it. So that boy, he rode me over on his horse. 'Course his horse ain't much better than that hardheaded mule. That dang animal still thinks it's in the war. Least little thing and off he goes like he was leading some battle."

"He…rode you over?" Sayer asked, trying to concentrate on the part that interested her.

"I reckon I made him," Rorie confessed.

Sayer looked at her doubtfully, and Rorie shrugged.

"Is he leaving now?"

"Can't say for sure," Rorie said obscurely. "I'm hoping he'll go get my cow. Want me to ask him?"

"I want you to help me up so I can find—where Thomas Henry—" But the room began to spin again as she made the attempt on her own, and she fell back against the pillow. "I don't—" She reached up to touch the place that hurt so on her forehead.

"I reckon you fell and hit your head, honey. I reckon you ain't been eating—ain't been sleeping either, most likely, what with the girls as sick as they was, and the chore to get to the spring and back was too much for you."

"Thomas Henry…"

"He ain't here, Sayer," Rorie said. "And we ain't wanting to wake the girls," she added, looking directly into Sayer's eyes.

"I know what I saw!"

"You *saw* what you hoped," Rorie said. There was something in her voice, something fearful, that made Sayer let it go. She turned her face away, and she didn't press her anymore. She lay there in her narrow bed, her mind filled with dread, trying to understand. She had thought she might not recognize him when he came home, but she had. She had!

She must have slept again, despite her need to look for the man she was still certain she had seen. She was aware suddenly that she wasn't alone, and when she opened her eyes, Amity was sitting on the bed beside her.

"Shh," Amity whispered, holding a finger to her lips. "They're asleep." She held an oddly folded handkerchief by each of two corners, and she leaned closer so Sayer could see it better.

"What is it?" Sayer whispered in return.

Amity made a small sound of exasperation, a sure sign that she was on the mend. Her hair had been combed and neatly braided, and her face was clean. She was thinner, apparently because of the fever she'd had, but she looked so much better than she had yesterday. Or was it yesterday? Sayer realized suddenly that she didn't actually know.

"Two babies," Amity said. "See them in the cradle?" Once again she held the handkerchief closer to encourage Sayer to take another look and perhaps this time note the two rolls in it that must be what Amity called "babies."

"Where did you get them?" Sayer asked, still whispering.

"Jeremiah made it. He used to make them for the little girls when they came to the orphanage. They never had any dolls or anything until maybe later when the Sisters would make them one."

Orphanage? What orphanage?

"He made Beatrice one, too. She's pretending like she's too old for playing with handkerchiefs, but she likes it. He's going to show us how to make one for ourselves when he gets a chance. All you need is a hanky and that's one thing we've still got."

Sayer frowned. "Who is Jeremiah?" she asked in a normal voice.

"He's cutting wood today," Amity said, pointing out the window. "The woodshed was almost empty. Rorie thinks somebody's been stealing it. Do you think somebody's been stealing it? The mountain's got trees down everywhere. Why would somebody steal our wood?"

"I don't know that they would," Sayer said, but she was very afraid that she did. Both why and who.

"Jeremiah told Rorie we ought to make it harder to get to."

"Did he? What else did he say?"

"Beatrice!" Amity suddenly called to her sister instead of answering. "Sayer's awake!"

Sayer looked to the bed on the other side of the room, expecting Beatrice to be there, but she wasn't. She was coming in from the porch.

"Oh," Sayer said in surprise. "Look at you! You're up and you're all well. How long have I been asleep?"

"We've been well for days. You haven't been asleep very much," Amity said before Beatrice could answer, swinging her handkerchief back and forth as if she wanted to keep the tiny pretend babies rolled up in it quiet. "You just didn't know anything. You didn't even know who we were. Jeremiah said you shouldn't sleep too long even if you didn't know anything. So we woke you up and woke you up. But now you woke up all by yourself. Thomas Henry's not here," she added pointedly. "Is he, Beatrice?"

"No," Beatrice said. "You thought he was, but he wasn't. Jeremiah thought it was because you hit your head—but then he wasn't sure if it was *all* coming from your head or if you caught the fever like we had—or both," she added with a sigh. "I say it's both— You don't think Thomas Henry is here now, do you, Sayer?" She was looking at her with such a concerned expression that Sayer reached her hand out to her.

"No," she said, trying to sound convincing. "I'm so sorry I worried you."

Beatrice came to her then, crawling up the foot of the bed so she could sit on her other side, and Sayer hugged both girls hard.

"We were scared," Beatrice said. "When you didn't know us. We told you and we told you who we were, but you just wanted to look for Thomas Henry."

"I'm all right now," she said, hoping it was true. "Is Rorie still here?" She was certain she was right about that at least, that she'd seen and talked to Rorie Conley.

"She's here—and her cow. Jeremiah went and got it—he said that animal was contrary enough to make a priest swear. Anyway, we got milk now—and butter. Rorie went looking for eggs a while ago. Jeremiah cut her a walking stick so she could. It had a gall on it at the top and he cut a face in it so she could see where she's going," Amity said, laughing. "She thinks he's crazy, and she thinks she can find where those hens that got stolen might be nesting. She said they weren't stolen for keeps—just scattered around."

No, Sayer thought. *Not for keeps. For the worry and the hunger losing them would inflict.*

"Then I think I better get up and see about making us something to eat," Sayer said. But she realized as she said it that she might not be physically able to accomplish such a major task and that there might not be anything left for her to cook.

"Jeremiah made us cracker pudding," Beatrice said.

"I like cracker pudding," Amity said. "It's got sugar and raisins."

"Where did you get sugar and raisins?" Sayer asked.

"I didn't get them," Amity said. "Jeremiah did. He had them on his horse. Can we eat it now?" She looked at Sayer hopefully. "He said it's for all of us."

"I...suppose so."

"It's in the pie safe. I can set the table," Beatrice said. She crawled to the foot of the bed to get out and walked a little unsteadily over to the cupboard where Sayer kept the everyday crockery. The Royal Doulton china, the gilt and rose-patterned dishes that had belonged to her mother and the only thing Sayer had left of her own family, was kept packed in two boxes of sawdust out of harm's way. She still remembered the rare Sunday dinners when her mother had brought it out, and she was proud to say that she'd taken good care of it in the intervening years. A few chips here and there, but not a single piece broken, not even when the set had been shipped to her after she'd married Thomas Henry. She was still surprised that her aunt had gone to the trouble to locate the boxes of china in her big attic and send them on.

"Sayer!" Beatrice said sharply, and Sayer looked at her, realizing then that she'd been inattentive long enough to scare both girls.

"I see the tin cups are clean—use those for the pudding," Sayer said quickly. She managed to sit on the side of the bed, then to stand without any accompanying dizziness. She made it to the washstand and looked at herself in the dim mirror.

"Oh," she said softly. How unlike herself she looked. Her aunt Cecelia had made certain that Sayer understood she was no great beauty, but even taking into account the poor quality of the mirror and the patch of her hair that had been cut out around the gash in her scalp, she thought she had never appeared as bedraggled as this.

There was water in the ewer, and she poured some in the basin and pulled the privacy curtain for modesty's sake. She stared at her reflection in the mirror again. Clearly she should have been worrying about whether Thomas Henry could recognize *her* instead of the other way around.

She bathed as best she could, taking her time lest she run out of energy before she'd finished. The process was tiring, but not overly so. She had a slight headache that was mostly tenderness around the place where she had fallen. She had no memory of that, either. She remembered Rorie offering her things to eat, and she must have actually eaten them. She would have been much frailer otherwise. And she seemed to be thinking clearly despite the fact that the girls had said she hadn't known them. She had no idea how well she'd functioned during all that time. She gave a quiet sigh. There was no way of knowing anything when she apparently couldn't rely on her own memory of recent events—what little there was of it. It seemed that she was destined to have gaps in her ability to recall important things in her life.

Eventually, she put on a worn work dress hanging on a nearby peg. It had always been too long, and now it seemed even more so. The hem dragged the floor, but she couldn't worry about that now. The dress was fresh and clean, and for that reason alone a joy to put on. Rorie must have washed it for her. Sayer would never be able to repay Rorie Conley for the kindness she'd shown her and the girls.

She realized suddenly that someone had cut and frayed new sweet-gum twigs and put them in the small pewter vase where she kept the ones to be used as toothbrushes. *The phantom Jeremiah?* she wondered. The cutter of wood and the maker of cracker pudding? The man she must have mistaken for Thomas Henry?

She used one of the sweet-gum twigs to brush her teeth with salt and she felt the better for it, then combed out her hair and braided it into a single braid that hung down her back. She could hear the girls whispering to each other as she worked.

I'm afraid, she thought suddenly, and for once she was certain she could name her fear.

Jeremiah.

Who was he and what was he doing here? Rorie and the girls seemed to trust him, and Sayer didn't understand that at all.

When she pushed the curtain back and stepped out, both girls were still sitting at the table, the place where she herself needed to be as quickly as possible. Despite her good start, her legs were feeling wobbly now, and she managed to make it to a chair before they buckled under her.

"Harder work than I thought," she said to them, trying not to seem so breathless. Still, everything considered, she was actually feeling nearly like herself again. She realized that while the girls had set the table with the tin cups and spoons and gotten the cracker pudding from the pie safe, they hadn't yet eaten.

"Is it that bad, or aren't you hungry?" she asked.

"We wanted to wait for you," Beatrice said. "It's been a long time since we all sat at the table together."

"Yes," Sayer said. "It has."

"But I want *all* of us to sit at the table. I want Thomas Henry to come home," Amity said. "We *need* him. Why isn't he coming?"

"I don't know, Amity," Sayer said. "He might have a long way to come. We'll just have to be patient."

"I don't want to be patient," Beatrice said. "I want my brother. Everything would be all right if he was here. Do you think he forgot us?" She abruptly looked away and wiped at her eyes.

"No," Sayer said. "He hasn't forgotten us. Thomas Henry would never do that." She reached to take each of the girls by the hand, and when their circle was complete, they bowed their heads. "Thank You, Lord, for Your mercy…for letting us sit down together again," she said. "And thank You for Rorie Conley's good help."

"And for the cracker pudding," Amity added. "And Jeremiah."

"And please, Lord, keep Thomas Henry safe. Amen," they said in unison, because it was their custom. They had long ago agreed that they should ask only for that because anything else would be selfish in light of so many other families who were waiting for someone they loved just as they were. Thomas Henry had to do his duty, and if he couldn't be at home with them, then the thing they wanted most was that he should stay safe from harm.

"Taste the cracker pudding," Amity urged. "You'll like it."

Sayer took a tentative spoonful of the gray soggy mass and put it into her cup. She took a bite of it, and then another. It was quite…edible, though "pudding" was perhaps an overly generous description.

"See?" Amity said, filling her cup and digging into hers. "I told you it was good. Jeremiah says you learn to make strange things out of strange things in the army."

"He doesn't know the half of it, does he?" Sayer said, thinking of her own efforts to make coffee out of roasted acorns and bacon fat according to a recipe in an Alabama newspaper someone had nailed up on the wall in the general store down at the crossroads. "I do like this, though—"

"You in the cabin!" someone suddenly yelled from the outside. "Hey, in there!"

Sayer knew the voice, and her heart began to pound with apprehension. "Both of you stay inside," she said quietly.

"But what if you don't—"

"Beatrice, do as I say!" Sayer said sharply. "I will talk to your Uncle Halbert. I don't know who he has with him and I mean for you and Amity to stay in here. You are not to come out unless I call you."

Sayer got up and stood by the chair for a moment to make sure she was steady enough to face down Halbert Garth. She could hear a horse blowing—several of them—but no one was talking. She realized that the musket was no longer on the pegs over the mantel. She had no other weapon—but Halbert and his friends didn't need to know that.

"Get me a tea towel, Beatrice," Sayer said, and Beatrice ran to the sideboard to find one. She brought it back immediately, and Sayer took the only big spoon she had out of the table drawer. She stuck the bowl end up her sleeve and covered the rest of the spoon and her hands with the towel, as if Halbert Garth and his company had interrupted her in some task—or perhaps not. She would let them worry about what she might have concealed.

"Open the door, Amity," Sayer said. "And close it right behind me."

"Well! Sayer!" Halbert said as soon as she stepped outside. "I heard you was…sick."

"Not I, Mr. Garth," she said, trying to keep her eyes on the two other men with him without seeming to do so. She didn't recognize them, but she recognized their lack of respect as they looked her over. "The girls had a bad fever. They're up and around now. What brings you all the way up here?"

"Had some reports of bushwhackers up this way," he said. "We come to see about it."

"All three of you?" Sayer asked because even she knew it would take more men than that to put a body of deserters and bushwhackers on the run.

Halbert Garth ignored her thinly veiled sarcasm. "And I'm wanting to know if you've had word from Thomas Henry."

"No," she said. "But I expect to."

"Do you, now?" He spat tobacco juice in a high arc. "Seems to me like he ain't coming back. I've made me some inquiries. Can't find anybody in the Highland Guards what knows why he ain't turned up yet."

"That doesn't mean he won't. I thank you for going to all that trouble for us, Mr. Garth. I'm sure Thomas Henry isn't the only one delayed. I was just telling the girls that we had to be patient. Don't you agree?"

One of the other men gave a snort of laughter, which he immediately choked off because of the look Halbert gave him.

"Now, you listen to me. You ain't going to last another winter up here," Halbert said. "You know that. I'm still willing to take over this property. I'll even give you money so's you can settle down in another place—of course the amount is going to come down every time I have to come back up here and make another offer. You take what I'm offering now and you'll get a good price. All we have to do is have Thomas Henry declared a casualty of the war and me the executor. That won't be no problem. I'm his next blood relative. You can go on back where you come from. Take them girls with you—"

"They're your kin, too, Mr. Garth. As for your taking over this land, I don't believe that's what your father wanted," Sayer said. "And I know it's not what Thomas Henry wants."

"Thomas Henry is dead, woman, and you know it!"

"If he is, I still won't be handing the Garth land over to you. Not ever. Thomas Henry learned a good deal from your father. I know he has a will, and I'm sure you're not in it. And there's nothing you can do about it."

"What makes you so sure he filed that will? Wills get misplaced all the time. This is *my* land! Mine! I'm the oldest son! If you think you can hold out against me—"

Halbert broke off so abruptly, both of the men with him turned in their saddles to look at him. But Halbert's attention was elsewhere. He was looking at the man on horseback who had just ridden around the side of the cabin and halted not far from the edge of the porch. Sayer could just see him out of the corner of her eye, but she didn't turn to look at him. She kept her eyes on Halbert, and from the look on his face she knew that he was as surprised as she was. The man didn't say anything; he simply waited, with complete confidence in his right to be there.

Halbert's two followers looked at each other and then to Halbert for guidance, but Halbert was focused now on Sayer.

"Who is this, then?" he asked, his eyes narrowed. "You done got yourself a step-husband?"

Sayer could feel her face flush at the insult, and she struggled to stay calm and not give Halbert the satisfaction of knowing how much the remark had offended her. He wanted her to be offended. She had no doubt about that.

The man rode forward then, straight toward Halbert,

letting his mount walk directly into Halbert's horse, causing it to shy away and Halbert to work hard to rein it in.

"Maybe you'd rather say something to me, Mr. Garth," the man said quietly.

Halbert smiled. "I'm just saying how it looks. That's all."

"Then maybe you ought to work on that. It's not good for a man's mind to abide in a place so low."

They stared at each other.

"Either of you men fight in the war?" the man suddenly asked without taking his eyes off Halbert.

Neither of them answered.

"That's what I thought. I believe you should know that I did, and the three of you are nothing to me. I won't even break a sweat—except for digging the hole to bury you in. You understand me, don't you, Mr. Garth?"

His voice remained quiet and calm, and his message was all the more unsettling for it. Halbert attempted a smile again, but didn't quite make it. Still, he wasn't ready to concede his ground.

"It ain't right—you being up here with her alone. She's my kin. I'm obliged to see she don't shame the Garth name—"

"Well, if that don't take the cake," Rorie said, hobbling up from the nearest stand of trees, stick in one hand, basket in the other. Sayer nearly smiled, not because of her timely arrival but because of the face on the walking stick. And the basket Rorie was carrying appeared to be heavy with what Sayer hoped were foraged hen eggs.

"Ain't nobody brought shame on the house of Garth

so far but you, Halbert," Rorie said, setting the basket on the ground. "I heard tell that's why *your* name ain't on the deed to this land. You might have forgot all about that, but I ain't—and nobody else around here has, either, I can guarantee you that. Since they ain't no bushwhackers here as far as I can tell, I reckon you better be looking someplace else."

"One of these days you are going to push me too far, Rorie Conley," Halbert said, jabbing his finger in Rorie's direction.

"I know, Halbert. And I can't hardly wait. Of course, it'll be a little one-sided, unless you bring your friends there with you. Sorry you all can't stay for supper. Might be too chancy for a man your age, what with the girls so soon past being sickly. As for Sayer being alone, she ain't. So don't you go fretting yourself about that. *I'm* here—as you can plainly see—and so is my cow and my mule. Been here the whole time, and that's the pure truth. What have you got to say about that, Halbert Garth?"

"You had better be staying out of my business!" Halbert said to her, clearly ignoring the man who had initially challenged him. He glared at her for a moment, then wheeled his horse and rode off the way he'd come, his two henchmen following close behind.

Sayer immediately sat down on the edge of the porch, her head bowed, breathless with the effort it had taken to stand up to Halbert.

"Are you going to faint?"

She looked up into the face of the man who had made the inquiry, the man whose name she could only guess, and shook her head.

"Say something, then."

"I...don't understand."

"Say something. Something sensible would be help-ful."

"Who *are* you?"

"Very good," he said. "That was as sensible as can be. But what were you going to do with this?" he asked, taking the spoon out of her hand.

"Make them wonder," she said.

"Well, you made me wonder, too. I thought you had Rorie's revolver."

"What would Rorie be doing with a revolver?"

"She brought it over in a basket in case she needed to shoot me with it."

"She didn't, I see," Sayer said.

"Well, not yet."

She kept glancing at him; it was too unsettling to look at him directly because he had apparently been roaming around in her life for some time now, only she couldn't remember any of it.

"I thought if you had her gun, you must know how to use it. I can tell you one thing for sure. I wouldn't have been nearly so bold if I'd had any idea you were planning to beat them to death with a spoon."

She laughed at the remark, suddenly and without warning, when the situation didn't warrant any kind of mirth whatsoever on her part. This man was a stranger and the confrontation with Halbert was nothing to laugh at.

But it had been so long since she'd laughed, and it just...got away from her.

The door behind her suddenly opened, and both girls

rushed out and grabbed on to her before she could protest their disobeying her and before she could grow any more uncomfortable about her own behavior.

"I'm all right. *We're* all right," she said to them, kissing each of them on the forehead.

"I'm thinking later I might like to fry us up some taters and onions and crack a couple eggs in it," Rorie said, stepping up on the porch. "Fighting with Halbert Garth always makes a body hungry. Come on, girls, I'm needing help now." She shooed Beatrice and Amity into the cabin, and Sayer didn't miss the look she gave the man who must be the mysterious Jeremiah as she went inside.

But Rorie popped right back out again in the cricket-in-a-hot-skillet way she had. "I reckon you ought to be introducing yourself," she said, looking at the man hard. "We both know why *I* can't do the introducing." And that said, she went inside again.

"She never beats around the bush, does she?" the man said.

"Never," Sayer agreed.

She waited, glancing at him from time to time, noting that he wasn't quite bearded or clean shaven. He had spent a lot of time outdoors. His face was tanned and his hair streaked by the sun.

He came closer, and he kept looking at her, staring into her eyes as if he were searching for something he needed but hadn't yet found. She could see that his hair color was similar to Thomas Henry's, but he had very blue eyes, which were nothing like Thomas Henry's at all. If she'd seen his eyes the day she had fallen down at the spring, she would have known.

But then perhaps she had and perhaps Rorie was right. She had seen only what she'd hoped.

"Yes," he said, still looking at her. "I think you're back."

Sayer looked away then, afraid suddenly of what might be the consequence of his having declared that her lucid self had returned.

"My name is Jeremiah Murphy, ma'am. I—"

"Is my husband dead?" she asked abruptly, clearly surprising him with the directness of the question. "Is that why you're here?" She supposed that he had thought she would need to hear whatever bad news he had brought piecemeal—and she had no doubt at all that the news was bad. But more delay was the last thing she needed. She had been waiting month after month, year after year, first for a letter or some word of him, then for Thomas Henry himself, and she couldn't bear to wait any longer.

"Is that why you've come here?" she asked again.

He hesitated, then looked into her eyes again. "Yes," he said with a bluntness of his own.

She made a small sound and looked away, clutching at her skirts in the great effort it took to stay upright and in control.

"I'm sorry, ma'am," he said again. "To bring you such bad news."

"It's what 'Jeremiahs' do," she said.

"Ma'am?" He was looking at her again, clearly ready to revise his earlier opinion regarding her having returned to her right mind.

"Jeremiah. In the Bible. He brought bad news to the people of Judah—about their coming destruction. I'm afraid you've done the same to me." Her voice quavered, regardless of her determination to sound as if she were not about to fall weeping onto the porch boards. She could feel how hard he was looking at her, but she didn't say anything else for fear it would sound even more amiss.

"I see this isn't the time for us to talk, ma'am—you aren't well enough yet. I shouldn't have said anything—"

"I have a right to know."

"Yes, ma'am. But I will still take my leave. When you're stronger—"

"I want to hear what you've come to say. I want to hear all of it, Mr. Murphy."

"Not now," he said, and he walked away, leaving her sitting with her spoon and a tea towel.

Big scared eyes.

Just like Thomas Henry had said. What he hadn't said was that, scared or not, she would stand strong. Maybe he didn't understand that about her. Maybe all he knew was that marrying him would both rescue her from the kin who didn't want her and put her directly into Halbert Garth's way.

Jack half expected Sayer to come after him, to hang on to him and try to keep him from leaving the way Elrissa had done. But she didn't, and he kept walking, his fists clenched in a vain effort to keep his hands from shaking. The war was over; and so should this affliction—whatever it was—be, too, he kept thinking. At least he didn't cry. He knew soldiers who were overtaken by fits of weeping when they least expected it.

He was grateful for that, just as he was grateful that he hadn't come undone when he was facing down Thomas Henry's uncle. Father Bartholomew would be pleased that he could find gratitude in such a bad situation. He wouldn't be pleased, however, at how ready Jack had been to kill a man, if not three of them.

When he was on the blind side of the cabin where no one inside could see him, he went down on one knee, his head bowed, ultimately sitting on the ground with his back against the log wall, his arms folded hard against his chest as he struggled to stop the shaking. Sweat poured from his body, and he forced himself to put his mind to remembering the poem again, the upstairs porch with his orphan family on a warm Saturday evening, the last remnant of the life and the people he would never know again.

God save thee, ancient Mariner…from the fiends
that plague thee…plague thee…thus…
God save thee….

When the shaking finally passed, he got up again, and after a moment to be sure that this latest episode was truly over, he walked a little unsteadily toward the mule he'd left tied to an anchor post in the split-rail fence.

He kept thinking about Halbert Garth's so-called visit. When he'd realized that there were three horsemen in the front yard, he'd held back and listened for a time to the exchange between Sayer and the man clearly in charge, standing carefully under the open-sided lean-to shelter at the back of the cabin, trying not to rattle the gourds hanging down from the eaves. His thinking was that he could stay where he was and no one would have to know about his presence at the Garth place, but in no time at all, he realized that he was in that class-room again and that he was going to have to intervene in some way. Thomas Henry Garth had done him no favor by dying in his arms.

Jack wanted to think that *he* had nothing to worry about in the aftermath of the encounter, that Halbert Garth couldn't possibly know who he was or why he had come to these mountains. At worst, he'd made him-self another enemy, one who could get in line behind Farrell Vance.

He untied the mule, led it to the barn and retied it to the hitching post. He had no trouble finding the horse harness. The only plow in evidence was standing out in the fallow field on the slope to his left, he supposed where somebody had left it. Thomas Henry? No, he decided. It didn't look weathered enough. But if he had left it, it was good that Jack intended to use it or at least move it someplace else. Sayer didn't need that kind of constant reminder that Thomas Henry was perma-nently gone.

"You as hardheaded as Rorie says?" he asked the mule as he worked to get the tack and harness on. "Well, I'm hardheaded, too. Anybody who knows me can tell you that. And before you decide to give me your ver-sion of a plowboy's nightmare, you'd best remember this. You won't be the first mule I ever took a bite out of. Men like Farrell Vance saw to that."

He got the mule harnessed with no more than the expected degree of resistance. Jack might have been a store clerk before the war, but he'd been one of the orphanage's intrepid boy farmers for a long time before he ever wore a dress shirt and suit to work. The orphanage had to rely mostly on what their child workforce could grow and raise for its daily bread. There was nothing in the long process from seeding to harvest or egg to chicken he hadn't done. He'd taken his turn in the orphanage kitchen, as well. And the laundry, both the washing and the ironing. And the infirmary as a patient and as a bedside nurse. He suddenly smiled. With the skills he had acquired as an orphan combined with the things he had learned during four years of war, he truly must be the jack-of-all-trades people talked about. He was even a master of a few of them. All in all, it was reassuring to know that, given his diverse training, he should never starve.

"What are you looking at?" he said to the mule, because it was seriously considering where to bite him.

He gathered up the reins. "Yaaa!" he said as masterfully as he knew how, sending the mule forward toward the field he hoped to improve.

Getting a mule into harness was one thing. Getting it attached to a plow and of a mind to pull it over hard ground was an entirely different matter. But it gave Jack something real to concentrate on. The mule did understand the concept of "gee" and "haw," and in time, a truce of sorts was established in their battle of wills. The mule would at least plow a row or two before they had to discuss the merits of doing such a thing again. It occurred to him that his recent army experience could have been worse—he could have been drafted to be a mule skinner. He had been taught to never hate one of

God's creatures—Father Bartholomew had read them *Moby Dick* on the upstairs porch to make his point. But Jeremiah decided somewhere after the third or fourth row that if he ever did, he'd start with a mule—this one.

But even as hard as the animal was to manage, Jack's mind still wandered to the place he would just as soon it not go.

Sayer Garth.

Thomas Henry had said she was pretty. She was definitely what he would call pretty, too, not polished up and expensively arranged and unapproachable like Elrissa, but pretty in her own…soft…way. There was something about her. The eyes—he'd been forewarned about her eyes. Still, she didn't seem fragile, regardless of having suffered a blow to the head or being half-starved, likely for years. She didn't seem delicate at all—except for her petite size—but he still had felt an unwelcome inclination to take care of yet another orphan—of *her*. He wasn't going to take the job on, of course. Strictly speaking, he hadn't actually made any promises to her husband. If there was a promise at all, it was one made by proxy on behalf of someone named Graham.

Had Thomas Henry said that Graham was dead? Jack couldn't remember. It didn't matter. A false promise he had agreed to in order to give peace to a dying man couldn't be binding. Thomas Henry's mind had been somewhere else entirely at that point, and he had completely lost his awareness of the enemy soldier who had given him a drink of water from his canteen.

Jack was firm in his conviction that he would stick to the plan he'd devised on the road to Knoxville and then refined on the hard trek toward Jefferson. He would give

Sayer her husband's letters and his personal belongings with all due courtesy, as if he weren't her husband's sworn enemy, and hers as well if the truth be told. And he wouldn't behave as if he were on the run and he had a motive for showing up in this high, lonesome place other than to give her some peace of mind. He would tell her the things her husband wanted her to know and not tell her the things he didn't. Then he would go on his merry way and try hard to attend to his own decidedly significant troubles, leaving one dead Rebel soldier to go to his reward with a satisfied mind.

He hoped.

And what of his widow?

He could ask and answer that question in the span of one breath. Sayer Garth, big sad eyes or not, was *not* his concern. But another question immediately arose. What, then, was he doing out here fighting with a plow and a hardheaded mule?

He looked around because someone had called his name—Rorie, standing at the edge of the field.

"Come and eat something," she called. "We got enough for you."

He waved her away and walked on, sending the mule to the far end of the row. Rorie was still waiting when he came back around.

"I *said* come and eat with us," she said when he was close enough.

"You know that's not a good idea."

"Ain't *my* idea. It's hers. She wants you to."

"She must still be addled, then. I just told her her husband is dead."

"I don't reckon you told her anything she didn't

already know in her heart. That Thomas Henry was as faithful to her as the day is long. He wouldn't be silent all these weeks without a bad reason. So come and eat."

A bad reason, Jack thought. *A very apt way of putting it.*

"No," he said.

"You ain't got the shaking now," she said, and he looked at her sharply. "I told you before. You ain't the first no-name soldier to turn up in these mountains." She gave a small shrug. "Some of them might even have been kin. And some of them might have been underfoot long enough to where a body gets so they can just look at one of them and tell when one of them shaking spells is coming on—or did you think you was the only one to have that kind of aggravation? Besides which, I ain't hearing you deny it."

"There are a lot of things you're not hearing," he said pointedly, and she laughed her cackling laugh and punched his arm.

"I reckon they is, Jeremiah. I reckon they is. It's getting too dark to plow. Unhook that ornery creature and come to the table. I left you a bucket of water on the porch so you can wash the dirt and sweat off you. If we got to suffer your company, you might as well smell better than you do now."

"I told you I'm not coming," he said, certain that he meant it. "She's not well enough," he added around the mule's decision to challenge his authority again.

"Maybe not. Maybe her heart is broke all to pieces, but she went and put the good china on the table anyway. The china what come from her own mama's house—the mama what died when she was just a little girl and left her at the mercy of that hateful aunt of hers. Most treasured thing she owns and here she is, wanting to honor you with it. You going to walk yourself away from a kindness like that? And then there's them two little girls. Somehow *they* got the idea you hung the moon."

She was looking at him in that forceful way she had, but it wasn't going to do her any good.

"Funny thing about that there china," Rorie said after a moment. "Sayer had two boxes of it. Ain't got but one now. She reckons somebody done took one of them. Ain't but one time that I know of when she wasn't here—well, she was *here,* but she didn't know nothing. None of them did. Them girls was too sick, and she was knocked out cold down yonder at the spring. You want to know what I reckon?"

"No," he said, and for once she seemed to accept something he said as fact. She turned and began walking back toward the cabin. He watched her go, still trying to hang on to the rambunctious mule. He knew exactly what she "reckoned," and she knew he did. There was a good chance Sayer Garth hadn't slipped and hit her head after all.

"You're not always going to win!" he called after her.

"I know, Jeremiah," she called back, chuckling to herself. "I just do my best. Leave the rest to the Good Lord."

But she stopped then and turned around to look at him. "She needs to do this, Jeremiah. She ain't ready to face the bitterness of what you told her yet, that's all. She knows she's got to be strong for them girls, and she needs a little time and something to keep her hands busy until she can hold up under it. You ain't never been in a situation like that, I reckon."

Jack expected more conversation, but that apparently was the last of it. She walked away for good this time.

"What are you looking at?" he said to the mule.

He decided, after both the mule and his own mount had been watered and hobbled to graze, that the cooking aromas coming from the cabin were what made him change his mind. He knew Sayer Garth had little in the way of provisions, but there had apparently been enough to make bread. He could smell it baking, and it had been a long time since he'd had hot bread. He more or less convinced himself that that was reason enough to accept the invitation.

The mule appeared to be as content as a mule would ever allow its cantankerous self to be, and there was nothing left for him to do—except cede the field. He went into the barn and got his only other shirt out of his saddlebag. It was clean, but that was the best that could be said of it. It was clear to him now that he was going to follow Rorie's most recent commands even beyond the letter. He was going to wash up and put the shirt on, and then he was going to go see for himself why this woman, distraught or not, wanted him at her table. He'd seen her face when he'd told her Thomas Henry was dead. He might as well have stuck a dagger in her heart—and she was still getting out the good china and inviting him to dinner. He had never understood Southern women, not in all his four years of war and breaking into their houses and barns and either stealing or burning whatever he could find, if not the house and barn right along with it. And it didn't look as though he was ever going to. Things—people—women—who wouldn't bend were supposed to break, but so far he hadn't seen any evidence of it. He supposed that Sayer Garth and Elrissa Barden had that in common, despite their political differences.

The bucket of water was still on the porch where Rorie had left it, along with a thin square of flannel and a small sliver of brown soap. He made good use of all of them, pouring the last of the water over his head. He didn't have a comb or a straight razor. He just had to do the best he could. The smell was gone; he did know that.

He scraped the mud off his boots, took a deep breath and stepped up to the door. It opened before he could knock on it.

"Jeremiah!" the girls said in unison. They grabbed him by the hand and pulled him inside. Sayer was standing in front of the hearth, and he studied her closely for some sign that he should go back out again.

"Please, Mr. Murphy," she said, her voice quiet and controlled. "Come sit down. Everything's ready."

He hesitated, watching as she placed a serving bowl just so on the table, then he glanced at Rorie to gauge her reaction to Sayer's now knowing his last name. He would also have liked a little guidance from her regarding the situation in general, but for once in their short acquaintance, she had no helpful gestures and nothing to say.

The table was indeed set with some of the finest china he'd ever seen. Royal Doulton, he thought, the kind he'd special ordered from New York for some of Lexington's wealthiest families. He had even personally delivered and unpacked the china himself. They had thought it was a service Mr. Barden extended only to his most important customers, but it had actually been Jack's idea—a way to keep them from claiming that some piece had been broken in transit, thereby acquiring extras for which they would not have to pay. He had learned early on that such ruses were an all-too-common practice among the newly rich who had had to claw their way to the top rung, and one that Mr. Barden never seemed to suspect. But, thanks to Jack, once they had signed the delivery slip, the store was protected from that kind of pilfering.

"We didn't think you were coming," Amity said, smiling up at him.

"I said you would," Beatrice told him. "Because you've been plowing. People get hungry when they plow."

"Do they?" Amity asked him. "I've never plowed. Beatrice hasn't, either, so I don't know how she thinks *she* knows."

"Yes, they do get hungry," Jack said. "Thirsty, too."

"See?" Beatrice told her with considerable satisfaction. "We want you to sit here, Jeremiah."

He had no choice but to sit down in the chair both of them were pulling him toward, the one they had apparently already decided should be located at the end of the table and between the two of them.

Sayer sat down at the other end of the table with Rorie to her left. It occurred to Jack suddenly that the girls must have put him in Thomas Henry's place. He looked at Sayer, ready to get up again.

"It's all right," she said, apparently realizing his discomfort.

He very nearly complimented the look of the table, then thought better of it as he remembered she was missing half of the china set he was seeing. It was enough that he was sitting in her husband's chair. She didn't need to be reminded of yet another loss.

"We hold hands when we say grace," Amity said, retaking his left hand firmly in hers. Beatrice took his other hand.

"Will you say grace for us, Mr. Murphy?" Sayer asked, looking at him directly for the first time since he'd arrived.

"Yes, ma'am," he said. Prayers at mealtimes had been yet another of his many duties at the orphanage. He had never minded saying grace, and it occurred to him as he bowed his head and repeated the familiar words, how long it had been since he'd done this.

"Amen," he concluded, and the others joined in.

"We have apple water to drink, Mr. Murphy," Sayer said. "Will you have some?"

"Yes," he said, accepting the pitcher Beatrice passed to him. He had no idea what apple water was or how much he should pour into his glass. He didn't want to take what little food he knew they had. There was a platter of flat baked bread, which was neither biscuit nor loaf, and some honey and a very large main dish of fried potatoes, onions and eggs. He suddenly smiled. A bowlful of his cracker pudding had also been added to the table. What he wouldn't give if Ike and the rest of them could see it served in such a fine piece of chinaware.

He didn't know that he'd ever eaten with an audience before, but it seemed that he was doing so now. Four pairs of female eyes seemed to be trained on him—

until he realized that they were waiting for his opinion of the food.

"This is the best I've had to eat in a long time," he said, looking at Sayer. She looked down at her plate, her dark eyelashes standing out starkly against her pale skin. He didn't think he'd said the wrong thing, but he still felt as if he had. There was nothing to do but keep eating.

Eventually, the novelty of his presence waned, and he was able to enjoy the food with less attention.

"Where are you from, Mr. Murphy?" Sayer asked, finally looking up at him again.

"Kentucky," he said without thinking. It was no wonder Father Bartholomew always caught him when he was at the orphanage. The first order of his mind didn't seem to run to escape plans, hiding and ruses, no matter how dire the situation. Without Ike's and Father Bartholomew's help, he likely would have never gotten out of Lexington. And yet, here he sat at this sad woman's table, perpetrating the biggest ruse of all.

I'm not Thomas Henry's friend. Or yours, he thought, but still he kept looking into her sad eyes whenever she would let him. He had no difficulty now understanding why Thomas Henry had been so beguiled.

Fortunately for him, she didn't seem to think it amiss that a man from Kentucky would have had an association with her Confederate Army husband.

"I had heard that many Kentucky men joined Southern regiments," she said. "Have you been home yet?"

"I have, ma'am."

"Good. I wouldn't want to think that we…kept you from…from your…"

She trailed away. She had come too close to the real reason for his being here. Or what he'd led her to think was the real reason.

"Do you like the table, Jeremiah?" Amity asked, tugging at his shirtsleeve. "We set it just for you. It's got my mama's tablecloth—"

"My mama's, too," Beatrice interrupted.

"—and Sayer's mama's dishes and glasses," Amity continued, undaunted. "Do you like the plates?"

"I do," he said, realizing that he now had the opportunity to steer the conversation elsewhere. Unfortunately it was to another painful place. "I like the tablecloth and the dishes," he blundered on. "I believe those are Royal Doulton, are they not?"

Sayer looked at him in surprise. "How is it you know chinaware, Mr. Murphy?"

"I used to clerk in a dry goods store. Before the war."

"Reckon he learned to plow there, too?" Rorie put in, making them both smile.

"Ah, no. That I learned elsewhere."

"When you used to be an orphan," Amity said firmly. He had forgotten that he'd mentioned that phase of his life to her.

"I still am an orphan, Amity," he said.

"Everybody's an orphan," she said with a sigh.

"Not *everybody,* silly," Beatrice said.

"Everybody *here,*" Amity said with the quiet confidence of someone who knew when she was right.

"That's a fact, young-un," Rorie said. "Everybody here."

"Jeremiah, do you care if there is a child at the table?"

Beatrice asked, looking at Amity and apparently meaning to exclude herself from that particular age group.

"Only if they start throwing things," he said.

"Do you mind if we—the child—is heard and not just seen?"

"Not as long as she—the child—doesn't interrupt her elders," he said, hoping he wasn't running afoul of any domestic rules. "Unless the house is on fire, of course. I would take it as a great kindness if you were to let me know in plenty of time to get out," he added, making her giggle. He thought it best not to mention how long it had taken him to learn *his* table manners when he was at the orphanage.

He took a sip of the apple water. It tasted like... apples. "This is truly a very fine meal," he said when Sayer looked in his direction. "I thank you for inviting me."

"You're welcome, Mr. Murphy. May I ask you... what...the orphanage was like? When I was a child, after my parents died, I was very afraid of the idea of being sent to one," she added quickly, as if he might think she had overstepped social decorum and was prying into something he would prefer to keep private.

Jack looked at her for a moment before he answered, wondering who had used that fear to terrorize her. He had no doubt that someone had. "It was...strict. There were rules to follow—the days were very organized. Which was what most of us needed—order and discipline."

"Army orders weren't nothing new to you, then," Rorie said around a mouthful of bread.

"No. Just the guns," Jack said.

"Were you happy there, Mr. Murphy?" Sayer asked.

"He weren't happy in the army," Rorie said. "I can tell you that."

"That's the truth," he said agreeably. "It was lonesome at the orphanage for a while. All orphans are lonesome at first."

"That's why you made 'babies in a cradle' out of handkerchiefs for the little girls," Amity put in.

"Yes," he said.

"What did you give the boys?" she inquired with obvious interest.

"A string ball—or the beginning of one. String was easy to come by and making the ball bigger gave them something to do so they wouldn't dwell on their new situation."

Amity had no more questions, possibly due to the kick Beatrice gave her under the table, and he thought the topic of orphan life exhausted until he glanced at Sayer. She was clearly waiting for him to continue.

"It was better there later," he said. "After you got to know everyone and you learned what was expected of you. There are a lot of things to get used to. You even had to get used to having three meals a day and most definitely had to get used to helping to cook it and clean up afterward."

"You had to *cook?*" Beatrice asked incredulously.

"Miss Beatrice, have you not sampled my very fine cracker pudding?" he teased, and she grinned.

"The hardest part about orphan life was having people taking an interest in your welfare whether you wanted them to or not. No more roaming around doing as you pleased.

"I think we must have been like a…different kind of family—but it was still a family. We took care of each other and we took care of the institution. Everybody had chores. Everybody learned how to survive in the world—literally and, it was hoped, spiritually. I'm grateful for the time I spent there. I believe I'm a better man for it." He smiled slightly. "At least some of the time."

"Perhaps I worried for nothing," Sayer said quietly.

"I believe it would depend on the orphanage, Mrs. Garth. There are likely some better than Sa—than where I was, and I'm certain there are some much worse."

Sayer didn't say anything more and he thought he had done little to reassure her about orphan life. She sat either nibbling at her food or pushing it around on her plate. He glanced at Rorie, who seemed to need to say something at this point, but for some reason known only to her, she didn't say it. Rorie Conley *not* saying whatever she had in mind to say was not what he would call heartening.

But the meal continued pleasantly enough, despite all the adults trying not to say anything that might lead them to acknowledge the deep emotional pain that was like another living being in the small confines of the cabin. He didn't want to think about the girls being told that their brother had been killed. He had seen enough sorrowful children in his life. It seemed to him that Rorie must indeed be correct in thinking that Sayer Garth needed to postpone the inevitable until she could bear their grief as well as her own.

The meal was ending, and the children were clearly

fading rapidly. And Sayer—he didn't know what was happening with Sayer. She was obviously struggling now to concentrate on the conversation around her and on her duties as hostess, and whether she was about to be overcome by some last remnant of her head injury or by her profound sorrow—or both, he couldn't say.

He did the only thing he knew to do. He stood up. "I'll go now and put the animals up for the night."

"Does that include you, Jeremiah?" Rorie asked with a grin.

"I expect it does. Thank you again for the fine meal, Mrs. Garth. Mrs. Conley."

Rorie raised both her eyebrows at the "Mrs. Conley," the way most women would have if he'd called them by their given name rather than the other way around.

"I reckon you'll be sleeping somewhere close by tonight. Out yonder on the porch maybe," Rorie said, looking at him hard.

He hadn't considered sleeping at all, but he thought to say so would only underline the possibility of Halbert Garth's return. He had no doubt that there was a chance Garth—or the men he'd hired—might come back, particularly if they were the ones who had stolen the other box of china, and he intended to be ready.

Rorie was still looking at him. Her gaze pointedly shifted to the well-set table, then back to him. He knew perfectly well what she was trying to tell him, but it was clear from her expression that she thought he'd turned simple-headed again and had completely missed the detail she was willing him to grasp.

"Yes," he said finally, but his focus was on Sayer. She was very pale.

"Mrs. Garth, are you—?" He was about to ask if she was all right, but another hard look from Rorie made him think better of it.

He said good-night to both sleepy girls instead and stepped outside, instantly alert for any sound that might indicate that someone was about. But he only heard the usual night sounds—crickets and a whip-poor-will's song that couldn't help but remind him of the night Thomas Henry had died. Incredibly, being here with Sayer and his sisters was making him feel as if he'd actually known the man. It was…unsettling.

After a moment, he walked out to remove the hobbles from the mule and the horse and put them in their stalls. Nothing seemed amiss outside the barn, but on the inside he nearly fell over something blocking his way. An empty wooden box turned on its side with a pile of sawdust scattered on the ground around it.

Chapter Five

When thou liest down, thou shalt not be afraid…

But Sayer was afraid. She lay in the dark with her eyes open, the news of Thomas Henry's death weighing her down until she thought she might suffocate under it. She was exhausted from trying to be quiet and not disturb the others. She could hear the girls' steady breathing and Rorie's fitful little snores. They were all sound asleep, and she couldn't stand it any longer.

She sat up and quietly put her feet on the floor, resisting the urge to get up and run. She had to get out. She needed air and solitude, regardless of the hour, but she forced herself to find her dress and brogans and put them on. She was well aware that if Rorie and the girls awoke, it was better to look sleepless, rather than mad with grief.

She didn't go to the front door, because Jeremiah might be on the porch and might take exception to her leaving the cabin at this hour. She went to the other door instead, despite the struggle it would take to open it. It led to the open-sided lean-to out back, a roof supported by cedar posts that offered shade and some shelter from the elements for work best done outdoors. The bar had always been hard to shift. It was yet another chore Thomas Henry would have seen to when he got home.

She had to work a long time before the bar finally gave, and she stood perfectly still for a moment to make sure she hadn't wakened anyone. Then she cracked the door open and slipped outside.

The air was fresh and cool; a strong breeze blew down from the higher ridges. She had no idea what time it might be. She thought that it must be close to dawn because she wasn't in pitch-black darkness. She could just make out the shapes of things around her.

But it didn't matter to her what the hour might be. She walked a few yards away from the cabin and looked up at the night sky. There was no moon; she could see a few stars. And how quiet it was around her, save a distant rumble of thunder from time to time.

"Where are you?" she whispered, looking up at the sky again, not knowing if she meant Thomas Henry or God Himself. The truth was that she felt abandoned by them both. "Where are you? Where *are* you!"

She began to walk, to stumble aimlessly around the property that Halbert Garth wanted so desperately. What else would he do to take it? Kill her? And the girls? She didn't know enough about property law. She had no idea whether Thomas Henry's will would protect them from his uncle or not. All she knew for certain was that there was no comfort here. None. There was no place she could go to feel closer to him. It was true that Thomas Henry had lived here, but they had never lived here together. She had no memories of a life with him. It would be as if he—they—as a married couple—had never existed. She had far more memories of Jeremiah Murphy in this place than she did of Thomas Henry.

She wandered too close to the barn, and Jeremiah's mount gave a soft rumble and began to blow and stamp. She went inside, feeling her way along until she reached the horse.

"It's too early to feed you," she whispered, gently stroking its soft nose. It leaned forward to breathe in her scent. "Rorie says you were a soldier, too."

She was tired suddenly. Too tired to walk around. Too tired to commiserate with a horse. She went back outside, ultimately heading toward the big shade tree where she had sat many long hours diligently pushing a threaded needle through green bean pods and sweet apple slices so they could be hung up along the eaves in the loft space to dry. There was a half-log bench to sit down on, but she sat in the girls' rope swing instead, swinging back and forth, slowly at first, and then higher and higher the way she had as a child, feeling the wind on her face. And some part of her stood aside, watching.

Chastising.

Your husband is dead and you're swinging.

She abruptly stopped the swing. She wasn't a child anymore. She was a widow. A widow who had never been a wife.

"I've been waiting for you," she whispered. "The way you used to wait for me. Where are you?"

The anger had gone out of her, and she gave a wavering sigh.

Every sigh is a prayer.

Who had told her that? Her aunt? Rorie? No. It was Thomas Henry's mother. How strong her faith had been, and how accepting she was of whatever happened—her illness, her son going into harm's way, her widowhood. Sayer wished Mrs. Garth was still here. Her prayers were always so meaningful and eloquent, the kind God listened to. Mrs. Garth—the true Mrs. Garth— had never prayed in snippets and fragments and sighs the way Sayer did.

Sayer realized suddenly that she wasn't alone.

"It's me," Jeremiah said, before she could become alarmed. She had forgotten that he might be in the barn—or had he been sleeping on the porch as Rorie had suggested?

She didn't say anything, expecting that once he had identified himself, he would walk away from her as he had earlier. But he sat down on the bench under the tree instead. She could barely make out his features in the semidarkness.

"Don't worry," he said. "I'm not going to ask you if you're all right."

She didn't ask him to explain what he meant, but he continued as if she had.

"I'm afraid Rorie will hear me and turn me wrong side out."

"Very wise, then," she said. "Though I don't know why she would object."

"I believe she thinks it's not a sensible question for anyone to be asking—me, in particular. And she's right. A question like that doesn't do anybody any good. I expect the answer is always…unreliable, especially among strangers."

Sayer thought about this for a moment. "People who don't have things well in hand don't like to be asked how they are, strangers or not," she concluded.

"No, they don't," he agreed. "At least not in my experience."

She wondered on what occasions he might not have had things well in hand, but she didn't ask for fear that one of them might involve the circumstances surrounding Thomas Henry's death.

"I...don't know what we would have done without Rorie," she said, not because she wanted to encourage the conversation to continue, but because it was a truth that needed to be stated.

"She's very fond of all of you."

"She...mentioned that she forced you to bring her here."

"It was an interesting trip," he said, and Sayer felt the smile more than saw it. She thought that he didn't smile often, though she couldn't have said why she had come to that conclusion. She supposed it was because of the reason for his being here. Bringing bad news to someone, even a stranger, didn't encourage smiling.

He didn't say anything more. He just sat there, looking at her, she thought, and perhaps waiting. It occurred to her that he might finally be willing to tell her about Thomas Henry.

"Where did he die?" she asked quietly, surprised by how calm her voice sounded. He had been right after all. She hadn't been ready to talk about Thomas Henry before.

He took his time in answering, but she didn't sense any reluctance on his part. It was more that he was trying to get things straight in his mind before he said anything.

"Virginia," he said when he was ready. "We weren't close to any towns—it was wilderness mostly and some unplowed farmland. Fields that should have already been planted but weren't—because of us. Armies either trample a crop into the ground or steal it. There were no landmarks so I don't really know where it was. It was one of those times when we just…"

"Just what?" she prompted when he didn't continue.

She could hear him take a breath, and she realized suddenly that telling her about Thomas Henry was going to be hard for him, that the incident was perhaps more to him than just an accumulation of facts he was obliged to recount.

The wind was picking up; the storm was coming closer. She could hear the thunder rumbling across the ridges and down the mountainsides, smell the rain in the air.

"Just run into each other," he said. "There's no planned military strategy or anything like that. It starts out small. Our skirmishers find their skirmishers or vice versa. Sometimes it doesn't amount to much— just bloodying each other's noses and moving on. And then sometimes…it's a battle royal. Either way, though, when a minié ball finds you, it is just as deadly…" His voice trailed away.

"He was shot?" she asked after a moment.

"Yes."

"Where?"

"I'm…not sure. It was dark when I found him."

"Like it is now?" she asked, urgently needing to know what must seem to him a meaningless detail.

"After sundown. Not just before dawn."

"Could you not have...done something?"

"No."

"How can you be sure—if you didn't know where he was wounded?"

"I'm sure," he said, his voice flat and emotionless.

After a moment she found that she believed him despite his unwillingness to convince her.

"When did it happen?" she asked next.

"A day or two af—" He abruptly stopped.

"When?" she asked again because she wanted— needed—him to answer the question.

"It was in April," he said.

"Oh," she said softly. "Oh..."

April. The war ended in April.

"Don't do that," he said. "It won't do you any good to start grabbing on to the 'if onlys.' Every soldier dead on the battlefield has got a big pile of those. It's done. You can't change what happened—are you listening to me?"

"Yes. Yes, I'm listening," she said, but she wasn't, not really. She was thinking how different things might have been *if only* the skirmishers had "just happened upon each other" later, after Lee had surrendered.

She looked at him. "He's dead. Thomas Henry has been dead all this time. How could I not—?" She didn't finish the thought. It was painful to think that he had died months ago and she hadn't sensed it, hadn't felt his absence in the world, *her* world, and she should have. He was everything to her. He had saved her from living with people who didn't want her. He had given her the promise of a new life, of somewhere to belong and a family of her own.

"Did he suffer?" she asked abruptly.

"No," he said.

The answer came too quickly.

"That's not the truth, I think. One cannot be mortally shot and not be in pain."

"Yes, Mrs. Garth, they can," he said. "Sometimes emotions are running so high it's a long time before a wounded man feels it."

"Emotions from the battle, you mean?"

"Yes. The battle. Danger…concern for comrades."

"Do they ever speak of their families?"

"That comes…later."

"When they know they are dying."

"When they are afraid."

"Did Thomas Henry know he was…?"

"He did. He wanted me to tell you that and that he wasn't afraid to die. He said he knew how hard you had prayed for him—"

"It didn't help, though, did it?"

"It did where it mattered. He said he knew you'd prayed for him to be ready if he fell, and he was. It was…important to him, I think, for you to know that."

"Did you know him a long time?" she asked, because it suddenly mattered to her whether or not Thomas Henry had died with a close comrade at his side.

"No. It was more that I was…there."

"Not friends, then."

"There is always a bond between soldiers, ma'am. The strength of it isn't measured by time."

Tears were running down her cheeks now; she sat

with her head bowed, as if she thought he could see them in the darkness.

"He wanted me to tell you what happened to him. He was afraid you wouldn't know otherwise. Information gets lost in the confusion of battle. Men get lost from their companies. It can take a long time to get it straightened out, if ever.

"He said to tell you not to grieve and to tell Beatrice and Amity they weren't to cry. He didn't want that, the three of you being sad. The one thing, the only thing, I think he truly regretted was not being able to see you again in this life."

"He said that?"

"Yes."

"Was he buried there? Where he fell?"

"Yes."

"Could you find the place again?"

"No," he said.

No.

A sob escaped her lips, but he didn't try to intervene. He made no attempt to soothe her. He offered no words of comfort. He simply let her weep.

"What—else?" she managed to ask.

"He wanted me to give you some letters. He said he hadn't been able to mail them. I brought his personal belongings, as well. There's not much, but I have them in my haversack—we need to get out from under this tree," he said abruptly.

He gave her no chance to object. He pulled her to her feet and hurried her to the shelter of the lean-to just as a loud crack of thunder rumbled across the sky overhead and the rain began to fall. She stood next to him out of the downpour, not looking at him as the wind whipped her hair about her face. She kept wiping at the tears with the back of her hand.

"You need to go inside," he said, and she shook her head.

"I don't want to wake them—Beatrice and Amity. I can't…" she said. She didn't try to elaborate on whatever she had intended to say. She took a deep breath and asked the one question on which her acceptance of all he had told her hinged.

"Who buried him?"

"I did," he said, and with that remark he took away her last hope that it still might have been some kind of mistake.

She needed to sit down suddenly, and she moved to a small stool she had used for milking when they still had a cow. She sat down on it, her arms folded tightly over her breasts as if there was no one to comfort her but herself.

"I'll go now," he said. "Leave you to your private thoughts."

She nearly asked him to stay. She didn't want to be alone, and that was the only explanation she had for even thinking such an inappropriate thing. She knew that except for handing over the letters and Thomas Henry's personal belongings, he had accomplished the charge that had been given him. She knew that he was free now to go on his way and she shouldn't want to cling to him. He was a stranger—but he was as close to Thomas Henry as she could ever be again.

He hesitated, then left the lean-to. She could hear his splashing retreat to the barn. She didn't have to struggle to stay ahead of the tears now. The grief she felt, despite Thomas Henry's wishes, was overwhelming. Incredibly she felt a sudden flash of anger, as well. How could he not know that his death would be devastating to her? To all of them? Grief was the only thing she had left, and it was *hers* to endure as best she could. He had gone off to war and died for a cause she didn't begin to understand. He had no right to try to deny her the need to mourn him. How else could she learn to endure the terrible loss she felt if she didn't cry?

She leaned forward, her hands covering her face, and finally let go, rocking back and forth as the storm raged around her. She didn't know how long she cried. It was nearly sunup and no longer raining when she finally lifted her head and wiped her face on the sleeve of her dress. She felt too unsteady to stand, but stood anyway.

Remarkably, Jeremiah was nearby, sitting on an upside-down barrel, his back to her, she supposed because he didn't want to intrude. She looked at him, at the resigned set of his shoulders and the back of his hair. Rorie had told her that his hands sometimes trembled, the way her own nephew's had after Gettysburg.

"What terrible things you must have seen," she said, not realizing until he abruptly turned toward her that she'd spoken out loud. He looked so stricken for a moment that she very nearly reached out to him.

"It's what war is, ma'am."

She nodded and took a deep breath. It was time now to do the most difficult thing she had ever done.

I need Your help…please…

The back door opened suddenly, and Rorie stepped outside. Sayer didn't avert her face. There was no hiding the fact that she'd been crying for what must have been hours from anyone as astute as Rorie Conley.

"I reckon you better come on in now," Rorie said to her.

"Yes. Are the girls awake?" she asked.

"Awake and eating that there cracker pudding they're so fond of," Rorie said. "You best splash a little water on your face before you come in. Crying ain't becoming to no woman no matter what causes it."

Rorie went back inside, and Sayer scooped water from the rain barrel at the corner of the cabin and splashed it on her face. She didn't know that it helped her appearance, but she felt somewhat better afterward. She looked up to find Jeremiah watching her.

"If you'll wait, I'll get the letters," he said.

She nodded and stood under the lean-to until he returned with what was left of her life with Thomas Henry Garth. He placed the objects into her hands—the tobacco pouch and clay pipe bowl that had belonged to Mr. Garth Senior; the letters she had written with the cedar pencil, all tied up with the ribbon Thomas Henry had taken from her hair on their wedding day; his letters that had never been mailed; and what she recognized was her mother's Bible. She clutched everything hard against her chest. She could feel the tears sliding down her face again, and she bowed her head, struggling hard for control.

"We—thank you—Mr. Murphy," she said, looking up at him again. "Thomas Henry—and I."

Chapter Six

"I reckon people will be coming up here today," Rorie said.

"Why? No one knows about Thomas Henry yet," Jack said.

"It ain't Thomas Henry they'll be interested in. It's who's staying up here with Sayer while he's gone. *That's* what they'll be wanting to know about. It's for sure Halbert's got the word spread around by now. Probably made some big announcement at the crossroads general store and left out the part about me being here. I reckon we all better get ready for it, and by that I mean *you* ought not be underfoot when they get here."

He gave her a look, but he didn't say anything.

"They'll be wanting your whole life story," she said by way of explanation. "And I've done had the feeling for some time now, you ain't all that inclined to tell it. I can tell you right now, people around here ain't a bit shy about asking whatever they want to know."

"Yes, I know all about that," he said pointedly.

"Well, yes, I reckon you do, Jeremiah. But I was thinking you could go on over and see about my place today, if you was of a mind. Unless you're moving on now that you've done told Sayer about her man."

"I thought I'd stay on and finish plowing under that cornfield stubble and do the haying," he said. "And there's some other work that ought to be done."

"Noticed that, did you?"

"Now, don't start up with me. I'm not simple-headed *all* the time," he assured her.

Rorie continued talking, giving him the list of things she wanted him to bring back from her place and where to find them. Jack was only half listening.

"What exactly is a step-husband?" he asked abruptly when Rorie handed him an empty sack to take with him.

"Why in this world are you asking me that?"

"Because Halbert all but called me one. I may not know what the precise meaning is, but I know an insult when I hear it."

"How come you don't know what that is?"

"Because I don't. I'm not from around here. How would I know?"

"I reckon because you are one—ain't that why you're on the run?"

"I'm not—" He stopped, remembering her aversion to lies just when he was about to tell a rather large and complicated one. He'd done enough lying—especially if Father Bartholomew was right and omissions were the same thing as untruths.

"So what is it?" he persisted.

"It's when the lawful husband leaves and another man comes to the house as soon as he sees he's gone. Husband steps out. Somebody else steps in. He's the—"

"Step-husband," Jack finished for her. All in all, it

was a more precise term than he would have thought. "It's a good thing for Halbert I didn't understand."

"Why? Ain't that what you are?" Rorie asked bluntly. "That woman trouble I'm thinking you got yourself into," she elaborated in case he'd forgotten his own missteps in the past few seconds.

"Not…exactly," Jack said, persuading his mount to exhale so he could tighten the saddle cinch. He might have stepped in when he was reasonably sure Elrissa's lawful husband had stepped out, but he'd had no designs on her other than to salvage some remnant of his pride. He gave a quiet sigh. But he might as well have had, considering the outcome.

"I do declare, Jeremiah Murphy, if you don't get more interesting by the minute. *'Not exactly.'* One of these days I'm going to make you tell me what *that* means. Now you better get going before you get caught in the cross fire."

"Is Sayer telling the girls?"

"She's done told them. She was ready to do it. No need to put it off."

"Are they—?"

"She's reading them parts of them letters you gave her. I reckon it's going to help all three of them, especially now that they got that likeness of Thomas Henry you brought. Maybe it'll help you, too."

He frowned at that last remark, baffled by something she'd said once again.

"Now do you reckon you can find them taters I told you about?"

"I can find them—it's one of my more recent skills— finding crops people think they've got hidden."

"And the cabbages? I need some to wrap my knees."

"Those, as well," he said despite the fact that he had no idea about the way she meant to use them.

"You wrap cabbage leaves on your bad knees, and they feel better," she said in case she needed to clear up any confusion.

"Cabbage," he repeated.

"That's right. You're going to come back with them, ain't you? 'Cause if you ain't, if you're heading on out of here now that you told her about Thomas Henry and you got the chance, I'd just as soon you leave them right where they are and don't take them with you."

He looked at her, seeing what could only be worry in her eyes.

"I'm coming back," he said. "With everything you sent me for—unless I get simple-headed again somewhere along the way or this horse gets to thinking it's in another cavalry charge."

She grinned, but the grin quickly faded. "I'm scared, Jeremiah."

"About what?"

"About Halbert and what he's saying. One time there was this here woman what lived up on Little Smoky Ridge. They put her in the Jefferson jail."

"For what?"

"For what he'll say Sayer is doing. With you. That poor woman went to jail and they took her young-uns."

He didn't say anything.

"Gives you something to ponder over," she said.

"Well, it explains why you're so determined to get me out of the way today."

"Does, don't it?"

"What's to be done, then?" he asked. "About Halbert and his tale-bearing?"

"You got the whole day to yourself. You think of something."

"What are you trying to do, Rorie—give me a reason not to come back?"

"No," she said. "I might know you'd up and miss what's right in front of your face. When you go from here, I'm giving you a reason to take her and them young-uns with you. Sooner or later, one way or the other, Halbert *will* have this here land. Every bit of it. He might have to do something so bad he'll get hisself hung for it, but he'll have it. I believe that in my heart, Jeremiah. I *believe* it."

"Sayer loved—loves—Thomas Henry."

"Well, he ain't here, and he asked you to take care of her, didn't he?"

"Not…exactly," he said for the second time, and she gave him an exasperated look at having to hear that tired excuse again.

"Don't matter if he did or didn't—*exactly*. He wanted Sayer kept safe. We both know that. I reckon you're a man who could do it—keep her safe."

"She's got roots here."

"I told you she weren't born and raised here. Her only connection was Thomas Henry and he's gone."

"She's not going to go riding off with me."

"Why not? You got a wife or two stuck somewhere?"

"No."

"Well, then. One thing I know about step-husbands. They are silver-tongued devils, and that's a fact."

Jack mounted the horse. He had nothing to say to

that. Silver-tongued devil or not, he would have to say if asked, that Rorie Conley was just as crazy as he'd thought the first day they met. Crazy—and sharp as a tack.

He rode past the cabin windows on his way out. He could see Sayer sitting at the table, apparently still reading the last words Thomas Henry had written.

Keep her safe.
Easier said than done.
You think of something…

He was more concerned about the "something" Rorie had thought of.

Take her and them young-uns with you when you go.

He couldn't do that. He was in trouble with the law. And he couldn't stay—for the same reason.

He had known women in Lexington to be sent to jail for immoral behavior—there was a good chance his own mother had been one of them. And he'd heard of women being rescued by the Magdalene societies. But one thing he knew for certain, those women were nothing like Sayer Garth. He had no idea whether or not Thomas Henry's uncle would actually drag Sayer into court, but the threat of it would likely be all the leverage he would need. And if it did come down to some legal proceeding, he didn't know if Rorie had enough standing in these parts to be believed or not. He thought one thing was certain. Sayer wouldn't sacrifice Amity and Beatrice—and see them go into an orphanage somewhere—no matter what the consequences.

But Thomas Henry's uncle and his lust for the Garth land had nothing to do with him, and that was the truth of the matter. He had done what Thomas Henry had specifically asked *him* to do, despite his lapse into thinking Jack was the soldier he called "Graham." He had delivered the letters and had repeated the dying words—most of them. Unfortunately, there was another truth: he didn't want to go from here. It had nothing to do with his need to hide from Elrissa Vance's jealous husband. He wanted to be in this place, despite the guilt he felt for inserting himself into the lives of a dead enemy's family. He wanted to stay because of Sayer herself—and the fact that he just couldn't seem to break his long-standing habit of looking out for orphans.

We thank you, Mr. Murphy. Thomas Henry and I…

He didn't want her gratitude. He wanted…

What? That was the question, and it was as troubling as what Rorie had suggested Halbert Garth might do to Sayer.

And that was another thing. He didn't think of her as "Mrs. Garth" even when he called her that. She was "Sayer" to him and had been since the night Thomas Henry Garth had died.

Sayer.

It was an unusual name for a woman, one he'd never encountered before and one that suited her well. She, too, was unusual. He could see it, just as her husband must have long before he was ever her husband.

And here was yet another of Father Bartholomew's Biblical truths, living and breathing right before his very eyes. The priest had spoken to the boys often about the importance of marriage and family, not from the pulpit, but during their Saturday-evening gatherings on the upstairs porch. *A good woman is more precious than rubies,* he said in that subtle way he had, *and a man will know immediately when he has found her.* That part must be true, Jack thought. Thomas Henry had apparently seen Sayer's value even when they were still children.

Such a man is very fortunate indeed, Father Bartholomew had told them, *because she is a gift from God, one to be respected and cared for. And, more importantly, they should be thankful for her and should make certain to cherish her, for that was the way to fewer abandoned children in this world.* "Abandoned children" was the hook that always caught their collective attention. It was something the priest and his young charges understood only too well.

Jack didn't remember what he had thought of these particular words of wisdom at the time, especially from a man who had never married. Not much, apparently, or he would have realized what a wrong path he was taking in proposing to Elrissa Barden. When he thought about her now, his last visit to her and his having to go on the run, he marveled at his own stupidity. He wondered if she was still living in Farrell Vance's house or if she'd finally found some man gullible enough and ignorant enough of her husband's authority to help her escape. For a brief moment, he felt sorry for the man, whoever he might be—and for Farrell Vance. For all his money, he wouldn't tame Elrissa Barden unless she chose to be tamed. She had no fear of consequences when it came to obtaining her heart's desire, and Jack didn't for one moment entertain the idea that she might regret the lie she had told.

But there was no point in feeling sorry for anyone,

even himself. It was a waste of time. If he'd learned nothing else after four years of war, he'd learned that.

A young captain in the Orphans' Guild suddenly came to mind. He hadn't lasted long despite his being a brave man with a remarkable military mind—or maybe because of it. He was one of the "if onlys" Jack had been thinking about when he told Sayer about Thomas Henry. *If only* the captain hadn't refused to take cover when the cannonballs were flying. *If only* a cannonball hadn't fallen at his feet.

If you get yourselves in a hot spot, don't think about what you can't do, he had told them earlier that day. *Think about what you can—and do it. You* will *find* something.

"Something," Jack said aloud, causing some unrest and anticipation in his mount. "Easy, old man. No battles today," he said, reaching out to pat its neck. "At least not that kind."

He came to the path that led down to the old buffalo trace Rorie had told him about and he headed in that direction, despite her forceful plan for him to go to her cabin. He had something else in mind now, a "something" that might suit his dead captain, but likely wouldn't suit Rorie Conley at all.

It occurred to him as he headed east on the trace that this was the only access road to the Garth cabin and that he might encounter the very people who, for Sayer's sake, he was supposed to evade. But the ride down the mountainside was uneventful. He didn't meet anyone along the way, and he thought that perhaps Rorie had been wrong in her expectation that Sayer's neighbors would be arriving at some point to judge her behavior today.

The nameless crossroad was about what he expected—a general store housed in a two-story wooden building, with a blacksmith and farrier's shop close by. As he came nearer, he could see a livery stable beyond the general store, one that likely catered to the stages going to and from Jefferson, and attached to that, what looked very much like a jail.

The blacksmith was clearly in demand, busily clanging away on a section of red-hot iron as Jack rode past. Little boys played marbles in the dirt at the side of the road, and a collection of men, young and old, sat on benches and straight chairs on the front porch of the store, likely refighting the war and bemoaning the fate of the newly conquered South. A few days ago Jack would have said that the South deserved whatever it got, but since he'd met Sayer and Thomas Henry's little sisters, surprisingly, he no longer felt that way. His need for vengeance for the thirty-six tin cups on the dining hall mantel at the orphanage was clearly dependent upon his not knowing these people by name and sharing a sit-down meal with them. It was especially dependent on never having looked into a pair of dark, sad eyes.

All of the men watched with interest as he approached. He knew that the crossroads would be the center of all manner of public and private business for miles around, and that his arrival was likely now at the top of the list of community concerns.

He took his time dismounting and tying up the horse, and he touched the brim of his hat in a general acknowledgment of them all as he went inside. One of the men got up from the bench and followed him, either the proprietor or the one designated to find out who Jack was and what kind of dealings he had in mind.

Jack had always liked general stores, finding them much more interesting than the more refined and much more limited Barden's Dry Goods version. He liked the heady mixture of smells—all pleasant, for the most part—and the mystery of what might be lurking on the shelves, things that would give him pleasure. The floor had been heavily oiled over the years, and fresh sawdust had been put down. It squeaked as he walked around looking at the shelves, which must be helpful to the proprietor—no one could lurk about the place without him knowing it. Jack could feel the other man's watchful eye on his every move. Most of the shelves were stocked with merchandise, which didn't necessarily indicate that business was good. It was more likely that the stock the owner had managed to acquire before the South was completely closed off by the blockades and the Army of the Potomac had never been sold. Still, the items he picked up and inspected didn't seem shoddy.

He walked over to look at a number of posters tacked up on the wall near what must serve as a post office window.

"You expecting mail?" the man asked.

"No," Jack said, keeping his attention on the posters, relieved that none of them seemed to pertain to him.

"If you are, it might come here, but it's more likely to be delivered to the courthouse in Jefferson. The clerk of court would have it. You'd have to go there and ask."

"I'm not expecting mail," Jack said.

"You looking to buy something?" the man asked.

"Flour, sugar, raisins, molasses, bacon," Jack said. "For a start."

"You got money or you aiming to barter?"

"Money."

"I have to see it first."

The risk was great—no one likely had silver coins in these parts even before the war—but Jack pulled a small bag of silver dollars out of his pocket and opened it just enough for the man to see he had the means for them to do business.

"How did you get these?" the man asked.

"The usual way," Jack said.

"Whatever you buy, if you don't spend all of a dollar, I can't give you no money back. You'd have to take credit."

"Credit will do."

"You are planning on staying a while, then." It wasn't quite a question, but either way, Jack ignored it.

"I'd need your name. For the ledger," the man said, still trying.

"Let's see how far we get first. I'm going to look around. I'll tell you when I see something I want. You keep a running list—tell me how much I'm spending as I go. You might as well know I've got a good idea what things cost and I'd appreciate it if you don't jack up the price just because you know I can pay."

Jack knew such a remark would likely offend the man, whether he was honest or not, but Jack needed to establish that he wouldn't be cheated.

"You got people around here?" the man asked as Jack began searching the shelves in earnest.

"No," Jack said. "Some gun oil. And a pot of honey—one of these small ones."

"Friends, then, I reckon," the man said as he jotted down the additional items.

"No."

"Then what's your business here?" the man asked, clearly no longer willing to dance around what he really wanted to know.

"I'm here by request—how much have I spent now?"

"Five dollars and ten cents. Whose request?"

"Add six sticks of peppermint candy to that and tally it up. Wrap each one separately."

"Whose request?" the man asked again as he reached for the lid on the peppermint-stick jar.

Jack could hear some shuffling on the porch out front that either meant their audience was trying to get closer to the wall in order to hear better, or they were letting go of all pretense and coming inside for a better view.

"Thomas Henry Garth's," Jack said. Jack handed him six silver dollars. "Put the money that's left down as credit for Mrs. Garth."

He could hear the men from the porch come to a halt somewhere behind him.

"You know Thomas Henry?" one of them asked immediately.

"I just said I was here by his request," Jack said. "Or did you miss that part?" He was smiling when he said it, and several of the men laughed.

"Caught you out, didn't he, Dan?" the store owner said.

"Yeah, he did. But I wasn't the only one with big ears. Thomas Henry in a bad way?"

"No."

"Dead then, I reckon," the man named Dan said.

"He is," Jack said.

"I always liked that boy," one of the other men said, a veteran, Jack thought, because he was missing his lower left arm. "His daddy, too. Man of his word, Mr. Garth Senior was, ain't that right, Benton?" he said to the store owner. "And Thomas Henry was just the same. I don't ever know of him doing somebody wrong."

The conversation picked up among the men, mostly recounting things they remembered about Thomas Henry and his family, the kinds of things Sayer should hear, Jack thought.

"You know for a fact he's dead?" Benton, the store proprietor, asked quietly as the discussion of Thomas Henry Garth's personal merits went on around them.

"I do."

"You know his uncle? Halbert Garth?"

"We've met," Jack said.

"I reckon you'll think this ain't none of my business, but don't take offense at what I'm going to say. Somebody better get to Jefferson—find the lawyer up there to see if Thomas Henry filed a will. Ain't but one lawyer in Jefferson as far as I know and I'd be wanting to get to him before Halbert hears Thomas Henry is gone," he said, his voice still low. "Halbert Garth can make things happen. You understand me, son?"

"Why are you telling me this?"

"People here think a lot of Thomas Henry, me included. And I've known Sayer since she used to come in here when she weren't no more than this high." He demonstrated just how high that would be with his hand. "Thomas Henry, he swept the floors in here and cleaned out the horse stalls and run errands for me just to earn enough money to buy her candy. We used to tease him something terrible about having a sweetheart, but he didn't care. He earned what money he could and then he waited for her to come in here with that bossy cook they had up at her uncle's big summer house— the woman was always buying up whatever fresh vegetables I had. Those people of Sayer's, they liked a full set table, I reckon.

"Thomas Henry, he acted like he weren't interested in either one of them until the cook got busy going through the baskets and bad-mouthing what she found so she could drive the price down, and he called Sayer over to the candy jars and told her to pick out whatever she wanted. She was so happy about that—lit up like sunshine on a cloudy day. It was like she couldn't believe her eyes and couldn't believe somebody would do that for her. Didn't happen but that once, though," he said. "Her aunt found out about it and put a stop to it. That boy moped around here for weeks because she couldn't come down to the store with the cook anymore. Now I reckon you're here to satisfy a worry Thomas Henry had about his wife and his little sisters, and I think getting to Jefferson is one way to see that boy rests in peace. *That's* why I'm telling you."

Jack didn't say anything.

"I'd go now if I was you. I'll box up these supplies you bought. They'll all be here when you get back. You don't have to worry about that."

Jack reached for the wrapped sticks of peppermint lying on the counter and borrowed the store owner's pencil. He wrote a name on each piece and gave five of them back to him.

The last peppermint stick he put into his pocket.

Chapter Seven

I'm still waiting, Sayer thought. *Still watching. Still listening.*

But it wasn't Thomas Henry she was waiting for, and there was no use pretending otherwise. It had been five days since Jeremiah left to fetch Rorie's potatoes and cabbages. When he hadn't returned by the third day, Sayer decided not to sit and wonder about his absence any longer. She did the only thing she could do. She took Beatrice and Amity and carefully walked the distance to Rorie's cabin, looking for him along the way in case he'd had some kind of accident on that war-scarred horse of his—or worse. He had already crossed swords with Halbert, and Halbert wouldn't forget it.

"Why didn't he *tell* us he wouldn't be coming back," Amity kept wondering as they walked along. "He likes us, Sayer. I know he does. Why didn't he tell us? Then we'd *know* and we wouldn't have to look for him. I'm *scared* to look for him. I looked and looked for Thomas Henry, and he—"

"Don't talk about Thomas Henry!" Beatrice cried,

close to tears. "He's dead! We're supposed to be looking for Jeremiah, so look!"

But there was no sign of Jeremiah anywhere along the way, and no sign that he had found the potatoes and cabbages Rorie was supposed to have buried somewhere in her yard. She had told Sayer how to find them, but her directions regarding where they were supposed to be were of no help at all. Rorie had apparently put a lot of planning into *not* making her straw-lined storage mounds high enough to be conspicuous. There were no elevations in the ground that looked out of place, and no visible drainage ditches to keep the rain from running in. None. Rorie must have dug deep instead, so deep that no one else but her would have the slightest chance of finding them.

Sayer and the girls had tramped back and forth over the ground, looking for soft spots or hard spots—anything—until they were in danger of having to return home in the dark if they didn't leave right away—and in worse danger of having to tell Rorie they couldn't find her secreted vegetables. Frustrated and weary, they had had no choice but to give up and return home empty-handed.

As expected, Rorie was not happy, especially about the cabbage, and her unhappiness continued, punctuating all their meals and chores and meager rest times from start to finish.

"I ain't surprised *you* couldn't find them, Sayer, but he said he could, on account of stealing so much during the war—well, that ain't exactly what he said, but that's what he meant. I *told* him what I needed that there cabbage for," she said yet again. She suddenly straightened up from the washboard she was bending over and slapped the pillow slip she had been scrubbing down hard. "Well, he's done up and beat me, that's what he's done. And I'm tired of being in a dither about it. He ain't coming back, Sayer. And that's the truth of it!"

Sayer didn't say anything. She'd learned in the past few days that Rorie didn't always welcome outside participation in her broadsides, even if she seemingly asked for it.

"Did you hear what I said? He ain't coming back!"

"There's no reason why he should," Sayer said quietly because she didn't want the girls to hear her. She concentrated on trying to spread a bedsheet on the privet hedge to dry, swatting at a wasp determined to bob in the air around her face as she struggled with the corners. But the sinking feeling she experienced upon hearing Rorie's most recently revised opinion of the situation—that Jeremiah Murphy wouldn't be coming back at all—was something she hadn't anticipated, despite the fact that she had already come to the same conclusion. She had told herself that she had no reason to hope—she had learned the hard way what a difficult thing *hope* could be. It required believing in the unseen and complete acceptance that she was exactly where God intended her to be. Here. Alone.

"Whatever he might have owed Thomas Henry, I believe he's repaid," she said.

"Well, he owes *me* a word of farewell at least," Rorie said. "So's I don't turn around looking for him every time I hear the least little racket. It's bad enough I have to listen out for Halbert and that good-for-nothing trash what follows him around night and day. I know that there orphanage Jeremiah was in learned him better than that—just up and disappearing when he *told* me right to my face he was coming back here. That's what he said—made a joke of it. He said he was coming back unless he got all simple-headed again or that dang horse of his thought it was in another cavalry charge. He said he'd get me them taters *and* the cabbage, and he'd be back."

"Why do you suppose he…?"

"Oh, I don't know," Rorie said impatiently before Sayer could finish the sentence. "Weren't no reason for him to say he was coming back if he didn't intend to do it. I asked him straight out if he was taking his leave now. He said he weren't—my knees is paining me something fierce!"

"I'll scrub the clothes. You sit down," Sayer said.

"Are you trying to make me feel useless, girl?"

"No, I—"

"I want my cabbage! And I want to clap that boy upside his head, too, while I'm at it. Making me worry like this. I'm too old to be worrying about some dang *man*."

"Somebody's coming, Sayer," Beatrice called from the porch, her voice sounding listless and defeated as it had since the morning Sayer had told them about their brother. And finding no trace of Jeremiah on their walk to Rorie's cabin hadn't helped.

Sayer stood on tiptoe, trying to see down the path, her heart sinking yet again because the new arrival wasn't a man on horseback. It was a wagon, one pulled by a brace of mules and loaded down with something, judging by the progress it was making up the steep incline. A number of men and women followed behind

it on foot. There were no children in the party, a fact
that didn't bode well for Sayer.

"Well, it looks like they finally got here," Rorie said.
"I didn't think it would take them so long once Halbert
lit a fire under them. Of course, I didn't think it would
take so long for somebody on a horse to go over to my
place and get my taters and cabbages, neither— Are
you ready for this?" she suddenly asked, nodding in
the direction of the approaching visitors.

"Yes," Sayer said firmly. "I am. There's nothing I
need to explain about Jeremiah Murphy being here, not
to anybody, especially not to Thomas Henry's friends
and neighbors."

"The preacher and his wife, too," Rorie noted in the
event that Sayer had missed their presence in the group.

Sayer gave a deep sigh, knowing for certain that she
was indeed expressing a prayer this time. She thought it
was good that she and the girls looked reasonably presentable, though if she were truthful, their clean dresses
and neatly braided hair had nothing to do with Rorie's
anticipation of the arrival of these people, and everything to do with the hope that Jeremiah hadn't left them
for good and he would keep his word to Rorie and come
back again.

She glanced at Rorie. "Are you praying?"

"I am," Rorie said. "And I ain't stopping until they
get here. Maybe not even then."

"Good," Sayer said.

"You ain't done nothing wrong, honey."

"I know. But they're not like you. They'll be afraid
to go against whatever Halbert has told them."

"Well, then, we just have to get ourselves to remembering what happened to Goliath and have a little faith."

Sayer gave a weak smile, and Rorie reached out to pat her gently on the arm.

Beatrice and Amity came to stand beside her, and the three of them walked out to meet their visitors, waiting quietly until the wagon rolled into the yard and the people on foot caught up. Several of the men immediately began to unload it.

Mrs. Tomlin, the preacher's wife, reached Sayer first. Sayer had always felt a certain kinship with the woman, because neither of them was mountain born and raised.

"We brought your supplies with us, Sayer, honey," she said, fanning her sweaty face with her hand and trying to catch her breath. "That Benton was going to let them sit around down at the store, but I said no. Sayer and the girls would be needing these."

"Supplies?"

"All the things Thomas Henry's friend bought the other day."

"Oh," Sayer said vaguely, exchanging a look with Rorie.

The preacher's wife looked up at the sky. "Beautiful day," she said. "One of the first things I noticed about the high country. The sky is always so fine the higher up you get, don't you think?"

"Closer to God, I reckon," Rorie put in.

"Yes, that's it exactly, Mrs. Conley," the preacher's wife said. She turned her attention back to Sayer. "I am so sorry to hear Thomas Henry has been killed, my dear," she said with no preface to warn Sayer of what she was about to say. She realized then that Jeremiah had been doing more than buying supplies.

"When Benton told me about it, I just sat down and cried. You and Amity and Beatrice—you all have been waiting so long for him to come back from the war. Little Amity used to tell me at church about how she'd go stand on the path down to the buffalo road or there in the cabin by the window to watch for him. So sad. So very sad. We would have been up here sooner, Preacher Tomlin and I, but we wanted to give you the time to tell the girls and everything. And it's good Mrs. Conley's here. You don't want to have to go through something like this alone. I think—"

"Where do you want the boxes, Sayer?" Willard Perkins interrupted to ask.

"Oh…" Sayer began, still trying to process everything the preacher's wife had been saying.

"Don't be worrying her with things like that, Willard," Mrs. Tomlin said. "Just take them into the cabin. Put them on the floor somewhere out of her way. She and Mrs. Conley will see to them later."

Willard took the wooden box he was carrying and did as he was told.

"Will you try to bring Thomas Henry home, Sayer? I know it would be a dear price to do it, but maybe your uncle would arrange it for you. As I recall, he was very fond of Thomas Henry," the preacher's wife said gently. She put her arm around Sayer's shoulders, and without warning, Sayer could feel the tears coming, just when she had believed she was all cried out.

"I don't—know where he—" She took a deep breath. "I can't—"

She stood there, tears rolling down her cheeks. There was nothing else to say. It seemed she would never get used to it—the sudden realization that Thomas Henry was lost to her. But she knew in her heart she wasn't crying just because of that. She was crying because of her own shortcomings, for her failure to be the kind of wife—widow—Thomas Henry deserved. Thomas Henry was dead, and she was consumed with worry about another man, not because of his friendship with her deceased husband, but because of the man himself, the man of rare smiles who teased Rorie mercilessly and who made handkerchief dolls and cracker pudding. The man who stood up to Halbert Garth.

"We were afraid that might be the situation," Mrs. Tomlin said. "Oh, here's my husband to have a word with you, my dear. I believe what he has to say will give you comfort." She moved away, but she kept a discreet distance, just in case Sayer's weeping worsened enough to unsettle him and she needed to intervene.

Sayer furtively wiped away the tears and forced herself to look directly into Preacher Tomlin's weather-beaten face. The years of circuit riding from mountain community to mountain community to perform whatever church services were needed had left him as brown and leathery as any farmer. His tanned face stood in stark contrast to his snow-white hair.

"Sayer, I'm here to hold a memorial service for Thomas Henry," he said without prelude. "I am about to go on my circuit ride again, and if you're up to it, it is my intention to leave you with the comforting memory of the people who cared about him paying their respects to him and to his family. If this endeavor seems rushed to you, I do apologize. It's because I don't know when I'll find another opportunity. I'm setting out early the day after tomorrow. There are a lot of weddings to be performed since the war ended and the boys started coming home. It might be months before I get back this way again. I was wondering if we might gather in Mr. Garth Senior's private place of prayer?"

Sayer frowned. "I...don't know where that is."

"It's up on that ridge yonder," Preacher Tomlin said, pointing toward the steep slope on the west side of the cabin. "Beyond the line of trees. I can find it all right, I believe. I helped him clear a path to it when I first came here to preach. I believe he paid me a true compliment in showing it to me. It was his own place to pray—a kind of natural alcove on a huge outcropping of rock overlooking the valley. Do you know your Bible verses, Sayer? Psalm 46? Verse 10?"

"'Be still and know that I am God,'" Sayer said, recalling it from memory. Every cabin in these parts had Preacher Tomlin's list of favorite Bible verses tucked away in the family Bible, and Mrs. Garth had been no exception. Sayer had read them to her over and over in the final month of her life.

"That is exactly right. Be *still*. And *know*. I believe this to be such a place for that experience because one is encouraged to do just that. It wasn't significantly overgrown even back then, and I don't expect it to be now—very rocky ground, you see. I anticipate finding it much the same. It was Mr. Garth Senior's idea of what a church ought to be—God-made instead of man-made. Not that he didn't do his part for the one we all built down below for the rest of the community. This was his personal place of worship, if you will, and I would have to say it is one of the most holy 'churches' I have ever been in. Incredible beauty—one ridge after another all the way into Tennessee. He said it was a place where you could see God's handiwork with your own two eyes, and when he went up there—when *we* went up there—well, it makes you forget your troubles, and we need that today, don't we? I'm certain we can accomplish access in no time at—"

He abruptly stopped talking because, incredibly, Jeremiah Murphy was riding slowly into the yard, nodding to the men and touching the brim of his hat to the women as he passed—as if he were completely unaware of their keen interest in him and he hadn't been the topic of all their conversations since his purchases at the general store.

"Jeremiah!" the girls cried, breaking away from Sayer and running to greet him.

"This is Thomas Henry's friend, I believe?" Preacher Tomlin said, studying Jeremiah with as much interest as the rest of his party.

"Yes," Sayer said, watching as Jeremiah rode on toward the barn.

"I am very eager to speak to him. Excuse me for a moment, Sayer."

"Well, this ain't what I was hoping for, I can tell you that," Rorie said at Sayer's elbow as soon as the preacher was out of earshot. "Now what are we going to do?"

"Nothing," Sayer said. "It's too late."

"I swear I don't know what's wrong with me. I keep thinking I have to make some kind of big fool plan to move people around where *I* think they ought to be—

when it's clear I ain't no good at it. Just look at this! We might as well have sent out play party invitations and served Jeremiah up on a silver platter. And I reckon they'll pick him clean—drag him back to them things what trouble him so and make his hands all shaky. All we need now is Halbert showing up—but that weren't no suggestion," she added, looking heavenward. "Jeremiah!" she suddenly yelled in one of the stronger versions of her voice, hobbling past the preacher to get to the head of the line. "I'm wanting to have a word with you!"

Sayer stood watching Jeremiah, who had been leaning down to speak to the girls, both of whom were all but bouncing up and down with delight at his return. She saw him grin at Rorie's well-heralded approach—though he was trying hard not to. He immediately headed her off by holding out the sack he had tied to his saddle. Rorie eyed it suspiciously, then snatched it away and looked inside. In a moment, she gave a happy cackle of laughter—apparently forgetting all about her earlier threat to clap him upside the head.

Jeremiah dismounted, despite his proximity to Rorie, and waited for Preacher Tomlin to reach him. He had yet to even look in Sayer's direction, but the relief she felt at his safe return was nearly overwhelming. He was so tired; she could see how weary he was. She wanted to talk to him, to make sure he was all right. She wanted to make him sit down at the table so she could feed him. She wanted him to sleep, to rest.

And oh, dear Lord, she wanted him to *stay*.

"It's an admirable thing," she heard Preacher Tomlin say in his booming back-pew voice. "The kindness a hardened soldier is capable of when it comes to his comrades. I suppose it was a pact you and Thomas Henry made—each would see to the family of the other if one of you fell."

"Not quite. I am an orphan, sir," Jeremiah said.

"Ah. That is a shame. You certainly seem comfortable in the role of big brother to Amity and Beatrice."

Sayer stood there, wanting to join the conversation, wanting to say that Jeremiah's remark didn't do him justice. He had a family—orphans made their own families—and that his family was every bit as real as anyone else's was, perhaps more so because of the hard work it must take to maintain it.

But she stayed where she was because Jeremiah suddenly looked in her direction. And it was as if no one else was there but the two of them, as if Amity and Beatrice weren't all fidgety with the effort it was taking them not to interrupt his conversation with Preacher Tomlin; and four women weren't headed in Sayer's direction to speak to her now that the preacher had walked away; and poor Willard wasn't still going back and forth carrying boxes and sacks from the wagon. And Rorie—Rorie wasn't shamelessly admiring her fresh supply of cabbage.

Sayer abruptly turned away. Thomas Henry was dead. It was wrong for her to feel so relieved—happy— to see Jeremiah Murphy. He was all but a stranger to her, someone she knew very little about, and he would soon go again. She knew that. Only, the next time he wouldn't come back.

When she looked in Jeremiah's direction again, his

conversation with Preacher Tomlin had ended, and he was leading the horse to the water trough.

"Now, you needn't worry about feeding all of us, Sayer," Preacher Tomlin was saying as he approached. "We have brought plenty of picnic baskets, all of them full to the brim. We shall have our service and then we shall break bread together in our remembrance of Thomas Henry. We'd best get started," he called to the men. "You, too, sir, if you would be so kind as to join us when your horse is seen to," he called to Jeremiah.

Jeremiah gave him a short nod, and led the horse into the barn. After a time he came out again carrying the axe Sayer had tried to keep oiled and sharpened and ready for Thomas Henry to use when he came home.

"Gather around," Preacher Tomlin said to the group, and Sayer was suddenly surrounded by sympathetic people who didn't hesitate to heed Preacher Tomlin's command. The women pressed in on her, embraced her, murmured kind words about Thomas Henry, kissed her cheek and briefly took her hand.

And kept her from saying anything to Jeremiah.

She couldn't see him, but she could *feel* that he was near. She realized suddenly that Preacher Tomlin was praying, and she bowed her head.

"…Your words are beauty. Your words are truth and mercy. Your words are justice and forgiveness and comfort. We are come to You now in this time of sorrow, offering You our gratitude because we know Your words help us to believe. Bless all of us here and this endeavor we are about to begin. Comfort our dear Sayer and Beatrice and Amity—and Thomas Henry's loyal

comrade, Jeremiah—in their loss that they may hear
Your words and understand…"

Sayer continued standing with her head bowed for a
moment after the prayer had ended. When she looked
around, Jeremiah was no longer there. She spotted
him walking up the hill with the rest of the men. And,
ignoring the women around her, she watched until he
had disappeared among the trees, and she couldn't see
him any longer.

*They went looking for me. All three of them went
looking for me.*

Jack didn't know why that bit of information from
Amity surprised him so, but it did. It just hadn't
occurred to him that they might think he was absent
from them because he was hurt. At worst, he thought
they might think he'd simply gone.

Sayer.

He had been very careful not to give the people
standing around her cause to think that there was anything between them when there wasn't. He didn't want
to seem overly familiar, and he didn't want to show
how glad he was to see her. He didn't know if they
were inclined to believe Halbert Garth, or more likely,
whether they were too afraid of Halbert to treat Sayer
kindly regardless of what they believed.

But finally, when he did look at her, it took his breath
away. As far from her as he was, he still got lost in her
sad eyes. She hadn't expected to see him—ever; he
could tell that, and it was a startling realization to suddenly be mindful of the fact that he didn't want to be
responsible for ever making her unhappy again.

The preacher—Tomlin—was nothing like Father Bartholomew, but he was just as competent at managing a captive work crew. Jack busied himself chopping down saplings that had managed to take root in the rocky ground. The haft was well-worn and comfortable in his hands, and it was yet another reminder of Thomas Henry. The axe had been a good choice of tools. No one approached him for conversation while he was swinging it.

But he couldn't chop forever, and eventually he would be at the mercy of the men around him and their burning questions regarding who he was and where he had come from and his assumed pact with Thomas Henry. Surprisingly, though, the ones he had already encountered at the general store didn't seem inclined to press him for new information. And the ones he hadn't met before had nothing to say beyond the initial introductions. He supposed that the reason they were all gathered here must have put a damper on their curiosity. It was time to pay their last respects to Thomas Henry Garth, and unlike Jack, they had all known him well.

Eventually, after some brush was burned to drive the snakes away, Preacher Tomlin was satisfied that the access to the huge flat outcropping of rock and the rock itself were in an acceptable condition for a memorial service. As the others turned to go, Jack stood looking at the vista Thomas Henry's father had apparently used to communicate with his God.

"I see you are a man who appreciates God's handiwork," Preacher Tomlin said behind him.

"It's a beautiful place," Jack said.

"Are you a godly man, Mr. Murphy?" he asked, and Jack gave a short laugh.

"I've spent the last four years of my life killing other men for reasons I still don't understand, Preacher Tomlin. I don't feel very…godly." He turned and looked the preacher directly in the eyes.

"You've lost many who were close to you." It wasn't a question.

"I have—and it doesn't make me feel kindly toward the Deity."

"I see you are a plain-speaking and honest man," the preacher said after a moment. "It's a very good thing to be. Our Lord is very fond of honest men. I believe you are well on your way to finding the godliness you seek."

Jack would have told him that he wasn't seeking godliness, but the man turned and walked away, leaving him standing with a mountain range at his back and his protestations unvoiced. Honest? There was no honesty in his even being here. He was simply doing what he had done all his life. He was trying, by whatever means available, to survive.

Jack joined the group, and they all walked through the trees and back down the steep slope to the cabin. He didn't see Sayer outside as they approached, and he didn't miss the intensity of his disappointment. He knew what a difficult event this must be for her, and for a moment, he wished that Father Bartholomew were here. Father Bartholomew would know precisely what to say to her to give her the comfort she so desperately needed.

But that wasn't possible. He would never see him or the others ever again.

Several cedar buckets of cold water from the spring

had been left for them on a long makeshift table near the porch, and the men all shared a communal dipper to drink their fill. What was left, they poured over each other's heads to cool off. There wasn't much hope of any of them looking presentable after that. Even Preacher Tomlin accepted a good dousing. Once again Father Bartholomew came to mind, and Jack tried not to smile at the unlikelihood that the fastidious priest would allow someone to empty a bucket of water over his head. Father Bartholomew would certainly have wielded an axe if needed, but he would have stopped short at losing control of his dignity.

The cabin door opened, and Sayer and the rest of the women came out. She looked so sad.

And so achingly beautiful.

"If you would escort Sayer, Mr. Murphy," Preacher Tomlin said.

Jack had no choice but to offer her his arm. He thought for a moment that she wouldn't take it, but she did. His sleeves were still rolled up. He could feel the warmth of her hand through the cloth, and her fingertips where they touched his bare skin. She looked up at him and gave him the barest of smiles. Amity caught his free hand, and Beatrice took Sayer's. Together, they began the walk back to the place where they would give Thomas Henry his final goodbye.

"Rorie's going to stay behind with Mrs. Mitchell and put the food on the table," Amity said, looking up at him. "Mrs. Mitchell's knees hurt, too."

"I see," Jack said.

"Do your knees hurt?"

"No," he answered.

"Mine, neither. I'm glad. I don't want to wear cabbage."

This was not the time to laugh, and he had to work hard not to. He realized that Sayer was affected by Amity's remark, as well, because she suddenly squeezed his arm.

But the moment passed, and the solemnity of the occasion rolled over them all. There was no talking, only birdsong and the wind in the treetops and the bright blue sky of a late-summer day. He realized suddenly that many of the women were carrying flowers that must have been brought up from someone's garden down below, and one of the men carried a fiddle. He glanced at Sayer from time to time as they made their way, but her head was bowed, her eyes on the rough, newly cleared ground.

"It's not much farther," he said quietly to her at one point, because he could feel her pace slowing with the steepness of the climb, and she nodded.

And the same thought kept going around and around in his mind.

I shouldn't be here….

Sayer's hand on his arm tightened again as they cleared the trees, and the wide vista of the Blue Ridge mountain range beyond came into full view, one ridge after another far into the distance. It was like standing on the edge of the world, and clearly, she found it breathtaking despite having lived here.

"I didn't know," she whispered. "Thomas Henry never told me."

"Maybe it was his father's special place. Maybe he only showed it to Preacher Tomlin."

Amity was holding on to his hand with both of hers now, and he leaned down to speak to her.

"It's all right," he whispered. "You're not close to the edge. You won't fall."

She gave him a grateful look, but she didn't let go. One of the women stepped forward to give her and Beatrice some flowers to hold. Amity hesitated, then finally let go of his hand to take them.

Jack didn't know what the memorial service would entail, but it was soon apparent to him that these people were well acquainted with the rituals held for the loss of a loved one. Several of the men spoke of their relationship with Thomas Henry. One told of the struggle Thomas Henry had had with "certain people" to get permission to marry Sayer before he had to leave with his company and go off to war.

"Wouldn't take no for an answer," the man said. "It didn't matter how many hard looks Mrs. Preston give him. Sayer's uncle, now, he was all right with it. He knowed they weren't nobody for Thomas Henry but Sayer from the time he weren't nothing but a boy. I don't reckon Sayer knows about this, but Thomas Henry, he up and told that rich man what his intentions was before he even had a beard to shave. Sayer's uncle said for him to come back and talk to him when he had a house and land of his own. And that's what he did—"

Jack stopped listening. He didn't want to hear any more about Thomas Henry Garth and his long-standing love for Sayer. He didn't want him to be any more real than the man whose face he could barely see in the darkness of the battlefield, the man whose daguerreotype he had avoided. He turned his attention toward the mountains and the wisps of clouds caught there like delicate white flowers in a beautiful woman's hair. He would think about other things, other places. He had good memories to dwell on, despite having grown up in an orphan asylum and surviving a war.

But he could still feel her warm hand on his arm.

Suddenly, Preacher Tomlin was asking him something, jarring him back into the place he would rather not be. Jeremiah looked at him blankly.

"Would you be so kind as to say a few words?" Preacher Tomlin said, apparently repeating the question he'd only just asked.

Jeremiah cleared his throat. "I… Yes. I will."

He managed to get through it, and apparently he was the last speaker, because Preacher Tomlin nodded to the man with the fiddle. The man began to play. The intro to the song was one long and mournful note, and when it died away, a woman began to sing, her voice filled with all the sorrow and regret of the occasion. He glanced at Sayer. She was weeping without making a sound, and the silence of it made it all the more heart-breaking and poignant. She stared straight ahead, the tears sliding down her cheeks. After a moment, she let go of his arm to wipe them away.

Bright morning stars are rising…
Day is breaking in my soul….

And then it was over. With one final gesture, the careful placement of the many flowers they had carried onto the outcropping of rock, these people sent Thomas Henry Garth's soul to its rest.

As they walked back down to the cabin, Sayer took his arm again, and Beatrice and Amity went on ahead. They were quiet and well behaved, but still it was as if some burden had been lifted from their small shoulders and they could be little girls again. Jack barely remembered what he had said about their brother, except for the one truth in the midst of it—that despite the sad circumstances, it was a privilege to have met Thomas Henry's friends and family.

Preacher Tomlin said a prayer of thanks when they all had gathered in the yard, his last of the day before everyone ate. This time Jack found himself actually listening. The ritual of prayer had been such a part of his life at the orphanage, but he had deliberately let go of that aspect of his faith. He had let go, and he'd found nothing to replace it.

Apparently it was the custom that the men were served first, so there was no time for anyone to start up a conversation with him. Jack found himself going around the table and filling his plate with ham and cheese and corn bread and pickles, but he didn't pile it high enough to satisfy the women who supervised the process. It took a considerable amount of charm on his part to convince them that he had a sufficient amount of food and that he would not starve.

"Will you let the poor man be and let him eat in peace," one of them finally said, shooing him along. He made it all the way to the porch with the plate and a glass of apple water before his hands began to shake.

"No!" Rorie hissed in Sayer's ear because Sayer had seen the sudden change in Jeremiah's demeanor, and she would have followed after him when he abruptly left the group. Rorie stepped firmly on the hem of Sayer's skirts to emphasize just how unwise she thought such a move on her part would be.

"Too many eyes hooked to too many wagging tongues," Rorie whispered. "And he don't need you. Not now."

Sayer looked around her. Surprisingly, Jeremiah's sudden departure had caused barely a ripple. She supposed that they attributed it to a soldier's need for the privacy to vent his sorrow—except that he had told her himself that he hadn't known Thomas Henry very long.

But whatever it was, Rorie was right. He didn't need her. Of course he didn't need her. She knew that. What she didn't know was why she had been so determined to go after him despite how it might look to the people around her.

"All right," she said to Rorie, and after a moment of intense scrutiny, Rorie stepped off her hem.

The meal concluded more quickly than Sayer expected, hurried along by the increasingly persistent rumble of thunder in the distance and the growing threat of rain. The food not eaten was packed up and taken inside the cabin—a parting gift from Preacher Tomlin and his congregation. Goodbyes were said amid renewed condolences and blessings, and all the while Jeremiah's plate of food and glass of apple water sat on the porch edge in mute testimony to his absence. Beatrice and Amity had relocated themselves to sit on either side of the plate and were taking turns shooing the flies away.

Sayer waited until the party of mourners was well down the path to the buffalo road before she picked up the plate and glass and took them inside. She set them on the table and covered them with a tea cloth until he could eat it. And she tried not to seem so preoccupied with his whereabouts, pouring the hot water from the kettle into a deep pan so she could wash the dirty dishes the women had already carried inside. Beatrice and Amity helped with minimal squabbling, but their illness had clearly left them without stamina, and they were once again drooping from the strain of the day.

"Go lie down and rest," she said, and for once they didn't protest. They took off their shoes and stretched out side by side on their bed and were asleep in no time.

"This was a hard day for them," she said to Rorie.

"Not just them," Rorie said, giving Sayer a look she couldn't read. She could tell with reasonable certainty, however, that Rorie wasn't referring to her.

"What do you mean?"

"Nothing," Rorie said. "Except *now* is a good time to go see about him."

"No, you were right before. I don't have to do that. He doesn't need me. I don't know what made me think he did."

"He didn't need you with the whole blooming church congregation watching and whatever Halbert's been saying floating on the breeze. But I reckon, if you'd take the time to notice, you'd see they ain't here now, are they?"

Sayer frowned and didn't say anything. She washed another plate, and then another, before she abruptly dried her hands on her apron.

"Take a bucket—say you're on your way to the spring so you won't look like you're all worried about him and tracking him down like a hound dog," Rorie said. "Men don't like that."

Exasperated by the suggestion that she needed some kind of ruse to justify her concern, Sayer headed for the back door—empty-handed.

"I'm telling you. It's the truth," Rorie said mildly.

Sayer hesitated, then returned and picked up one of the buckets. She knew nothing of men's foibles and wasn't likely to ever learn. Perhaps she did need something to hide behind, and an empty water bucket was as good an excuse as any.

"Take your time. I'll finish these here dishes," Rorie called after her as she opened the back door. "Leave the door open so's we can get a breeze through here!"

Sayer left the door ajar. The wind was picking up, though the thunder didn't sound any closer. Rorie would definitely have the strong draft she wanted.

Sayer didn't see Jeremiah anywhere at first glance. She walked to the barn, leaving the bucket on the ground outside. The horse and mule were in their stalls and decidedly interested in whether or not she intended to feed them. She didn't call out for Jeremiah. She climbed up the ladder a few rungs until she could see into the hayloft where she knew he slept on a cot Mr. Garth Senior had made for illnesses and visitors—when he wasn't sleeping rolled up in a blanket on the front porch. His belongings were there, but he was not.

She climbed down again, and because she had the bucket, she picked it up and began walking down the path toward the spring, remembering suddenly that Jeremiah had carried her bodily up this path the day she'd hurt her head. How happy she had been at that moment.

Because I thought he was Thomas Henry.

Well, she had no confusion about who he was now. She just—

Just what?

I just want to make sure he's all right. I want to see him for myself and make sure. That's all.

At the sharp turn in the path, she spotted him. He was lying on a flat rock that hung over the spring a few yards past the collecting pool, his hands behind his head. He gave no indication that he heard her coming. She thought that he probably didn't because of the wind stirring the treetops. Perhaps he was asleep.

And perhaps not.

"Don't worry," she said when he turned his head to look at her. "I'm not going to ask how you are."

He actually smiled, clearly remembering that he had said the same thing to her. "That's good to know," he said. "I'll even return the favor." He looked away and closed his eyes again.

She waited patiently with the bucket until he opened his eyes and looked at her.

"I'm all right," he said pointedly.

"I'm pleased to hear that. And do remember that I didn't ask."

He smiled again. "So you may think. But I believe I heard the question as clear as can be. Is that something all women do—ask without asking—or just you?"

"I couldn't say. It's not something I learned, so it may be a God-given talent. Something He thought we women needed—since men prefer us to be seen and not heard. Thomas Henry—"

"Don't," he said, sitting up. "Don't tell me anything

else about Thomas Henry." He was looking at her—staring at her—as if he wanted to make her turn away, but she didn't.

Blue eyes—not brown. Blue.

He seemed so…

She couldn't find a word for the emotional turmoil she could see in his eyes.

What terrible things he must have seen, she thought again, just as she had the night he told her the details of Thomas Henry's death, only this time she didn't say it out loud.

"Why not?" she asked after a moment.

"You need to fill your bucket and go," he said instead of answering.

"I'd like you to tell me."

"It's not something you'd want to hear."

She continued to look at him, and he gave a heavy sigh.

"This is a day for *you* to remember him, not me."

"I see," she said.

"I doubt that."

"I can see that you're worn-out with remembering," she said. "And I know it's not Thomas Henry that's troubling you, because you didn't know him that well. It's the others, I believe. The ones who were with you in the war. The ones who are gone now."

She stopped because she thought he wanted to say something, and surprisingly he did.

"A lot of us joined the army together," he said. "A merry band of orphans, or so we thought. But we were…cannon fodder because we wouldn't leave anyone behind if we were killed and because we would fight and fight hard. So many of us were lost, the generals shifted the ones who were left into another decimated company—in a different division. It never felt… right being with those other soldiers. None of them were from Kentucky and they weren't…like us. I still can't— That's the hardest part—"

"What is?" she asked, because he was suddenly lost in another place, another time, one far from the rocky overhang by the spring. The water spilled quietly into the collecting pool. A flock of crows settled noisily in some nearby trees and insects still buzzed in the air despite the coming storm.

He finally looked at her. "Believing it. Comrades— some still boys—some you've known since you were children. One minute they're there, alive, talking like always. Talking about the weather or how they're hoping for this or that—a letter, a chance to sleep, an apple pie. Fred, he was always talking about apple pies." He gave a sudden smile that just as suddenly faded. "And then Fred, and the rest of them, they're gone in the time it takes a heart to beat. You know they're gone because you've seen it with your own eyes, but you still don't… believe it. Even now I think I'm going to run into one of them somewhere."

"Yes," she said quietly.

He gave her a quizzical look.

"It's how I felt when my mother died," she said. "It was so…quick. I used to think she had to be in the house somewhere—in the next room or out working in her flower garden." She looked up at the darkening sky, then back at him. "I still remember her, though. Do you remember your mother?"

"No. Well, I have one memory. At least I think it's a memory."

"A good one?"

"Yes. I believe it to be."

"Will you share it?"

He looked at her a long moment. "I…made her laugh," he said, and Sayer smiled.

"How?"

"I told her where I thought the wind came from." He gestured toward the trees around them swaying back and forth in the wind. "I said the trees waved and they made the wind. And I was very sure about that."

"A quite logical conclusion," Sayer said, still smiling. "What did she say?"

"Nothing. It made her laugh. I don't think she laughed very often." He stopped and gave another heavy sigh. "I shouldn't be telling you any of this. You have your own sorrows."

"I did ask," she said. "Out loud. And if it helps you to speak of it, then I want to hear it."

"Nothing helps. And I can't extend you the same courtesy."

She looked at him—until he looked away.

Please, Lord, she thought. *Will You help Jeremiah find some kind of peace? All those warriors in the Bible—did You not help them when their hearts were heavy and sad like his?*

"Don't do that, either," he said.

"What?"

"I think you were praying for me just now. Don't."

"My prayers are mine, Jeremiah Murphy. But I am sorry about intruding. I don't want to do that."

She picked up the bucket and walked toward the collecting pool, stopping long enough to pick a few stalks of mint that grew near the water's edge. She crushed some of the leaves in her hand and savored the minty scent that rose from her fingers. Her mother had always put mint in her tea, and crushing the leaves was a way of conjuring her memory—something Sayer definitely needed today.

She stepped close to the collecting pool and filled the bucket, careful not to stir up the sand and mud in the bottom or to put more water in the bucket than she could carry without spilling it. When she lifted it out and turned around, he was standing there, waiting to take it.

"I can do it," she said. "I'm used to carrying water to the cabin from here."

The wind blew her hair across her face, and he reached out as if he meant to take the strand and tuck it behind her ear. But then he apparently thought better of it, and his hand fell.

"You don't have to carry water for me," she said, making an attempt to step around him and dropping the mint on the ground in the process.

He picked it up and handed it to her, and he didn't argue with her. He simply took the bucket from her hand. "I want to. And it's got nothing to do with Thomas Henry. After you."

She frowned and in lieu of getting into a tug-of-war over the bucket, she walked ahead of him up the steep path, trying not to dwell on his remark by being far more mindful of the possibility of snakes along the

way than she had been when she came down here looking for him.

"I think I'm going to ask how you are after all," he
said as they walked along. "I don't mean how you are
about Thomas Henry. I know you're sad about that. I
was wondering about that place on your head. How is
that?"

"Well, it doesn't hurt anymore, and I think I'm in
my right mind—most of the time. But I wouldn't ask
Rorie to bear that out, if I were you." She couldn't see
his face, but she had the distinct feeling that he might
be smiling again.

"I've got some good thick pieces of oak wood split,"
he said as they struggled to make the steepest part of
climb. "I think I can use them for steps along here. I'll
see to it when I've caught up with the plowing."

She stopped walking, disconcerted suddenly by the
domestic turn their conversation had taken. It was the
kind of conversation she imagined a man might have
with his wife. "Please. I've imposed on you enough.
You don't have to make steps," she said, looking into
his eyes. "You don't have to do the plowing. You've
done what Thomas Henry asked you to do. You're free
to go now."

"I can go," he agreed, "but I don't think I'd be free."

The ground was nearly level now, and he stepped
past her to carry the bucket the rest of the way to the
cabin. She watched him go, more disconcerted than
ever. She was certain that she didn't know precisely
what he meant by his parting remark—but then again
she was very afraid that she did.

She took a deep breath and looked up at the sky.

Beautiful, just as Mrs. Tomlin had pronounced it, but a storm was coming. If she'd learned nothing else in her life, she'd learned that there would always be a storm of some kind on the horizon. As she walked on, and in keeping with that conclusion, yet another problem came to mind.

Halbert.

She still had to worry about Halbert Garth. She was surprised that he hadn't come to the memorial service. She would have thought he would want to pressure her about handing over the land again, if nothing else. Halbert Garth wasn't one to let an opportunity pass him by, especially when she was certain to be at her most vulnerable. A chance to badger her on a day like today should have seemed golden to him. He wasn't the kind of man who would have been the least bit deterred by the presence of other people, especially people who had no authority and no power to cause him harm, and whose good opinion he would never crave. There was little doubt that he would have known that Preacher Tomlin and the congregation were coming up here. Isaiah said there was no rest for the wicked. Perhaps Halbert had other irons in the fire besides trying to steal away the Garth land, and he'd been busy with them.

When she reached the yard, Jeremiah was taking the water bucket inside, and he didn't immediately come out again. Sayer assumed that Rorie had pounced on him and by now had him seated at the table eating his delayed meal of ham and cheese and corn bread.

And so he was. He didn't say anything when she came in, and neither did she. She could feel Rorie's intense interest in the situation, and she stood awkwardly for a moment, then lay the mint on the edge of the table and set about finding a place to put all the supplies Preacher Tomlin's wife had ordered Willard to stack out of the way—supplies Jeremiah had bought, she suddenly remembered.

"If you'll give me a tally of the amount you spent for all this, I will repay you," she said without looking at him. "It may take a while. If you would give me an address where I can send the money after you leave—"

"You don't owe me anything. Thomas Henry meant for you to have it. You still have some credit down at the general store."

Sayer looked at him. She knew perfectly well that she was supposed to infer that this was somehow Thomas Henry's money he'd been spending, but that couldn't be. Thomas Henry had sent every penny home—when and if he got paid—and his paydays had been erratic at best during the last year of the war. Besides that, the money he would have gotten would now be worthless.

"I don't see how—"

"Best not to go looking a gift horse in the mouth," Rorie said from the rocking chair where she was sitting and rocking and smoking her pipe. "You decided yet how long you're staying, Jeremiah?"

"Until you run me off," he said easily because that was their usual banter.

"Well, that might be sooner than you think," Rorie said.

"I don't doubt it."

Rorie let him eat the rest of his meal in peace, and when he'd finished, he got up from the table.

"I hear tell Benton is wanting to have a word with

you. Sadie Mitchell, she told me that when we was putting out the food and waiting for the memorial service to be over," Rorie said as if she'd only just remembered it. "She said he's wanting to see you about something. He didn't tell Sadie what it was, though," she added with enough significance to suggest that this would be a good time for him to enlighten her at least.

But he chose to let the golden opportunity pass him by, and the promise of rain that had ended Thomas Henry's memorial service early arrived in a sudden heavy downpour. Sayer moved to close the back door.

"Thank you for keeping the meal for me," Jeremiah said, still not inclined to comment on whatever Benton might want, and he included Sayer in his appreciation. "If you'll excuse me now, I'll take my leave."

Sayer nodded in his direction, then moved the box she'd been emptying to the table. She wanted to sit down in the chair Jeremiah had just vacated because she was suddenly as exhausted as the sleeping girls. But she kept removing items from the box—a side of bacon, a large chunk of cheese wrapped in vinegar-soaked cloth, several pounds of beans, real coffee with such a tantalizing aroma that it made her stop long enough to sniff the cloth sack. How long had it been since she'd had coffee? So long that she couldn't remember the last time. There were several small, cylindrical packages in one corner of the box. Those she could identify by the smell, as well—peppermint sticks.

"That boy sure don't mind the rain, I'll say that for him," Rorie said, leaning sharply forward in the rocking chair so she could see out the window.

"I suppose after four years of war, you get used to it."

"Did you find out where he's been and what he was doing while he was gone?"

"No," Sayer said, placing the peppermint sticks on the table. The girls would be so happy to have these, not to mention Rorie. She handed her the one with her name on it.

"Well, look at this. Ain't nobody give me peppermint sticks since I was a young-un and I recited all my Bible verses in Sunday school." She tore off the paper immediately and began to eat it.

"You're not going to save it?" Sayer asked.

"At my age, putting things off ain't a good idea—especially when it's something you dearly want," Rorie said, taking a big bite and clearly savoring the taste. "Did you *ask* him where he went?" she asked around the candy.

"No, I didn't ask him," Sayer said, and Rorie gave a sharp exhalation of breath.

"Well, what did you think I wanted you to go see about him for?"

"I don't know," Sayer assured her. "You never said."

But that small but pertinent fact apparently carried no weight at all.

"We'll just have to corner him later, that's all," Rorie decided. "Or *I* will. I'm thinking you ain't no good at it. It must have something to do with Benton, though, don't you think?"

But she didn't wait for Sayer to answer.

"So tell me about the memorial service for Thomas Henry. I reckon I could have got up there if I'd used the walking stick Jeremiah cut for me and if I took it slow. But I figured I ought to be the one watching over putting the food out—since I'm staying here and all. Was Preacher Tomlin and the rest of them a comfort to you?"

Sayer didn't want to talk about whether or not she was comforted. All she could think about was that she had clung to Jeremiah's arm as if she were drowning. She began telling her about the outcropping of rock where Thomas Henry's memorial service had been held instead.

"The view of the mountains is so vast and open— Amity was afraid. It's good that Preacher Tomlin knew it well enough not to let the children in the congregation come. The little boys would have been daring each other to hang off the edge in no time."

"Did you have any singing?"

"Mrs. Tomlin sang 'Bright Morning Stars.'"

Rorie hummed it softly to herself for a moment. "I do like that hymn. I hate I missed it. She ain't like most of them women in the choir. She's somebody what can carry a tune. You know of anybody around here what sings better than she does?"

But Sayer barely heard the question. Her attention was taken by the sound of someone on horseback riding away from the cabin.

"I swan," Rorie said in exasperation. "There he goes again."

It was too soon to have heard anything from the Jefferson lawyer. Jack had given his sworn deposition that Thomas Henry Garth was dead, including all the facts of the battle itself, as he knew them. He hadn't realized that he would have to name his own regiment in the process, but the lawyer's clerk didn't seem to notice that Jack had been in the wrong army. A letter would have to be drafted to whoever was maintaining the military and enlistment records for the Highland Guards, the young man said. Supposedly, everything possible was being done to account for missing soldiers, and once the information Jack gave was verified to someone's satisfaction, then the will could be probated and given to Sayer.

But that could take weeks or more likely, months. Even so, Jack went to find out why Benton wanted to see him. He turned the possible reasons over in his mind on the ride down to the crossroads, mostly so he wouldn't think about Sayer. It was incredible to him that he'd actually told her about Fred and his constant longing for apple pie, much less his only memory of his vague and shadowy mother. He'd never told anyone about her. Not the other orphans, who were certain they knew everything there was to know about Jack Murphy, and not Father Bartholomew, whom he trusted with his life. He'd told Sayer, almost without hesitation, simply because he thought—knew—he could and that she wouldn't judge whatever he said. He had looked into her eyes and he had believed beyond all doubt that his secrets, the good and the bad, would be safe with her.

A good woman is more precious than rubies…

A man will know when he finds her…

Yes, he thought. Thomas Henry Garth had certainly known—or Jack wouldn't be here.

Despite the rain, there were a number of people about when he reached the crossroads, but their interest in his arrival was brief this time, he supposed because both he and his business here had been identified and categorized to everyone's satisfaction.

The benches and chairs on the general store porch were empty because the wind was driving the rain hard against the front windows of the building. Jack stopped long enough to beat the water off his hat before he went inside. Benton was busy with a customer, a woman Jack didn't recognize, one who apparently intended to wait out the rain in a rocking chair by the unlit potbelly stove. Benton, ever the wily storekeeper, offered her a sip of some newly opened blackberry wine while she waited—which she sharply declined.

"I'm temperance, Benton," she said stiffly. "You know that."

"I heard you wanted to see me," Jack said in the middle of Benton's immediate backtracking.

"I do," Benton said, clearly grateful for the interruption. "I was wanting to know if I need to be looking for...anything from Jefferson." He glanced at the woman who was now earnestly rocking in the rocking chair—and listening to their conversation.

"Yes," Jack said. "But I don't know how long it will take—" He stopped because two men on horseback had arrived and were coming through the door with a good deal more noise than was necessary. Jack could smell the O Be Joyful on them before they reached the counter and so could the woman in the rocking chair.

"Can I help you gentlemen?" Benton asked calmly. Apparently half-drunk travelers were nothing new.

"You got tobacco?" one of the men asked.

"You got money?" Benton countered.

The men exchanged a look.

"We can pay," one of them said, and Benton raised his eyebrows.

"It's not Confederate," the man said, glancing in Jack's direction.

"Then I got tobacco," Benton said. "And most anything else you might want as long as your money holds out."

"How's about some information?" the taller of the two men asked.

"What kind of information?"

"You seen any strangers hereabouts?"

"I've seen you two."

"Besides us," the taller man said with a flash of annoyance.

"We're a stopping place for the Jefferson stage," Benton said. "I see a lot of strangers—more than I care to, if I was to tell the truth about it. The traveling public these days don't buy much. And some of them you have to watch like a hawk so they don't walk off with half the shelf stock," he added pointedly just in case the two of them had thievery in mind.

"This here one is a ex-soldier."

"Union or Confederate?"

"Union."

"See a lot of them coming through, too. You know his name?"

"Murphy. Jack Murphy."

"What do you want him for?"

"Bounty—" the shorter man tried to say, but the other one interrupted.

"We just need to find him for somebody. You seen him or not?"

"Well, I don't know," Benton said, glancing at Jack. "Handing out your name ain't one of the requirements for doing business in my store. And I ain't one to ask questions that ain't none of my business. How much tobacco you want?"

The man bought his tobacco, looking hard at Jack as he made the transaction.

"You're that friend of Thomas Henry's what was in the army when he was, ain't you?" the woman in the rocking chair suddenly called to Jack.

"Yes, ma'am," he said, because the statement was close to the truth. He turned away slightly so the man couldn't get a good look at his face.

"I would have been at the memorial service, but my old man's poorly. I come down here to get him some stomach medicine. Did the weather hold? Up there on the ridge?"

"Yes, ma'am. Didn't rain until it was long over."

"Was his service nice? I hope it was nice."

"Yes, ma'am," Jack said again. "Some beautiful singing." He could feel the sweat running down the back of his neck.

"Oh, my, yes," the woman said as if she'd been there. "Thomas Henry would have liked that. I know he would. I sent all the flowers I had on the wagon with Preacher Tomlin. The late roses? The gladiolas and the strawflowers—and the dahlias. Did you see the dahlias? When I was a little girl, I used to walk by this old widder woman's house on the way to church every Sunday—Josephine, her name was. Everybody called her 'Finney,' though. She grew the prettiest dahlias—

all kinds of colors—and every time she seen me, she'd give me one. I do love my dahlias."

"They were beautiful, ma'am. I believe they meant a lot to Sayer and the girls."

"Will you tell them Mariah Grace asked after them? And say I'm sorry for their loss? Say I'll remember them all in my prayers."

"I will, ma'am," Jack said. When he chanced looking around, the two men had gone. He took a quiet breath in relief.

But Benton was still there, and he was looking at him with far more interest than he'd shown previously.

"I'll send you word by one of these wild young-uns what's always hanging around here if I get something from Jefferson," he said. "That way you won't have to come all the way down here…for nothing."

"Thanks," Jack said. "I appreciate it."

"Just trying to save you some time. You…tell Sayer you went to Jefferson?" he asked, lowering his voice so that the woman in the rocking chair couldn't hear him.

"No. There's nothing to tell yet. She's got enough to worry about."

"I hear tell it's going to take a lot of work to make that farm of hers right again. Might be some of the men around here can help you out when they get their own place caught up. The bachelors and the widowers around here, they'll be wanting to help, now that Sayer's free to marry again. You going to wait out the rain?"

"No, I'll be getting on back. Like you said—lot of work to do."

"You best mind how you go from now on," Benton said. It might have passed as a mildly obscure statement any other time, but not today. Today, it was fraught with something else.

Jack looked at him, and he could have jumped right in with both feet and asked what he meant, but he didn't. He turned and left, his mind more occupied by the notion of bachelors and widowers hanging around Sayer than how long it would take the two men who had just left to find out she had a protector. He couldn't think that Benton would be the only local they would ask in their quest to find a stranger.

Benton.

He seemed a good man but one who put his full concentration on making money, and he, like Jack, had heard the word *bounty*.

Chapter Eight

"I never let on to Sayer that I knowed about it," Rorie said.

Jack stopped midstroke in his search for a tender spot on the horse's knee. His first thought was that she had somehow acquired another message from Benton down at the general store, and for some reason she was hiding that fact from Sayer. He might have had a better idea of what the remark meant if he had actually been listening to her conversation, but he hadn't. Instead, he'd been savoring the cool morning breeze coming down off the mountain and trying to hear the song Sayer was singing as she did her household chores. He thought it was a hymn, but he wasn't sure. If it was, it wasn't like any he'd ever heard. He didn't let his mind dwell on the fact that he couldn't understand most of the words from this far away, even with the cabin windows and doors open, or that it was the singer herself—in a pink calico dress with many small flowers on it—who made him want to listen so intently.

Your company has been delightful
You who doth leave my mind distressed…

Pink calico. It was nothing like the dark green silk
Elrissa wore.

I go away, behind to leave you
Perhaps never to meet again
But if we never have the pleasure
I hope…

Sayer abruptly stopped singing, and Rorie was staring at him in that way she had. At that moment, she
likely knew exactly what he was feeling, but whether
or not she planned to discuss her observations remained
to be seen.

He went back to examining the horse's knee, forcing most of his attention to other, more pressing concerns. He was still going over and over the fact that two
men had come into the general store looking for him.
In the days that had passed since that nerve-racking
encounter, he had come to the conclusion that Elrissa's
husband must have bounty hunters following the stage
routes on both sides of the Tennessee border and asking about him at every community and crossroads they
came to. Even he would have to admit it was a good—
if expensive—plan.

Rorie was still waiting. He gave a quiet sigh. Whatever was on her mind, she had thrown the door to it
wide-open, but as usual, she was going to make him
come in after it. He'd have no peace otherwise.

"Know about what?" he asked.

"About that there place up yonder on the high ridge—Mr. Garth Senior's place," Rorie said. "I used to go up there a lot after my first baby died. First time I went, it was on his Burying Day. I knowed it was Garth land and I knowed Mr. Garth Senior didn't take kindly to trespassers. But I went anyway. I didn't want to ask if I could, neither—I reckon he would have said it was all right, but I just couldn't bear that, asking somebody if I could go on their land to grieve. I reckon that's why I didn't tell Sayer about it, too. Didn't want to seem… weak. Oh, I know women is *supposed* to be weak, but I always figured the fewer people what caught on when you was all wobbly, the better."

He looked up at her, still not understanding.

"I been thinking maybe you ought to go up there again," she said, clearly getting to the heart of the matter.

"Why?"

"You need to get a better hold on whatever's troubling you."

"Nothing is troubling me."

"It's a good place," she said anyway. "A prayerful place, like Preacher Tomlin said. Well, you been up there. You know what it's like."

"I'm not much for praying."

"I didn't say nothing about *praying,* now, did I? You don't always have to be talking God's ear off, Jeremiah. Prayer ain't just words and trying to sound all lofty like you ain't you. You think the Lord don't know when we got trouble and heartache? You just go up there where it's all quietlike, and you wait. You stand there in the pure beauty of what's all around you—maybe appreciate what a fine job He done. That's all. You don't talk if you don't want to. You're just there and ready—in case *He* wants to tell *you* something. It ain't that hard, even for you."

"Nothing is troubling me," he said again.

"Now, you know as good as anybody how much I hate a lie. You know I might have shot you dead if I thought you weren't telling me the truth that day you come to my cabin looking for Sayer."

"Might? I was sure you would—then. Don't think you'd shoot me now, though."

"Well, I ain't got my musket or my revolver handy *now*. I couldn't shoot you if I wanted to—but I can tell you the only thing what's keeping me from giving you a good hit upside your head is I know you believe what you just said about not being troubled—even when you catch your hands shaking like they do, even if you don't sleep, even if you got to work yourself to death so's you don't think on it. But *I* don't believe it, and you can put that in your pipe and smoke it."

"Don't smoke," he said, and in lieu of a hit upside his head, he got a good punch in the arm for it. He couldn't keep from laughing. "Don't you have somebody else to bedevil?"

"No, I don't," she assured him. "Might directly, though. Might need to go give Sayer a good talking-to here before long."

"About what?" he asked, no longer interested in the horse.

"Well, look at you," Rorie said. "You're listening to me now, ain't you?"

"No. Yes."

He waited, and when she still didn't say anything, he raised both his eyebrows, the way he might have at Ike when he was slow about getting to the point.

"You done a lot of work around here," she said when she was good and ready. "You're ever bit as good at working this here farm as Thomas Henry was—him *and* his daddy. But you and me both know you should have been long gone from here by now, on account of that other trouble you got."

"I don't think I ever said I had trouble."

"No, you said 'not exactly' and such as that—like I ain't been around men all my life and I can't figure out what that kind of dancing around something means. So why ain't you gone from here?"

"Halbert," he said without hesitation.

"You seen any sign of him?"

"Not since he and his men were up here looking for bushwhackers. The thing is, though, this horse knows when somebody is around."

"That there horse thinks the war is still going on, does he?"

"He does."

"Reminds me of somebody else I know," she said pointedly. "Go spend some time up yonder on the ridge like I told you. You're going to need help to figure out how to take Sayer and them girls with you when you leave out from here." And with that she walked away— without telling him why she had Sayer in her sights, too.

"Is she all right?" he called after her.

"Not exactly," she said without stopping, throwing what she apparently considered his favorite phrase right back at him.

"Rorie!" he called, and this time she turned to look at him.

"I'm sorry for your loss."

She frowned and seemed about to say something, but then she didn't. She nodded instead and continued on her way. He could hear her singing her own version of what must be a song as she went into the house.

My love lives at the head of the holler
She won't come and I won't foller...

"Is he all right?" Sayer asked as soon as Rorie stepped inside the cabin. She had been determined not to, but clearly she hadn't the ability to stand by her own decisions. She had been singing to keep her thoughts where they should be, and when that no longer worked, she had concentrated on listening to Beatrice and Amity chattering away until they went to fetch a fresh bucket of water. Then, she had taken Thomas Henry's letters out of her keepsake box and had been sitting at the table reading them—when she still had chores to do.

But no matter what she did, the only thing on her mind was Jeremiah. He was working sunup to sundown, trying to get the fields plowed and ready for the fall planting, putting the steps in the path to the spring, getting a winter's supply of wood cut—and she took every opportunity to talk to him if she could without seeming too bold. They had no serious conversations like the one they'd had down at the spring after Thomas Henry's memorial service. They only spoke of mundane things, crops, weather, the need to replace her missing livestock. They had finally done the haying—

a happy event for his horse and Rorie's cow and mule. It had taken days to do it, even with her and the girls helping. Sayer knew that he watched her as she raked the hay he cut into windrows, and shameless or not, she hadn't minded.

Of late she had been sending the girls out to the field to take him a hot midday meal, and it was all she could do not to go with them. Amity and Beatrice reported that he said thank-you, but he didn't stop to eat it while they were there. She had taken to packing as much food as she could into the pail because in the past week he hadn't joined them for the evening meal. If she happened to see him during the day, he didn't stop long enough to talk, but only nodded to her on his way to or from the barn. He wasn't sleeping. She could tell by looking at him. She didn't think he was eating much, despite the fact that every morning when she got up, the empty lunch pail was sitting on the corner of the porch.

"Is he all right?" she asked again because Rorie was clearly disinclined to answer.

"I swear the two of you is going to wear me out asking how one another is."

"He asked about me?"

"He did."

"What did he say?"

"He said the same thing you said, only he said 'she' 'stead of 'he.' 'Is *she* all right?'"

"And what did you tell him?"

"I said 'Not exactly.'"

"Rorie! Why did you tell him that!"

"I told him that because I didn't want to have to come right out and say being around him every day has got you thinking on him near about all the time. Pining over him, if you was to ask me."

"I am *not* pining over him," Sayer said, knowing her sudden blush was belying that fact with great eloquence.

"Well, what would *you* call it, then?"

"I'm a widow. I just lost my husband. I can't—"

"Can't what? Can't never let Jeremiah come to mind? Can't worry about him when you can see things ain't right with him? Can't feel all that gratitude for the things he's done for you and Beatrice and Amity sliding over into something else?"

"I just lost my husband!" Sayer cried.

"Husband in name only," Rorie said in that maddening, matter-of-fact way she had. "I know you loved Thomas Henry. I reckon everybody around here knows that. You'll always love him, honey—he's a big part of what makes you who you are. But he's gone. As a woman full-growed, you done already spent more time with Jeremiah than you ever did with Thomas Henry, and you know it."

Yes, Sayer thought. She did know it.

"I'm trying," she said after a moment.

"Trying what?" Rorie asked.

"Trying not to disrespect Thomas Henry's memory. Trying to be the kind of wife he deserved."

"You were the kind of wife he deserved. For four long years. You looked after his mama and you're still looking after his little sisters and his land. Besides which, I thought Thomas Henry said you and the girls weren't to grieve."

"Yes, but he didn't mean—" She sighed heavily and began gathering up the letters she'd been reading.

"Don't nobody know what Thomas Henry meant by that but him, and if he was hurt bad and dying, maybe even he didn't know."

"It's too soon," Sayer said.

"Some people might say so—people what's got plenty of money and plenty of time on their hands and no young-uns to look after. They can make rules and wait around forever when they don't have to worry how to make something out of nothing and where the next meal's coming from. One thing I know for certain sure. Hearts can't tell time. Hearts don't even know what time is. They feel what they feel when they feel it—and you can't talk them out of it even when it's wrong—which, to my way of thinking, this ain't."

Sayer could hear the girls coming back with the water bucket, and she didn't say anything more. There was nothing she could say. She hadn't been "letting" Jeremiah come to mind. The truth was that he was never out of it. Of course she could see how troubled he was. She knew the things he'd seen and done haunted him, even before he'd said anything. She prayed for him every single day—and not just sighs and vague, one-word petitions. She was worried about him and she told God so. And just like Rorie said, she could feel the gratitude she felt toward Jeremiah Murphy sliding over into something else.

"He ain't going to let Halbert hurt you again if he can help it," Rorie said quietly as the girls began to fill the pots on the stove with water so Sayer could begin cooking their supper.

Sayer looked at her sharply. "What do you mean, 'again'?"

"I ain't said nothing before because you had enough on your mind, what with being hurt and Halbert's big visitation and the news about Thomas Henry."

"Well, say it now," Sayer said.

"All right. Here it is, then. I don't reckon a army deserter or some bushwhacker sneaked in here and took that box of china when you and the girls wasn't looking. There ain't but one time I can see how that thievery could have happened and that was when the girls was so sick with the fever and not half knowing where they was. I don't reckon you just fell and hit your head down at the spring that day. I think Halbert had a hand in it."

"No. I— No, it must have been like you said. I was worn-out from taking care of them. I must have—"

"I was standing in the trees when Halbert and his men come up here looking for them pretend bushwhackers of his. I seen how surprised they was when you come out of the cabin. Maybe they only meant to scare you and you fell trying to get away from them, or maybe not. But I know this, you up and around and talking sense and not remembering what happened was the last thing they was expecting. What they was *expecting* was you being bed-rid and so scared you'd be ready to clear out and hand everything over to Halbert in a heartbeat, with or without something legal saying you could. He'd just bide his time till the taxes come due and he'd have the Garth land, free and clear just like he wanted."

Sayer shook her head. The thing she had been so afraid Halbert might be capable of—that he would actually harm her or the girls—had apparently happened.

"It doesn't make any sense. Why would he take the china?" Sayer asked, still hoping Rorie was mistaken.

"Because he knows what everybody else here knows—that there china belonged to your mama and it's precious to you. When a evil man finds out what's precious, he'll use it as a weapon. He'll show you what power he has by taking it away from you. Sometimes it's china plates. Sometimes it's…something else."

Sayer reached up to touch the place on her forehead.

"It's better if you know what's what," Rorie said.

"That's the problem. I don't know 'what's what,' Rorie. I don't know at all."

"You're just too believing for your own good, that's all. You are going to have to mind yourself. You might not fool Halbert with a big spoon next time."

"If Thomas Henry hadn't—"

"Thomas Henry is dead. And he owes Jeremiah a whole slew of debts he can't ever repay. So just maybe *you* can repay one or two of them for him," Rorie interrupted. "A kindness for a kindness."

"He doesn't come to supper and he doesn't stop long enough for me to even speak to him."

"Then corner him," Rorie said, matter-of-fact as always.

"Can we eat our candy?" Amity asked, apparently on Beatrice's behalf, as well, since Beatrice was still determined to seem disinterested in childish things.

"Not now," Sayer said.

"But when?" Amity asked. "We *never* have candy."

"I wonder who ate *my* peppermint stick, then?" Sayer asked.

"We had to," Amity assured her. "We wanted to save ours for later—and now it's later. Can we eat it?"

"No. I thought we'd all take Jeremiah his dinner today, and we'd have a picnic. You and Beatrice can eat some of your candy then—for dessert. That is, if Beatrice wants to eat hers."

"She does," Amity said confidently. "I *know* she does."

"Well, good. This plan should work out very well, then."

"It will if Jeremiah can stop and eat with us. Do you think he'll stop working and eat with us?"

"We can ask," Sayer said, hoping she wouldn't have to take Rorie's advice and corner him.

"I think he will. He likes us," she decided. "He likes orphans."

"Yes," Sayer said. "I believe he does."

Sayer spent the early morning picking the last of the green beans in the vegetable garden, and then making biscuits to go with the bacon Jeremiah had bought. She sliced onions and put them in apple cider vinegar, then she steeped some peeled apples to make apple water and had Amity and Beatrice take the jug down to the spring to chill until they were ready to go. As an afterthought, she made fried cherry pies. She had a good supply of dried cherries in boxes filled with straw stored under the beds. And, since Jeremiah's trip to the general store, she even had real sugar to sweeten them.

When the sun was high, she and the girls left the cabin. Rorie was sitting under the shade tree hard at work putting a threaded needle through green bean pods so they could be hung to dry. "No need to hurry back on my account," she said as they walked by her. "I ain't expecting to see you anytime soon—especially since all three of you is going in the wrong direction."

"It only looks like we're simple-headed," Amity assured her, and Rorie laughed.

"If you say so."

The walk to the field where Jeremiah was plowing was winding and long, but pleasant. What Sayer didn't expect was that they would startle him so when he saw them. Because they had had to fetch the jug of apple water from the spring, they had emerged from the woods behind where he was plowing, and he clearly hadn't realized that there might be a circuitous path through the trees that led from the cabin to the high field. She also hadn't expected that his horse would be hobbled nearby and equally disturbed, or that Jeremiah would be plowing with a sidearm stuck into his belt, one he promptly hid by pulling out the tail of his blue plaid shirt.

"Is it my birthday?" he asked upon seeing the large basket instead of the usual pail.

"No!" Amity cried. "It's a picnic! And we get to eat the peppermint candy today!"

"It seems to me it's taken you a long time to get to it," he said.

"We ate Sayer's first," Amity said. "She shares."

"I shared myself right out of the whole thing," Sayer said, and he smiled.

"Thank you for getting it for us. I didn't think I'd ever see peppermint candy again," Beatrice said in her grown-up way.

"You're welcome," he said, his formal tone matching hers.

"When *is* your birthday, Jeremiah?" Amity asked as he removed his hat and wiped the sweat from his face with his kerchief.

"Well, I'm not sure. Nobody seemed to know at the orphanage. When that happened, it was celebrated on the day we came to live there. If it didn't suit us, when we were old enough, we got to pick whatever day we wanted. I picked Christmas Eve."

"Why is that?" Sayer asked because she liked knowing these small things about him, about his life in the orphanage.

"I…thought it was a day when people try to be happy."

Sayer didn't know what to say to that, but she did know what he meant. She had always appreciated the peace and joy of Christmas Eve.

"I hope you don't mind if we stay and share the meal," she said, watching him closely for some sign that he did.

He gave her one of his "almost" smiles. "I can't think of anything I'd like better—as long as Miss Amity and Miss Beatrice save a biscuit or two for me."

Both girls giggled, and they moved out of the heat of the noonday sun and into the shade of the lone tree in the middle of the field where he had left the mule. Sayer and the girls sat on two of the nearby stumps, and Jeremiah sat on the ground.

"Amity, will you say grace?" Sayer said. "I believe it's your turn. And don't rush. The candy isn't going anywhere."

Amity sighed and did as she was told, clearly making this one of her best efforts for Jeremiah's benefit. As soon as she'd concluded the prayer that Preacher Tomlin had taught all the children, Sayer began emptying the basket. She could sense that Jeremiah was watching, but she concentrated on the task itself, only daring once to look at him. It was as if he had been waiting for her to do just that. She didn't—couldn't—look away.

A kindness for a kindness, she thought, knowing it was more than that.

"Are you hungry, Jeremiah?" Amity asked, breaking into both their thoughts. "We have bacon biscuits. I hope you're hungry."

"I am, Miss Amity."

"And we brought apple water. We put it in the spring so it would be *cold*."

"My favorite thing to drink. What have you been doing this morning?" he asked, turning his attention back to Sayer, but Amity answered for her.

"All this," she said, waving her hand over the food. "Sayer made fried cherry pies, too."

"Those are *my* favorite," Beatrice said. "My mama taught Sayer how to make them, didn't she, Sayer?"

"Yes, she did, and she was very patient with me. It took me quite a while to learn how to do it. The biscuits, too."

"Mama said Sayer could slay Goliath with her biscuits," Beatrice said, and he laughed.

"Not that bad, surely."

"Oh, yes," Sayer said. "That bad."

"We fed them to the pigs," Amity said with her mouth full. "They *liked* them."

"Well, these are really good," Jeremiah said, starting on his third one. "A pig would have a very hard time getting it away from me. I appreciate your bringing the picnic all the way up here."

"You're welcome," Beatrice and Amity said in unison, and he smiled.

"Father Bartholomew would approve of their manners," he said to Sayer.

"Father Bartholomew?"

"The priest who ran the orphanage. He expected civility at all times, no matter what. Got it, too, usually, in the classroom and out."

"There was a school? At the orphanage?"

"Yes. I didn't realize until I was in the army that I'd gotten a better education than most, thanks to Father Bartholomew. He was determined to make sure that we were well prepared to leave and go out on our own."

"You went to church, as well? Sunday school and preaching services?"

He looked at her thoughtfully. "Why do you ask?"

"You seem…"

"What?"

"You…seem like a person who…went to church."

"Not entirely heathen, then."

"No, I didn't mean— It's— I shouldn't—" She could feel her face growing warm with embarrassment and she looked down at her lap.

"Our souls weren't neglected, if that is what you mean. Regular church services were a big part of my upbringing," he said, apparently choosing to answer the question she hadn't quite managed to voice. "Father Bartholomew never missed an opportunity to teach us the Scriptures and how they applied to us—to real life. It was…helpful. Even when I didn't want it to be."

She looked at him. "Are you a heathen now?" she asked bluntly because she wanted—needed—to know, and she couldn't for the life of her have said why. She just wanted him to be…safe, physically and spiritually.

"Lost souls are important to you," he said.

She sensed no annoyance in the remark, but she didn't know if it was a way of avoiding her question or whether it was a statement of his opinion—and so she said nothing.

"Preacher Tomlin seems to think I'm in search of godliness," he said after a moment.

"Are you?"

"I don't know." He gave a quiet sigh and looked away toward the line of trees at the edge of the field. "Maybe I am a heathen. I have every reason to be. Maybe I'm just…mad at God. Or maybe I never had true faith in the first place. Father Bartholomew always said faith would come and then go if you're not careful. You have to tend it if you want to keep it. I…haven't done much tending of late."

"It doesn't show," she said quietly. How could any man be as kind as he had been to her—to all of them—and not have faith?

He was looking at her steadily, and he seemed about to say something more.

But he didn't, and the silence between them became awkward.

"What do you want to do now that the war is over?" she asked to keep the conversation going.

"Do?" he asked, as if he'd never once considered such a question.

"Have you got a sweetheart, Jeremiah?" Amity suddenly asked. "Beatrice wants to know," she added, the remark causing her sister to turn beet-red.

"I do not, Miss Amity," Jeremiah said. He took a long drink from the jug of apple water, Sayer thought to give Beatrice time to recover.

"Why not?" Amity asked the second he lowered the jug.

"Well, she married somebody else," he said, glancing at Sayer.

"Why in the world did she do *that?*" Amity persisted, clearly exasperated on his behalf.

"I went off to war. I wasn't around, and I think she must have gotten tired of waiting."

"Is your poor heart broken?" Amity asked earnestly.

"No, my poor heart is fine, Miss Amity," he assured her.

"Waiting is hard," Beatrice said quietly. "We waited and waited for Thomas Henry."

No one said anything, and the silence lengthened.

Sayer raised her eyes to find Jeremiah looking at her over Amity's and Beatrice's heads.

What is it? she thought. *What's wrong?* Whatever it was, she thought it had more to do with the still-hidden revolver than with an engagement gone awry.

"You're doing it again," he said, and she looked away. He was right. She was doing it again. She was asking without asking—because she had him cornered.

A flock of crows suddenly flew from one side of the field to the other.

"I didn't know you brought your horse up here," Sayer said, making the inane comment because she was hoping to resurrect the conversation and turn it in a different direction. The animal suddenly lifted its head and began to paw the ground.

"It settles the mule down," Jeremiah said absently, but he had become as alert as the horse, and he was looking in the same direction.

"Sayer," he said, his eyes still on the line of trees off to their left. "I want you and the girls to pick up everything and go back now. Don't hurry, and don't go back the way you came. Go straight down through the field to the cabin, and don't look back. When you get there, stay inside, and make sure Rorie does, too. Do you understand?"

"Yes, but—"

"Now, Sayer," he insisted, finally looking at her. "If Rorie gives you any argument, tell her…because I said so."

She hesitated, then got up from the stump. "You heard Jeremiah," she said. "Let's pack up the basket—and we're not in a hurry."

She expected a lot of questions from them both, but there were none. They were clearly afraid now as she herself was beginning to be. She kept glancing at him as they packed up what was left of the picnic, but his attention was completely taken by something only he and the horse sensed. Now and then he casually handed her something to put into the basket, but his eyes were on the line of trees.

He walked to the mule, and she realized that he was unhooking the traces.

"I have no regrets, Sayer," he said over his shoulder. "I want you to know that."

"Jeremiah—"

"Go," he said, still busy with the mule. "Now."

She picked up the basket and gathered the girls to her. They began to walk across the plowed field. She made a point of looking neither right nor left.

"Is Jeremiah going to get hurt?" Amity asked, clinging to her hand, trying not to stumble on the plowed ground.

"I can't say, Amity," Sayer said because she didn't understand the situation any more than they did. "I don't know what's wrong. But whatever it is, Jeremiah is ready for it, and we have to get out of his way so he doesn't have to worry about us, too."

"I'm going to pray," Amity said. "I'm going to pray *really* hard. I don't want Jeremiah to die, too. He won't, will he, Sayer?"

"Say your prayer. God will hear it," Sayer said instead of answering, but her own fears were rising by the minute.

"Well, I'm going to sing," Beatrice said, and she suddenly burst forth with the chorus of "Shall We Gather at the River." After a moment, Amity joined in.

"Yes, we shall gather at the riv-er…the beau-ti-ful, the beau-ti-ful riv-er…"

They kept singing until they reached the edge of the yard. She handed them the basket to carry between them. "Go straight inside and close the door. I have to get Rorie."

Rorie was still threading green beans under the tree, and Sayer moved as quickly as she dared in her direction.

"Well, that didn't take long. Didn't he like the biscuits?" Rorie asked before Sayer could say anything, her attention fully on working the needle through a bean pod.

"Something's wrong," Sayer said, and Rorie looked up sharply. "He told us to go back and to stay inside the cabin. *All* of us."

Surprisingly, Rorie reached for her walking stick and got up from the bench. "You help me carry this here pan of beans," she said, gathering up her needle and thread and the beans she had already strung.

"Sayer," Rorie said as soon as they were inside the cabin. "Tell me what happened."

"Nothing," Sayer answered. "Except the horse was upset about something."

"Oh, no, I was afeard of that. You young-uns stay away from them windows," Rorie said. "Sit yourselves down over there on the floor. Put that pan of beans between you and pick out the big ones for me—the ones I'm wanting to shell." She glanced in Sayer's direction. "You didn't see nothing at all?" It was more a recrimination than a question.

"No," she said. "There was nothing to see. I just…"

"Just what?"

Sayer looked at her. "I trust him."

Rorie nodded and hobbled to the bed and lifted the mattress. She removed the revolver she'd apparently hidden there. "Can you shoot a revolver?"

"I… It's been a long time."

"Well, now, that there is a surprise answer, let me tell you. I would have up and guessed 'no' and 'never.'"

"Willard Perkins used to come to my uncle's house to see the cook," Sayer said, trying to stay out of sight and still see out the window. "I think he wanted to court her—by showing her how good he was with firearms."

"That sounds like Willard. That boy never did have the sense God gave a turnip."

"He offered to let me shoot the revolver. I guess he thought paying attention to her employer's niece might impress her if his shooting didn't. I didn't know what to do. I wanted to try, but I was more afraid of my aunt than I was the gun. The cook said, 'Might as well be hung for a sheep as a lamb'—she knew she was too good a cook to be in any danger of being sent packing if my aunt found out. So I did it. Several times. Mostly because..."

"Because why?"

Sayer gave a quiet sigh. "Thomas Henry was there."

When she glanced over her shoulder at Rorie, the old woman was grinning from ear to ear, despite their increasingly worrisome situation.

"The things us women will do to get a man's attention," she said.

"It wasn't just that. I was like Willard. I wanted Thomas Henry to...think well of me, I guess."

"Well, he sure done that. Jeremiah wouldn't be here, otherwise. Pity we ain't got but the one revolver. You might know what happens when you pull the trigger, but I better hang on to it. Can you see anything?"

"No. Nothing."

She moved to the other window to get a different view of the slope and the woods. Rorie hobbled to the rocking chair and pulled it well away from the window with one hand. Then she sat down in it with the revolver resting on her knees.

"I hear something," Sayer said abruptly.

In only a moment she could identify it—hoofbeats, coming hard. The distressed mule arrived with as much speed as it could muster, dragging the harness traces in the dirt behind it. It didn't stop, but ran directly past the windows toward the barn. Several gunshots echoed from the direction it had come. And then another, and another, and several more in rapid succession.

Amity dropped the handful of beans she was holding and put her hands over her ears, then scrambled on all fours to get to Sayer. Sayer sat down on the floor with her out of the line of the windows and held her tightly. She reached out her hand to Beatrice. Beatrice hesitated, then crawled over to join them, hiding her face in Sayer's shoulder. Both children were trembling. And all the while, Rorie rocked slowly back and forth in the rocking chair, eyes closed, her hand on the revolver to keep it from falling.

Sayer strained to hear some sound coming from the high field where Jeremiah had been plowing. The only thing she heard was the still-panicked mule blowing and its tack clinking and rattling as it moved around the barnyard. She removed herself from the grasp of both children and stood up again to peer out of the window. She couldn't see anyone.

"I need to find out what's happened," she said to Rorie. "I can go the back way—through the trees."

"Not yet," Rorie said.

"He could be hurt—"

"Not yet. You got to give him time to get back down here," Rorie said. "He might have to circle around and we ain't wanting him to get here and find out you're off wandering around where you shouldn't be."

Sayer gave a quiet sigh and sat back down on the floor.

They all waited, hardly daring to breathe. Amity sniffed from time to time, and Mrs. Garth's oak kitchen clock ticked quietly on the mantel. Outside, the birds sang and the mule had yet to settle down.

"Do you think they heard the gunfire? At the cross-roads?" Sayer asked when she couldn't stand the quiet any longer.

"They heard it. Ain't nobody going to mistake all that shooting for rabbit hunting. Is the back door barred?"

"No," Sayer said in alarm without turning to see. She never bothered with the lock in the daytime when there was so much going in and out to do the chores that needed to be done. She should have locked it the minute they came into the cabin. She crawled on the floor to the back door, then stood and grabbed the bar, pulling hard. She couldn't budge it, and she kept trying until the stubborn lock finally slid into place. In relief, she rested her head against the rough wood of the door for a moment. Someone suddenly pounded on it, causing her to jump back in alarm.

"Sayer! Are you all right in there? What's going on?"

"Benton!" she cried, trying to work the lock again. "Wait—the door—" He must have pulled on the door from the outside because the bar suddenly slid back. She quickly let him inside. "We don't know what's happening—"

"Is everybody all right?" He was hatless and disheveled and not looking like himself at all.

"The mule's in a fair state, but we ain't hurt," Rorie called from her corner.

"Jeremiah was plowing—" Sayer tried to say, but Rorie interrupted.

"What are you doing way up here, Benton?" It was a pertinent question, Sayer thought, because Benton almost never left his store.

"I brought a letter for Jeremiah. I just come off the buffalo road when I heard the guns and it wasn't but a little bit till somebody took a shot at me. Dang near parted my hair for me."

"Jeremiah is up in the high field," Sayer said, trying again to tell him the thing that concerned her so. "We don't know if he's—" She broke off at the sound of more gunfire.

"I ain't got but one shot left in my revolver. You got any paper cartridges and mini balls?"

"There's near a full box of them in that there basket in the corner," Rorie said. "You better load up if you're going back out there."

"You got any other weapons?" he asked, glancing at the revolver on Rorie's knees.

"We got Mr. Garth Senior's musket. I put it out of the way when Sayer was all— If I can remember where it is, we got that," she amended.

"All right, then," Benton said, rummaging through Rorie's all-purpose basket. He put the box of paper cartridges and balls on the table and then reached into an inside pocket and handed Sayer an official-looking letter. "You better keep that here," he said as he began the process of reloading each empty chamber in his revolver. "I'll see if I can get up there where Jeremiah is. I left my horse a ways back so don't let it scare you if it comes wandering in. I took off through the high grass—didn't want whoever was shooting up the place to get a clear aim at me."

He stuck the box containing the remaining cartridges into his pocket and moved to the nearest window to chance looking out. "Where is he? Which way?"

"Up there. Just beyond the open meadow," Sayer said, putting the letter he had handed her on the mantel.

"Too much in the open," Benton said, shaking his head.

"You can get up there the back way. Go down to the spring. Beyond it there's a path though the woods. It leads to the edge of the field. You'll be in the trees most of the way."

Benton nodded and headed for the back door. "Lock this behind me, Sayer," he said as he stepped cautiously outside.

"You be careful, Benton," Rorie called. "You don't know who's up there."

"I'm afraid I do," he said as Sayer closed the door behind him.

Sayer struggled with the bar again and by leaning on the door hard, she finally got it pushed into place. "Rorie, where is the musket?"

"Well, just wait a minute. I got to think on it," she said, frowning.

Another gunshot sounded, this time much closer to the cabin, and the girls screamed.

"I remember—it's up there in the loft," Rorie said in a rush. "You don't have to climb all the way in. Just feel along the edge on the right."

Sayer climbed the ladder quickly, but she couldn't find the musket as easily as Rorie had indicated. She had to move all the way to the edge of the ladder rung and lean out as far as she could before her fingers touched the stock. She finally managed to drag it to her and get a good grip on it, but getting it down without falling was another matter. "Is it loaded?"

"It is," Rorie said. "So don't you go and drop it."

"I can take it," Amity said.

"No, you can't!" Rorie and Beatrice said in unison.

Sayer finally managed to carry it down safely, and she didn't like to think *why* Rorie had had to put it so far out of reach. What a trial she must have been to both Rorie and the girls in those days when she thought Thomas Henry had returned.

"What do you reckon Benton meant—he was afeard he knowed who's up there shooting?"

"Bushwhackers or deserters, I guess," Sayer said, but all the while she was thinking that, given what she knew now about her head injury, it was as likely to be Halbert's men as anybody. Rorie held out her hand for the musket, apparently deciding to take possession of both weapons despite Sayer's experience with a revolver, minimal though it may have been. Or perhaps it was *her* experience with Sayer and the reason she'd had to hide it in the first place that led her to take possession of it now.

Sayer hesitated, then handed it over to her.

"Could be that, I reckon," Rorie said. "More likely it's some sorry good-for-nothing what got wind of Jeremiah having money to spend down at Benton's. You know how quick word of that would get around."

"Maybe. But I don't think bushwhackers need a reason—" Sayer stopped, realizing suddenly that Amity was crying. She moved to sit on the floor between her and Beatrice again.

"Don't cry!" Beatrice said, reaching across Sayer to give Amity a push. "Stop crying! We have to be ready to help Jeremiah!"

"She's right," Rorie said. "We'll cry later if we got to, but right now, we got to be ready—just in case."

Amity lifted her head and sniffed loudly. "I'm scared, Sayer."

"I know," Sayer said. She glanced at Rorie for help.

"Now, what did that sweet mama of yourn tell you to do when you were afeard?" Rorie asked.

"I don't know!" Amity said, bowing her head again.

"She does, too," Beatrice said. "Psalm 91. Mama always said it to us when we were scared!"

"That's right. She did," Sayer said. "'Thou shalt not be afraid for the terror by night, nor for the arrow that flieth by day…'" she quoted. "Beatrice, you recite it for Amity. Help her remember."

"But she *does* remember. She's just being a baby!" She would have pushed Amity again, but Sayer caught her hand.

"Beatrice," Sayer said quietly, and Beatrice gave a sharp sigh.

Another gunshot sounded, one that was not nearly as ominous as the abrupt silence that followed. Sayer kept trying to hear something, anything, and it was all she could do to stay put with the girls on the floor. She was so afraid that something had happened to Jeremiah. After a few more agonizing minutes, she made up her mind.

"Take your sister's hand, Beatrice. Recite the Psalm for her, please."

Beatrice began to recite, her words forced and resentful at first, but then her tone softened, Sayer thought, because the beautiful wording had begun to invoke the memory of their mother.

"'There shall no evil befall thee...'" Sayer whispered along with her as she got to her knees. "'For He shall give His angels charge over thee...'"

She moved to the window and stood up. Not far off she caught a glimpse of a blue plaid shirt in the tall grass—Jeremiah. She caught her breath. He was moving in a direction parallel to the barn. Where was Benton? She couldn't see him anywhere, and she stood on tiptoe in an effort to get a better view. She realized suddenly that Jeremiah was empty-handed.

She turned and hurried to the back door, pulling hard on the latch to get it open again so she could see where he was going.

"What is it?" Rorie called, but Sayer didn't answer.

It took what seemed an eternity for the bar to finally give way. She cracked the door open slightly, but she couldn't see him now. The mule was still in the barnyard, and in her line of vision. It lifted its head and looked in her direction. She caught movement out of the corner of her eye and turned in time to see two men moving along the edge of the trees. Both of them were armed.

She looked over her shoulder at Rorie, panic-stricken,

not knowing what to do and trying hard not to alarm the girls. She took a deep breath.

"There shall no evil befall thee…"

What should I do! I don't know what to do!

"Under his wings shalt thou trust…"

She looked for Jeremiah again. She couldn't see him, but she could still see the men dodging from tree to tree. Clearly, they didn't know that he no longer had his revolver. The mule brayed loudly again and again.

"Beatrice, Amity," she said as calmly as she could manage. "I need your peppermint candy. Is it in the basket?"

The girls looked at each other.

"Is it in the basket!"

They nodded rapidly in unison.

"I need it to help Jeremiah," she said as she edged to where the basket sat on the floor, and began to search through it. She couldn't find it.

"It's not in here," she said, looking at both girls.

"Oh, I forgot," Amity said suddenly. "I put the sticks in my pockets—so it wouldn't get lost if we had to drop the basket and run."

She found the pieces after a moment of struggling with both her pinafore pockets and handed them to Sayer. Sayer quickly unwrapped them.

"What are you seeing out there, Sayer?" Rorie asked. "What's happening?"

"I need this, too," Sayer said without answering her questions. She took the revolver off Rorie's knees before she could protest. "I don't have time to explain."

She moved quickly to the slightly open door and looked out again. She could see Jeremiah now; he was much closer to the barn than he had been before. He was being run aground, she thought, by the two men she'd seen among the trees. He was unarmed and cornered with no place to go.

She stepped outside, holding the revolver in one hand down by her skirts and one piece of peppermint candy in the other. The remaining piece she had tucked into her apron pocket. She stood well behind the rain barrel at the corner of the cabin, hopefully out of sight, and she gave a soft whistle. Both Jeremiah and the mule looked in her direction.

"Sayer!" Jeremiah hissed at her. "What are you doing! Get back inside! Sayer!"

But, she gave another soft whistle and held out the candy. After a moment of wary interest, the mule trotted up. She fed it a chunk of the peppermint stick then caught hold of the bridle and began leading it toward where Jeremiah lay hidden, staying close to the mule's head and making sure to walk too far out instead of taking the shortest route to the barn. The promise of more candy kept the mule's attention long enough for her to be able to lead it where she needed to go. As she passed near Jeremiah, she bent low enough to place the revolver on the ground close to him without stopping. She didn't look in his direction. She intended to appear to the men she thought were certain to be watching that her only concern was catching the mule and getting it into the safety of the barn. As she rounded the water trough, she moved in front of the mule and led it the rest of the way to the barn. When she reached the barn door, she heard Jeremiah say her name.

"Couldn't find my big spoon," she said, still not looking at him. "Benton's here somewhere."

"Stay down. Get behind the feed bins," she heard him say as she was about to go inside. "And you and I are going to have a talk about this later."

Her knees were shaking badly by the time she got the mule into the barn. She cajoled it into the nearest stall with the second peppermint stick, but she made no effort to remove the harness. She closed the stall gate and the barn door, then peered through one of the cracks in the wall toward the cabin. The back door was now firmly closed.

"Jeremiah, be careful," she called, but she doubted that he heard. She could tell that he was on his feet and running now, but where, she couldn't tell.

She moved close to the large metal feed bins Thomas's father had bartered with the blacksmith at the crossroads to make for him, and all but collapsed on the dusty barn floor. The bins were perfect for keeping the rats out, and she could only hope that they worked as well for bullets.

She sat there wedged between them, still trembling. She pulled her knees up after a moment and rested her head on her arms.

Please. Please keep him safe, Lord. Whether he stays or goes, please don't let anything happen to him.

She thought of Thomas Henry suddenly.

Now, don't you go and forget me....

"I won't," she whispered. She heard more gunshots then, too many to count, and she closed her eyes tightly.

Jeremiah!

Please...

And then it was quiet again. She waited, looking around the barn, wall to wall, in the hope of seeing some movement outside through the cracks. She saw nothing but the streams of dusty, mote-filled sunlight pouring in. The mule brayed once, causing her to jump violently. She got to her knees, clinging to the lip on the feed bin, listening hard for something that would tell her whether or not Jeremiah was all right.

She heard a scrape along the barn wall to her left, and she jerked around to see. Someone was moving along it on the outside. She held her breath. After a moment, whoever it was stepped away. She couldn't tell where he was going and she didn't dare go to the wall to try to find out.

After a moment, she heard the back door of the cabin rattle—and Rorie.

"I'm telling you right now!" Rorie yelled. "Get away from that there door or die where you stand!"

Sayer had no doubt that she meant it, despite Rorie's having nothing but a single-shot musket.

"You hear me!" Rorie yelled. "I done put more than one man in the ground what interfered with me and mine. I ain't worried about adding to the tally!"

Sayer could hear movement again. The man came back along the barn wall and around to the front. She could hear the door creak as he slowly opened it. Had he seen her come in here? Or worse, had he seen that she hadn't come back out?

She stayed crouched down behind the bins, not daring to breathe. She could tell that he was inside now, walking carefully around and around where she was hiding. He stopped in front of the feed bins.

The mule brayed suddenly, but this time she didn't jump. It brayed again.

"Shut up!" the man said, and he went back outside.

Sayer waited, her forehead resting against the side of the bin, her heart pounding. She couldn't get up from her hiding place; he'd left the barn door open.

Where is he?

She couldn't hear him walking; he wasn't moving along any of the barn walls now. She breathed a quiet sigh of relief, but her relief was short-lived. Another gun fired, this time from the cabin itself. She moved to the barn wall despite her fear. She could see a man writhing on the ground near the front porch. He rolled over and got onto his knees, and after a moment of struggle, he stumbled off into the trees holding his bloody arm.

Sayer waited for a time then dared to step into the barnyard and run the distance to the cabin, heading for the porch and going inside through the still-open front door. Rorie was standing by the table calmly reloading the musket. She took it and went out onto the porch while Sayer tried to calm the crying girls.

"Well, look-y here. He's done dropped his firearm," Rorie called. "I reckon we got ourselves another revol— Shooting on the ridge!" Rorie cried on the heels of another round of gunfire.

She hobbled inside as quickly as she could, and Sayer closed the door behind her, then sat down on the floor again with the still-crying girls.

"Take the revolver," Rorie said, handing it to her. "I'm better with the musket. I'll watch the front door. You move over yonder, Sayer, where you can see them without them seeing you— I'm telling you, I thought we'd never get that back door barred after you went out. Good thing we did. I wouldn't have had as clear a shot if that scamp had tried to come in the back way."

Sayer nodded and moved quickly to the other side of the cabin. She had to leave the girls where they sat, because the only small space that might be safer was behind the wood cookstove, and it was still hot. She wished now that she'd learned Rorie's method of cooking. Rorie preferred using heavy iron pots with lids in the hearth and burying them in the embers rather than using the stove.

But there was nothing to do now but sit on the floor where Rorie had told her to sit and wait it out.

"Your ears is keener than mine," Rorie said to the girls. "You young-uns listen hard and tell me if you hear anything. And don't be wasting time crying. Jeremiah might be needing us again."

Jeremiah.

Please!

Sayer realized suddenly that Rorie had asked her a question.

"What?"

"I *said,* do you know how many of them there is?"

"I only saw two," Sayer said.

"Well, maybe there's only the one left what can try to get into the cabin."

The inside of the cabin grew increasingly hot and stuffy with both doors closed. Rorie sat nodding in her rocking chair—which could no longer rock, Sayer suddenly realized. Rorie must have had the girls stick a small piece of firewood under each rocker—she needed steadiness to wield a musket.

"I'm thirsty, Sayer," Amity said from the cramped space where she and Beatrice sat.

"Stay where you are," Sayer said. "I'll get the bucket—"

"Sayer," Jeremiah said from somewhere outside, and she scrambled to her feet and ran to fling open the door. He was standing near the porch, the revolver she'd dropped on the ground for him in his hand. And she was free to go to him this time; there was no Rorie standing on the hem of her dress and petticoats.

She rushed toward him and threw her arms around him without hesitation. He held her tightly, and she pressed her face hard into his shoulder.

"Is it over?" she said, still holding on to him. She didn't want to let go. He was safe, and that was all that mattered to her.

Thank You, Lord! Thank You!

"Yes," he said. "They've gone."

She suddenly remembered herself and let go of him and took a step back. He moved toward the porch, and she realized that he was limping.

"You're hurt—"

He gave her one of his quick, half smiles. "Fell over my own two feet dodging bullets," he said. "Must be out of practice."

Amity and Beatrice burst from the cabin and threw themselves on him before he could sit down. He suffered their hugs and listened intently to their excited report that Sayer had given all their candy to the mule.

"It's a good thing she did," he said, glancing up as Rorie came outside. She was using the musket in lieu of her walking stick. "How's your knee?" he asked her, likely because she was making such slow progress crossing the porch.

"Better than yourn, from the looks of it. You're bleeding. You best see to it."

"It's all right," he said. "Rumor is you shot somebody."

"People ought not try to open other people's doors without they've been given leave to," she said. "Where did Benton get to? Is he all right?"

"He's up in the high field. He's waiting for Willard and some of the other men to get here. He says they'll likely come in from that way. If they don't, you can tell them where he is."

"Are them men with guns still up there?"

"No, they took off through the trees."

"I can't reckon what they was after, myself. What are you planning on doing now?" Rorie asked.

He didn't answer her. "Are you sure you're all right?" he said, looking at Sayer.

"Yes. I'm— We're fine."

"I'm going to catch up with Benton."

"Your knee," Sayer said in the hope of keeping him longer.

"It's nothing."

But he didn't walk as if it was nothing. He stopped for a moment to let the girls hug him again, then made his way up the slope to the high field, still limping. He didn't look back.

"Well, come on," Rorie said behind her. "If them scalawags ain't around no more, we got to get some water from the rain barrel and set it to boiling."

"What for?" Amity asked.

"For Jeremiah. We're going to fill up the soaking tub out yonder behind the privet hedge. And if we can catch him, we're going to put him into it. It's what he's needing for that cut-up knee of his so he don't end up half-cripple— Well, come on," Rorie said when Sayer hesitated.

"I forgot to tell him about the letter," Sayer said. She looked around, hoping to still be able to catch sight of him, but he was no longer in view.

Chapter Nine

Benton stood waiting for him in the plowed field. Now that the battle was over, the horse stood calmly where it had been left. Everything around them was quiet and as it should be. During the war, Jack had always found it disconcerting—the quiet that followed a battle. Birds sang as if nothing had happened. Clouds moved overhead. Insects buzzed and swarmed—but for once, there were no dead and wounded lying on the field.

"Everybody all right?" he asked when Jack was close enough. "Everybody besides you, that is," Benton amended, looking at his face and then at his bloody knee.

"They're all right," Jack said, ignoring his scrutiny.

"What are you going to do now?"

The question of the hour.

"Try to find my revolver," Jack said, knowing that was not what Benton was asking. But whatever happened next, he'd need the gun. That one, along with the one Sayer had laid on the ground for him, plus the one Rorie had retrieved from one of the bounty hunters should give them adequate protection—he hoped. He was going to trust that bounty hunters were a greedy lot and would by no means want to split the reward more than two ways.

"They'll be back. Them or somebody just like them," Benton said, still pressing for some kind of plan. Jack had no doubt now that the man had suspected from the day the two men came into his store that he was the "Murphy" they'd been looking for.

Jack nodded, but he didn't say anything.

"Is Jack your real name, or not?" Benton asked bluntly, going in a different direction.

"My real name is Jeremiah."

He could feel Benton trying to decide whether or not to believe him.

"You only got two choices now, son," he said finally. "Hide in these mountains or go on the run."

"I should have left here the day I knew they were looking for me. I have to get away. I can't bring this kind of trouble down on Sayer."

"What kind of trouble would that be, exactly?"

Jack didn't answer the question despite Benton's apparent willingness to participate in the effort to keep him from being put into leg irons and taken back to Lexington—or shot dead.

"You got a bounty on your head, son. Now I'm asking you outright. What did you do?"

Benton was armed, and Jack had the distinct impression that whether Benton decided to ignore the regard he claimed to have for Thomas Henry Garth and his family and collect the bounty money himself, hinged a great deal on the explanation Jack gave now regarding his current difficulties.

He had Benton's full attention, but Jack wasn't nearly as guilty as it might seem, and he didn't look away. Benton would likely hear some distorted version of the situation sooner or later, and he might as well hear the truth from him.

"I got on the wrong side of a rich man," Jack said evenly. "And his…wife."

Benton was clearly expecting there to be more to the story than that.

"You kill somebody?" he asked finally.

"No."

"You do something you shouldn't have?"

"No, I *didn't* do something I shouldn't have."

"Well," Benton said in the absence of any further elaboration on Jack's part, "that worked out all right for Joseph when he was in Egypt, I reckon. You, I don't know about. When the others get here, I'm going to say it was bushwhackers as far as we know. I'd like to say it was Halbert Garth and them scalawags what run with him, but I reckon that's too big a lie to get away with."

"Lies don't come in sizes—or so I was always told." He'd also been told that deliberately withholding the truth was as much a sin as lying itself, but that hadn't stopped him from handing out half-truths ever since he'd come here.

"Depends on which side of the pulpit you're on," Benton said. "You tell Sayer about the rich man's wife?"

"No. No need to."

"Well, seeing as how the air still smells of gunpowder, I can't be agreeing with that notion. It ain't right to let her or the girls maybe get hurt, and her not even know the reason why. You can go on the run again, I reckon, but that ain't going to keep them from coming back here. If you ain't here when they do…" He didn't finish the thought. He didn't have to.

"Benton, this is my business."

"Maybe it is, maybe it ain't," Benton said. "If you decide to make a stand here or if you decide to go—either way—she ought to know what it's all about. That's all I'm saying. I reckon you can see for yourself I'm too old to be running up here every time people start shooting at one another. You got out of it today without much damage, but next time might be a different story—I got to go look for my horse. Ain't no telling where it got to by now. It don't stand where you put it like that one of yours does."

"Mine doesn't always stand, either," Jack said, thinking of the ride to Sayer's cabin with Rorie hanging on for dear life. If he'd had any idea what that ride would lead to, would he have still come looking for Sayer?

Yes, he thought. He would—which said little for his character. She would be far better off if she'd never seen his face. At least he'd told her the truth about one thing. He had no regrets.

"Looks like it does when you need it to. I'm going to look down at the cabin first. You see it up here anywhere, you catch it if you can."

"Benton," Jack called when he'd gone a few steps. "I…appreciate your help today. You didn't have to take that kind of risk, but you did. I won't forget it."

"It ain't easy to make a life in these hills, son. We have to rely on one another. I reckon it's enough for us that Thomas Henry sent you here. I meant to tell you—" He looked around suddenly as several men on horseback came riding through the trees. Jack immediately recognized Willard and one or two of the others. They were men he had met at Thomas Henry's memorial service and at the general store. Incredibly, their small company also included the two bounty hunters.

"Well, will you look at this," Benton said, walking in their direction. Jack took a deep breath and followed at a slower pace.

"Willard!" Benton called when they were close enough. "Where'd you find them?"

"They come busting out of the woods right up there along the buffalo road. Might have believed they was hunting if that one wasn't bleeding like a stuck hog. Far as I know, we ain't got no critters up here what shoot back." He grinned.

"I ain't the criminal here!" the wounded bounty hunter said. "*He* is! He's the Murphy we're looking for!" He pointed in Jack's direction with his bound hands.

"You just up and pick somebody with the same last name when it suits you?" Benton asked. "That don't seem like such a practical plan to me. Might be a couple more Murphys around here someplace. You two going to go shooting at them whilst they're plowing their fields, too? Besides which, one of you nearly got me when I was riding up the path. You think my name's Jack Murphy, too?"

"You want to press charges, Benton?"

"I do," Benton said.

"Then I reckon we'll take them on down to the crossroads and lock them up until we decide what to do with them. You got any objections to that, Jeremiah?" Willard said.

"No," Jack said.

"All right, then," Willard said. "Let's go. Benton!" he yelled as they rode away. "Your horse is in the pasture down yonder with Sayer's cow!"

Jack could feel Benton staring at him again, but this time he didn't look in his direction. He had done all the confessing he intended to do.

"I've got to find my revolver," he said, limping back up the slope.

"Good idea, son," Benton said. "Like I said—this ain't the end of it. Here—"

Benton took a cartridge box out of his coat pocket and tossed it to him. "Maybe this will hold you until you can get down to the crossroads for some more."

Jack gave him a nod and walked on. He stopped long enough at one point to get his bearings and to reach a conclusion. This thing might never be over as long as he was alive, but he was *not* going to just hand over his life to Elrissa's husband.

He found his revolver in the tall grass near the edge of the field, not far from where the horse waited patiently. He picked up the gun and limped the distance over to it and ran his hand along its sleek neck when it gave a low whinny.

"Old man, I hope you weren't thinking you'd have some peace when you threw in with me," he said. "Meeting up in a graveyard like we did ought to have given you some kind of hint." The animal gave another low rumble and tossed its head as Jack picked up the reins and swung himself into the saddle. He had only ridden a short distance when he turned the horse sharply and began to ride in a different direction, up the steep slope and into the trees. He didn't stop until he had reached the outcropping of rock where Thomas Henry's memorial service had been held.

He dismounted where small patches of grass managed to grow in the rocky ground, then he limped out onto the edge of the world.

Incredible, he thought, just as he had the first time.

He half expected to feel Thomas Henry's presence here, but he didn't. All he felt was nature—wind and late-afternoon sun and birdsong. And despite Preacher Tomlin's and Rorie's opinions, he didn't sense God's presence, either, at least not in the way he had as a boy when he'd gone to midnight services on Christmas Eve. He'd felt God then, in the last few seconds when his made-up birthday had ended and the Christ Child's began. But here, now, there was nothing but the mountains and his own abject misery.

Such wildly beautiful country as far as the eye could see. It was no wonder people wanted to live here, even if it was hard.

Be still, Preacher Tomlin had said. *And know.*

His mind went suddenly to the Psalm Father Bartholomew had often read to them:

Wherewithal shall a young man cleanse his way?
By taking heed thereto according to Thy word.
With my whole heart have I sought Thee:
O let me not wander from Thy commandments…

But he *had* wandered.
Thou shalt not kill.
He had most certainly trampled that one into the dirt.

He realized suddenly that he did feel something after all, but it had nothing to do with this place. He felt… Sayer.

Sayer.

The joy of having her arms around him when she found him alive and unharmed had been like nothing he'd ever experienced. He could have stood there like that with her forever. It had been all he could do not to say something he would have surely regretted. He'd wanted to *tell* her what seeing her every day, talking to her, sitting down to meals with her, meant to him and that he—

He gave a sharp sigh. She deserved so much more than Jeremiah "Jack" Murphy and the trouble and sorrow he had caused her.

Jeremiah, the bringer of bad news and destruction.

"I love her," he said out loud to the God he was still certain wasn't there. "I *love* her."

I don't know what to do!

In his mind he heard the words in Thomas Henry's anguished voice.

"I don't understand," Jack whispered. "Why? Why am I here? Was it Your plan for me to come into her life and make everything worse for her? What did she ever do to deserve that? Can't You see how good she is? How beautiful? I've put her in harm's way. I know I can't stay—and I can't go. I don't know what to do!"

His dead captain suddenly came to mind.

Don't think about what you can't do…think about what you can. And do it!

No, he thought. Not this time. He had single-handedly

managed to effect a situation that was the exception to the captain's hard-and-fast rule.

He stood there, staring at the mountain ridges just as Thomas Henry's father must have done, trying to find his way in the shambles of his life, exhausted of mind and body.

God save thee, ancient Mariner, from the fiends that plague thee thus...

Today, he had been saved. The bounty hunters were caught, detained. He had a little time at least to...

To what? He didn't know. But he was alive and Sayer and the others were safe. He was grateful for that, and he hadn't strayed so far that he couldn't say so.

He took several limping steps farther onto the overhang. He had to brace himself in the strong wind.

"I thank You," he whispered. The prayer—if that's what it was—was immediately snatched away and carried...where? To God's ear?

Are You listening? I'm here. Where are You?

Be still and know. Preacher Tomlin's admonition was clear enough, even for him.

He continued to stand there, his thoughts chaotic as they always were after a battle.

"Sayer," he whispered, and the love he felt for her once again washed over him. He had given Thomas Henry his word that he would help her, a token promise that had meant nothing to him that night on the battlefield. It meant something now. It meant *everything* now.

He bowed his head. "Help me, Lord," he whispered. "Please! I can't do it alone. If it *is* Your will that I'm here, I don't have to know why. I don't have to know what's coming. Just help me keep them all safe."

What was it Thomas Henry had said in his delirium? The fragment of a verse from the book of Psalms.

Jack looked out at the mountains, trying to remember, and it suddenly came to him. "…teacheth my hands to war and my fingers to fight…." Skills both he and Thomas Henry had once had. And David. God's warrior.

After a moment, he began to focus on the incredible beauty of this place. He was still troubled, still worried and afraid, but it wasn't the same somehow. He could feel the…determination rising in his heart, and he was grateful for it.

He looked up at the sky. "All right, then," he said, much as he had that night on the battlefield when he'd made the decision to answer Thomas Henry's desperate call. He would do the best he could to stay alert for whatever might come and to protect the people he loved. He had always done that, and he wouldn't stop now.

He turned and walked back to where the horse grazed among the rocks.

When he reached the cabin, Rorie informed him that, according to Benton, the bushwhackers had been caught. He could feel her watching him closely as she said it.

"Where is he now?" Jack asked as he dismounted. The pain in his knee escalated, and he had to grab on to the saddle to keep from falling.

"He got his horse and left."

Jack glanced at the musket propped against the wall

on the porch and handed her the box of cartridges Benton had given him.

"We going to need more of these or not?" she asked.

He looked at her without answering.

"That's what I was afeard of," she said. "This kind of thing ain't never over till somebody's dead."

He looked around because Sayer and the girls were coming out of the cabin. Sayer was carrying what looked like folded men's clothing, and the girls were trying not to giggle.

"I got the soaking tub ready," Rorie said at his elbow.

"What soaking tub?"

"The one you're getting yourself into," Rorie said, causing the girls to have to put their hands over their mouths. Clearly there was a conspiracy afoot, and he was in no mood for it.

He looked from Beatrice and Amity to Sayer—whose facial expression he couldn't read—and back to Rorie. He had no trouble reading *her* face.

"Get yourself on over there behind the privet hedge," she said. "You can't half walk as it is. We got to get that knee to where it'll heal. Soaking it—and all the rest of you right along with it—is the best way to do it. If we take the soreness out, you won't be favoring it. You favor it too long and it won't bend no more."

"I don't—"

"I ain't asking! I'm telling. You done caused me enough worry and aggravation today and I ain't going to set back now and let that knee of yours fester just so I can have some more. You can do what I say or I can lay hands on you and throw you in the tub myself. And don't you think I can't! I have had enough!"

Sayer walked up to him—when he wasn't prepared to have her so close. She looked so pretty to him despite the events of the day. He wanted to reach out to her, and he couldn't.

"I believe I'd listen to her, Jeremiah," she said, looking into his eyes. "These were Mr. Garth Senior's. He was tall like you. I think they'll fit." She pushed them into his hands, then turned and headed back to the cabin.

Beatrice and Amity ran up, each of them handing him a sock before running away again to catch up with Sayer.

"We still have what's left of the picnic. When Rorie says you're done, you can come and eat, if you want," Sayer said over her shoulder.

But she didn't wait for him to decide. She and the girls went back inside, leaving the door open. He could hear the girls giggling again, and Sayer shushing them. After a moment, Amity and Beatrice began to sing.

The clothes Sayer had handed him smelled of cedar. He glanced at Rorie.

"I have to stay ready. I can't stop for a soak—I don't know if—"

"I'm going to keep watch, Jeremiah. Me and that there horse of yourn. And Sayer and the girls, too. You can trust us. Ain't nothing going to get past all five of us. Well, go on," she said. "Before that there water gets cold."

"I didn't get ordered around this much in the army," he said, but he limped in the direction she was pointing.

He pushed his way through the hedge. There was indeed a long, troughlike wooden tub behind it, and a weathered straight chair with a big steaming iron kettle sitting on the wooden seat alongside a sliver of soap. Several pieces of flannel were draped over the back.

"Take your time," Rorie said on the other side of the hedge. "And don't be worrying, because I got my musket handy and I usually hit what I aim at. Now throw them dirty clothes over the hedge so's we can do something about them. Maybe me and Sayer can get the blood out and the knee patched."

He stood for a moment, looking at the tub. It was both inviting and a great source of aggravation.

"You see the soap?" Rorie called.

"Yes, I see it," he said, rolling the clothes Sayer had given him and wedging them onto the seat of the chair.

"You know what to do with it?"

"I used to. Maybe it'll come back to me."

"There's a little bit of honey on a strip of flannel there on the chair for you to bind your knee with when you're done."

"Where's the cabbage?"

"You don't need cabbage—and you won't if you do like I tell you," she said. "Now get busy!"

He shook his head and began to strip off, throwing each subsequent article of clothing over the hedge one at a time. The revolver he laid on the seat of the chair where he could reach it if he needed to.

"You're going to be glad you done this," Rorie assured him.

He didn't reply, mostly because he didn't want to have to admit that she was probably right. The water in the tub was much warmer than he expected, but he emptied the kettle into it anyway and got in, easing his

knee under the water eventually, sinking low and closing his eyes.

He was so tired. He could smell the evergreen smell
of the hedge, hear the birds chirping as they went in
and out among the branches. The girls were back to giggling, and Sayer was singing that song again.

I go away, behind to leave you
Perhaps never to meet again…

He closed his eyes and tried to let go of the strain of
the past few hours. What a joy it would be to live his
life here in this place—with her. A life without Farrell
Vance and Halbert Garth and all the battlefield ghosts
that haunted him.

Thomas Henry's life.

He suddenly thought of Fred and his apple pie. Were
there apple pies in heaven? He wanted to think so—

"Jeremiah," Sayer said quietly on the other side of
the hedge, startling him back into reality.

"What?"

"We're— I'm…glad you're safe."

"May I borrow the scissors, if you please?" Amity
said. She had already requested Sayer's small mirror
on Jeremiah's behalf and had taken it to him.

Sayer glanced at Rorie, who couldn't keep from grinning. The back door was open and she could just see
where Jeremiah was sitting on an upside-down barrel
under the lean-to roof trying to shave. Mr. Garth Senior's clothes had indeed fit him and fit him well. She

could also see the musket propped and ready, and the still-saddled horse standing quietly not far away.

"Scissors," Sayer repeated, turning her attention back to Amity.

"Yes, please," Amity said.

"What in this world does he want scissors for?" Rorie asked.

"He doesn't," Amity said. "I do. I tried to hold the mirror for him when he shaved, but I was too wiggly. So I thought I'd cut his hair—it really needs it. He's got all kinds of things in his saddlebags, but no scissors. So can I borrow them?"

"*May* I borrow them, and no," Sayer said.

"But I know all the rules," Amity said, looking hopefully at Mrs. Garth's wicker sewing basket where the scissors were kept. "Number one, don't cut yourself. Number two, don't get them wet. Number three, don't lose them. Number four, remember they are *not* supposed to take the place of a saw—Mama made that one when Thomas Henry tried to cut off some cherry-tree limbs with them—they weren't very big, but he got into trouble anyway, didn't he, Beatrice?"

"Yes—and you forgot one," Beatrice advised her.

"No, I didn't."

"Yes, you did. Be sure to put them back in the sewing basket—or else."

"Oh, yes. That's right. Or *else,*" she said.

"I'm glad you know the rules," Sayer said. "Do you happen to know how to cut hair?"

"You just…snip!" Amity said, showing Sayer how it was done with her fingers. She looked at Beatrice for support, but Beatrice apparently hadn't forgiven her for telling Jeremiah she wanted to know if he had a sweetheart.

"There's a little more to it than that," Sayer said.

"Well, can—may—I try?"

"No."

"Why not?"

"Because we got to be able to recognize him when you're done," Rorie said. "We ain't wanting to shoot him for a stranger. He's already come close enough to being shot today."

Amity gave a heavy sigh and went back outside.

"Those men are in the crossroads jail—why don't I feel like this is over?" Sayer said, more to herself than to Rorie.

"Because it ain't. Not by a long shot. All we done is live to fight another day. I'm telling you, it's getting hard to keep up with which Philistine to worry about."

Sayer could hear Amity and Jeremiah talking.

"Oh, no," Amity said at one point, causing Sayer, Rorie *and* the reluctant Beatrice to look toward the back door. In a moment, Amity came inside with the mirror and a slight frown.

"He doesn't look like Jeremiah since he shaved," she said. "He says I'll get used to it, but I don't know."

Sayer put the mirror away and when she turned around, Jeremiah was standing in the doorway. Amity was right. He didn't look like Jeremiah—at least not the Jeremiah they all knew.

"Say something so we'll know it's you."

He tried not to smile. "It's me," he said.

Sayer walked closer, looking at him closely. "Yes, I do believe it is. You look very dashing, Mr. Murphy," she said, her relief and her joy at seeing him translating into a sudden, mischievous urge to tease him. He clearly recognized her intent, but incredibly, he actually blushed.

"Come sit down," she said. "I'll get the bacon biscuits and the cherry pies."

"Thank you, but no. I need to be outside," he said.

"But you have to eat—"

"I have…things I need to see about. I'll take them with me."

Sayer was about to try again to coax him into sitting down at the table, but then she understood the implication of what he was saying. She wasn't the only one who didn't feel as if this trouble was over. They still weren't safe, and they shouldn't behave as if they were. She got the biscuits and pies from the warming oven in the woodstove and wrapped them in a tea cloth.

"Thank you," he said when she placed them carefully into his hands. When he turned to go back outside, Sayer went with him.

"No," she heard Rorie say to the girls, when they would have followed them. In a moment, the back door closed.

Sayer saw one of the revolvers resting on top of the barrel he'd been sitting on earlier. He picked it up and held it with the wrapped-up bacon biscuits and fried cherry pies. She had no doubt that the other one was likely tucked into his belt.

"Rorie says there aren't many cartridges left," she said quietly.

He nodded. "It may be we won't need them."

She understood that he meant the words to be both

truthful and of some comfort, but what would have helped her most would have been his allowing her to look into his eyes.

"Will you put all that down for just a minute and sit?" she asked when he finally did look at her.

He seemed slightly surprised to find that his hands were full. "No. I need to go."

"I would like to say something first. It would be easier if you weren't towering over me and I wasn't worrying about you dropping everything."

He didn't say anything to that, but he did sit down on the bench. "I'll...eat something now," he said, putting the revolver aside and taking a bacon biscuit out of the tea towel and holding it up for her to see. "I already know you saved me twice today. This may be the third."

"Did I? How?"

"When you brought me the revolver," he said. "And when you didn't let Amity run loose with a pair of scissors. And now you're determined to keep body and soul together with your biscuits and pies."

She couldn't keep from smiling. He wasn't smiling, however.

"What you did—bringing the gun out to me. It was dangerous. They could have killed you."

"I know."

"Then why did you do it!"

She realized that, even though it was over and done with and no one had been hurt, he was actually angry with her.

"I could see you from the cabin—I could see you were unarmed," she said. "And I could see them coming after you. I wasn't being impulsive or reckless. I was doing the only thing I could do."

He looked at her for a moment, apparently thinking about what she'd said. Then he sighed and began to eat.

"Still good," he said after a bite or two, and she smiled again. The compliment pleased her, but she had something she wanted to say to him, something she'd been thinking about ever since Benton had left.

"I'm sorry," she said.

"Sorry?"

"That you got dragged into so much more than Thomas Henry asked of you. You could have been killed today as well—when none of this is your problem. You're only here—"

"It is my problem," he said.

"No, Thomas Henry didn't mean for you to risk your life."

"It's my problem and it doesn't have anything to do with Thomas Henry. I have to go," he said abruptly. He stood up and rolled the tea towel into a ball.

"Jeremiah—" She caught his arm as he walked by her.

"You should go inside," he said. "Bar the doors. Don't leave the lamps burning and stay away from the windows."

"I'm…afraid for you."

"No more than I am for you. It's worse now that I know you're apt to take matters into your own hands."

There was nothing she could say to that. She let go of his arm.

"Wait. I need to get your letter. I forgot to tell you earlier."

"What letter?"

"Benton brought it. That's why he came up here."

"It's your letter, then," he said. "Not mine."

"I don't understand. Who would be sending you a letter for me?"

"I went to Jefferson to see about Thomas Henry's will. Benton thought it needed to be done before Halbert found out you were widowed and got himself appointed executor for Thomas Henry's estate."

She frowned. "Why didn't you tell me?"

"There was nothing to tell. I went, and I gave my sworn word that I was with Thomas Henry when he died. That had to be verified somehow, and the law clerk said it would probably take a long time—weeks or months—before the lawyer could do anything about it. I wasn't thinking there would be a letter from him this soon. When I got back from Jefferson, you were having the memorial service. I...thought you had enough on your plate without having to worry about something so undecided. I couldn't even find out for sure if he had a will."

"He did," she said. "He told me so." She kept looking at him, but he was avoiding her gaze again.

"I have to go. I'm going to be close by," he said. "Just not where I usually am. I'll know if you need me."

He put the tea towel with the food and the revolver into his saddlebag and mounted the horse, clearly trying not to let the pain in his knee make him wince.

"Sayer," he said, working to keep control of a horse that was becoming more and more agitated in anticipation of yet another battle. There was something in his voice, something she recognized. It had been there when he'd told her about his dead comrade's love of apple pie and about his one memory of his mother.

"What is it?" she asked, looking up at him, afraid for him all over again.

But he shook his head. "Nothing. Just...take care."

She waited until he had ridden into the woods before she went inside.

Chapter Ten

It was raining when Jack returned to the cabin, a steady rain that had begun after midnight and continued into the dawn. He rode the horse inside the barn and dismounted. He had kept watch all night. He hadn't slept, even when he was satisfied that there was no one lurking around the perimeter of the farm. He was soaked to the skin—Rorie could have saved herself all the trouble she'd gone to getting him into a tub.

"Don't unsaddle the horse."

Jack turned around sharply. Sayer was standing just behind him. He hadn't heard her come into the barn. Had she been inside waiting?

"What's wrong?" he asked, taking a step toward her. She immediately backed away. She was in the shadows now. He couldn't see her face.

"You ask me what's wrong? I can't—" She lifted her hand and then let it fall.

"Sayer, what is it?"

"You were in the Union army," she said, and he froze. It wasn't a question.

"Yes," he said after a moment.

"It was in the letter Benton brought—your sworn testimony. Did you think I wouldn't know which side the Army of the Ohio and the Army of the Potomac were on? You lied to me!"

"Sayer—no, I did not."

"How could you let me think that you were Thomas Henry's comrade!"

"I never said that."

"No. You said there was a 'bond'—soldiers have a 'bond,' that's what you said. What else would I think? Why did you come here! Tell me!"

"Because he asked me to."

"He wouldn't have done that if he'd known who—what—you were."

"He did know."

"I don't believe you! Did you rob him on the battlefield? Is that how you got his things? Did you come here to see what else he had to steal? Did they teach you that in the orphanage? I can't believe I—"

"He knew he was dying. He asked me to tell his wife what had happened to him—because he was afraid you'd never know. He told me to get his letters and the things in his blanket roll to her. Sayer…"

She was standing too far away, but she wouldn't let him get any closer.

"It must have been so…easy for you. *I* made it easy, didn't I? If you came because he asked, then why did you *stay?* That's what I don't understand."

"I can't…"

"Can't what? Tell me."

"I stayed because I wanted to," he said, putting all the other reasons aside and telling her the one that mattered.

"Everything you said about Thomas Henry's death—how can I believe what you said is true? How can I believe you were even there?"

"I was there. I talked to him. I buried him."

"Did you kill him, too?"

He didn't say anything, and she abruptly put her face into her hands.

"Sayer, I can't explain it—things happened and—"

She abruptly took her hands away and took a step toward him. "I don't want you to explain. I want you to go away from here. I want you to go *now!*"

She pushed past him; he could hear her splashing footsteps as she ran back to the cabin.

I'm still in that classroom, he thought. *I'm still having to choose, only this time, I don't know what the right thing is.*

Sayer!

Sayer stood with her back against the door, trying not to cry. She was wet to the skin and shivering. Everyone was still asleep, but they wouldn't be asleep for long. The girls would wake up full of questions about whether or not they could go outside now and when Jeremiah would be back.

The papers Benton had brought were still lying on the table where she'd left them. She moved quietly to relight the stub of candle she'd used earlier and sit down. She wanted to read Jeremiah's sworn statement again, though why she did she couldn't have said. She didn't need to. The words still swirled in her mind.

Sergeant Jeremiah Murphy… The Army of the Potomac…

Jeremiah was a Yankee soldier. Thomas Henry hadn't died with a comrade. He had died with his mortal enemy. At least she had sent Jeremiah away. It was the right thing to do; she knew that—and still her heart was breaking.

She picked up the legal papers, straining to read the elaborately formal handwriting in the dim light, forcing herself to continue past the point that had caused her such pain.

Sergeant Murphy's account of the aforementioned Thomas Henry Garth's death on the battlefield is consistent with that of another soldier of the Highland Guards who was also wounded, separated from his company, and lying nearby. Said soldier has given a written account of Corporal Garth's having sustained grave injury in the fighting earlier that day and having died of his wounds, and having been subsequently buried on the field in a marked grave by an unknown Union soldier....

Sayer stopped reading. The rain was coming harder, and the candle flickered as the wick burned low. She folded the papers and put them back into the envelope. After a moment, she got up and placed it behind Mrs. Garth's kitchen clock on the mantel, then impulsively reached for the clock key and wound it as tightly as she dared. The world didn't stop because Jeremiah Murphy was no longer on the premises, and the sooner she realized that, the better. Rorie could go home now; Sayer had no further need of a chaperone. Everything could go back to the way it had been for the past four years—

except that Sayer would no longer be waiting and watching for a man she knew now would never return.

She gave a wavering sigh.

"What's wrong?" Rorie said from the bed. Sayer looked in her direction. She meant to tell Rorie that she was fine, that there was nothing the matter, nothing at all, but she couldn't make herself say the words. She began to cry instead and she couldn't stop.

Rorie got out of bed and limped over to her. "What's happened?" she asked, putting her arms around Sayer's shoulders. "Jeremiah ain't hurt, is he?"

"He's gone," Sayer managed to say.

"Gone?"

"I sent him away."

"What in the world for?"

"He's been lying to us—to me. All this time, he's been lying."

"About what?" Rorie asked.

"He was a Union soldier, Rorie. He's Thomas Henry's enemy—our enemy—"

Rorie didn't say anything.

"Did you hear what I said! He's a Yankee!"

"I heard you. I reckon they might have heard you all the way down yonder at the crossroads, too. Good thing them girls sleep so sound."

Rorie let go of her and would have stepped away if Sayer hadn't caught her by the arm. "Did you know about this?"

"Not…exactly," Rorie said. She pulled free and hobbled over to the washstand and poured some water into the bowl. She began washing her face, Sayer thought, more to put her off than to begin her morning ritual.

"Rorie, what does that mean?"

"It means I asked him if he soldiered with Thomas Henry—the day he come up on my cabin looking for you. He didn't answer me. So then I asked him if he's the one what killed him." Rorie went back to washing her face.

"What did he say!"

"He said what I reckoned to be the truth. He said, 'I don't know.' Just like that. I still take it for the truth. I ain't never been in no battle, but I reckon I can guess what it's like—a lot going on and all of it having to do with cannonballs and bullets and bayonets and things like that what will kill you if you don't do the killing first. I reckoned whether he did or didn't come across Thomas Henry in the heat of the fighting, he was trying to do something for you and the girls now. I figured he was one of them things God does sometimes. You know, when He don't put our chances right out in the open where we can recognize them. Ain't you ever got to thinking one thing or another was the end of the world—and it weren't that at all?"

Sayer didn't answer. Until she'd read Jeremiah's sworn statement, she might have applied Rorie's concept to his being the one to come here to tell her about Thomas Henry, but not now.

"Well, maybe you ain't old enough yet to have seen that kind of thing. Most times it's a way to something we need, only we don't even know we need it. And that's how it was when Jeremiah showed up. I was all worried and wanting to get over here to see why you never hollered that morning, nor answered mine. He come as close to being shot as he ever was in that there war, and that's the truth. But then I knowed what he was really doing here. I knowed he was a opportunity—I told you I made him bring me over here."

"This is nothing like that," Sayer said. "Nothing—!"

There was a knock on the back door.

"Sayer," Jeremiah said quietly on the other side of it. "I want to talk to you."

"No," she said. "I want you to go."

"Then you'll have to let me say what I want to say. Afterward, I'll leave. Come outside."

Sayer hesitated, glancing at Rorie, who clearly wanted to make some comment.

"What is it?" Sayer asked her, more to delay than to know.

"Nothing much. Just…I'd listen to him if I was you," Rorie said. "He can't sway you if you've made up your mind about this. All he can do is leave you wondering if there wasn't something he would have told you that you're going to regret not knowing about. I say go out there and make sure your mind is settled. Once and for all."

Rorie reached for Sayer's shawl and held it out to her.

"Sayer," Jeremiah said again.

Sayer took the shawl and put it around her wet shoulders. She bowed her head for a moment and opened the door.

"It won't take long," he said when she didn't immediately come outside.

His horse was tied to the lean-to post.

Poor old thing, she thought, not knowing if she meant the rain-drenched animal or herself. She stepped outside. She didn't say anything, and she didn't avoid looking directly into his eyes. She was immediately struck by how weary he looked, just as he had been the day of Thomas Henry's memorial service when he'd returned from Jefferson—only then she hadn't known where he'd been or what he'd been doing. He was an enigma then, and he was an enigma now.

"What is it?" she asked abruptly, because she didn't want to think about how he had come to be so weary. If she did, she would only be adding to the burden of her obligation to him when it was already more than she could bear. "What is it you want to say?"

"I want to tell you the truth. All of it. I don't want there to be anything about me that you don't know."

"Why?"

"Because I need to. And because you need to know what kind of trouble I've brought you."

She frowned. "Trouble...you brought," she said, trying to understand.

"The men who came here yesterday. They weren't bushwhackers. They were bounty hunters."

"Bounty hunters? After deserters, you mean?"

"They were after me. There's a man who...wants me dead. I was on the run when I came here. I...still am."

"You came here to hide?" she asked.

"Not..." He stopped and drew a quiet breath. "Yes, I guess I did. But I didn't come thinking I'd stay. I came this way because I thought they'd be looking for me in the opposite direction. I still had the things Thomas Henry had given me and I decided to try to find you. He told me where his farm was—Ashe County on the North Carolina side. I meant to give them to you and leave, but you were hurt and the girls were sick—and then Halbert showed up. I thought you needed my help."

"Yes," she said. "How pitiful we must have seemed to you then—but not as pitiful as we are now. Why is there a bounty on your head? What did you do?"

"Nothing. I told you that the young woman I'd asked to marry me married someone else. I went to see her after I was discharged from the army. My pride was hurt. I wanted her to look at me and say why she'd changed her mind and never bothered to tell me. Looking back on it, it wasn't one of my better plans. She…"

He stopped and turned his face away as a strong gust of wind blew the rain through the lean-to. Sayer couldn't keep from shivering.

"Go on," she said.

"You're cold—"

"Please! Say what you wanted to say."

He looked at her for a long moment before he continued.

"Elrissa was…unhappy in her marriage. She wanted to leave her husband."

"With you?" Sayer asked when he didn't continue.

"When I left her house, I thought she understood that I couldn't—wouldn't—do that. I didn't realize how angry she was that I'd said no. In a fit of pique, she must have told her husband that I'd…" He stopped and gave a heavy sigh. "The maid in the house knows whatever Elrissa said isn't true, but she's afraid to speak up. She's one of the orphans, but Elrissa's husband is a powerful man.

"Father Bartholomew found out somehow that the watchmen who were looking for me had been paid off.

They weren't going to bring me in alive. He helped me get away. I don't even know if there were formal charges made. Based on what Father Bartholomew told me, I suspect her husband is handling this...privately."

"But now they know where you are."

"Two of them do. I want to think that's all—I don't believe bounty hunters share information if they can help it. They want all the money for themselves. But there may be others. You and Rorie and the girls will have to be careful."

"We have always had to be careful here," she said. "Is that all you wanted to say?"

"Not quite," he said, but he untied the horse and mounted, clearly still favoring his injured knee. "There's one last thing," he said, looking down at her. "You said you'd made it easy for me. Well, it wasn't easy—being here, seeing you every day, longing for the things I know can never be. I love you, Sayer. I love you with all my heart. You're the reason I've stayed." He hesitated, then, "Tell Rorie and the girls goodbye for me, if you will."

Sayer stood there, stunned. He gave her no chance to recover, no chance to say anything. He wheeled the horse sharply and rode away.

Chapter Eleven

Amity was standing by the window again, trying to peek around the edge to see outside.

"Amity, come away from there. What are you doing?" Sayer asked, but she already knew. Amity was keeping a vigil, watching the path for some sign of Jeremiah the way she had for Thomas Henry.

Neither of the girls had had much to say since she told them that Jeremiah had gone. She was grateful that she could tell them truthfully that he'd asked her to say goodbye to them and to Rorie.

Beatrice had but one question. "Why did you let him go?"

And Sayer had nothing to say to that.

"You should have *told* him!" Beatrice cried. "You should have said we need him here now that we don't have Thomas Henry. I'm afraid if he's not here! Can't we go and find him? Amity wants to look for him and I do, too. He would take us with him—I know he would. Why did he go!"

"It was time for him to go," Sayer said finally, not

missing the look Rorie gave her. But it was the truth, albeit just barely.

I love you with all my heart....

The words swirled in her mind ever since he'd said them. She had told Rorie once that she trusted him. She did—perhaps *still* did, in spite of everything.

I love you...

Did he?

No, of course he didn't. It was...something else, something she didn't understand. Had he come here intending to enact some kind of revenge? He'd lost so many of the young men who were his orphan family. It *must* be something like that—except that that didn't make any sense, either. In her heart she knew he was not a vengeful man.

All through the day Rorie kept looking at her as they did the chores that could be done without being too much in the open, but she waited until the girls were asleep that night before she finally said anything.

"You keep on working at it," she said. "Sooner or later you'll get to where you can turn his coming here into a bad thing."

"It is a bad thing. He lied."

"He cut wood," Rorie countered. "He plowed. He made it easier to get water from the spring. And he stood up against Halbert and his men."

"He brought his trouble here!"

"Well, I reckon I can't argue with you none there. He did do that. But he wouldn't have if he hadn't been willing to help you and the girls. I reckon you should be mad at me, too. I'm the one what brought him over here. If I'd shot him when I was of a mind to, just think how much better off we'd all be."

"That's not funny," Sayer said.

"I ain't trying to be funny, girl. Do you believe what he said?"

"About what?"

"About loving you, of course."

"You were listening?" Sayer cried, more annoyed than surprised.

"Yes, I was listening. I'm smack in the middle of all this, ain't I? I was wanting to know what he had to say, too. This declaration of his weren't no surprise to me, nor you either, and it ain't no use to pretend otherwise. He's felt that way near about from the first day he come here. That's how it happens sometimes, and that's why I—"

"Why you what, Rorie?"

"Nothing."

"I think you better tell me."

Rorie gave a heavy sigh. "Why...I told him he needed to take you and the girls with him when he left here."

"You told him that!"

"I did. Didn't you just hear me say his declaration weren't no surprise to me?"

"Well, *I'm* surprised. I'm surprised he stayed at all after that." She tried not to ask the question that was straining to be asked, but she couldn't help it. "What...did he say?"

"He said you loved Thomas Henry, and you wouldn't go with him—which ain't the kind of thing a man would say if he didn't want you to do just that."

"Rorie—"

"You weren't born and raised here, Sayer. You ain't tied to these mountains."

"The girls were," Sayer interrupted. "And I love the mountains just the same."

"More than you love Jeremiah? Even if you do, it ain't going to matter one whit to Halbert Garth. Thomas Henry wanted to make sure all three of you were safe from him. You know he did if he asked a soldier what was his enemy to see about you. I don't know of a better way to do that than for you to go away from here with a man what says *and* shows he loves you."

Sayer frowned and turned away. She went to the washstand and poured water into the basin, using the same delaying tactic Rorie had when she didn't want to discuss a matter. She washed her face, unbraided and brushed her hair the one hundred strokes just the way her mother had taught her to do. And when she was finished, Rorie was waiting.

"So what are you going to do now?" she asked.

"Do? Nothing. He's gone."

"Is he?"

Sayer looked at her.

"I swan, Sayer, if you don't beat all sometimes. You think a man like Jeremiah Murphy is going to come right out and say in front of God and everybody he loves you, then ride off and leave you to fend for yourself? Ain't you been paying any attention at all to what kind of man he is?"

Sayer couldn't keep her mouth from trembling.

I love you with all my heart....

The problem wasn't that she didn't believe him. The problem was that she did. She believed every word of it.

"What are you going to do?" Rorie asked yet again, gently this time, too gently for Sayer to withstand.

She covered her face with her hands and showed her, crying again as if her heart would break.

"Well, I don't know what good you think *that's* going to do," Rorie complained in exasperation. "I'm going to put myself to bed. You should, too. If you'd quit that crying and get yourself some sleep, maybe you'd have good sense in the morning. You ain't got much now, if you want my verdict."

Sayer didn't want her "verdict." She turned away as Rorie climbed into bed in her work dress. She had taken to sleeping fully clothed since the bounty hunters' raid, and the girls had followed suit. Jeremiah had told them they would have to take care, and being ready to run for their lives no matter the time of day seemed to be the best they could do.

Sayer didn't go to bed. She went to the shelf where she kept the keepsake box that held Thomas Henry's letters and her mother's Bible. She took the Bible out, knowing she couldn't light a candle to read it without illuminating the inside of the cabin for anyone who might be watching. All she could do was hold it, and she would have to take comfort in that. She carried it over to Mrs. Garth's rocking chair and sat down, the Bible in her lap, her fingers caressing the now-worn leather binding. It had been her most precious possession, far beyond that of the boxes of Royal Doulton china. The Bible had been every step of the way with her mother and with Thomas Henry. He had said in more than one of his letters how much it had meant to him to have it.

She began to rock slowly back and forth, feeling

the confines of the cabin closing in on her just as she had the night Jeremiah had told her Thomas Henry was dead.

I can't sleep! I can't think!

No. It was more that she didn't want to think.

What was it Jeremiah had said?

I'll know if you need me....

And then he'd hesitated. She'd known immediately that something was wrong. Had he meant to tell her all his dark secrets then?

She gave a quiet sigh. It wouldn't have mattered if she'd found out about his being in the Union army earlier; she knew that. She would have sent him away in any case. If Rorie was right and he was still here, then she was afraid for him. And if he was gone, then she was still afraid for him, much more than she was for herself.

She suddenly remembered a verse from Proverbs, one she'd read so many times to Mrs. Garth.

Trust in the Lord with all thine heart
And lean not unto thine own understanding...

"I'm trying, Lord," she whispered. And then, "Please keep him safe."

She must have dozed off in the chair. When she opened her eyes, she was still holding the Bible. The night was fading, but the sun had yet to rise over the mountain ridge. She got up stiffly and put the Bible back into the keepsake box. As she did so, her fingers touched the daguerreotype of Thomas Henry. She hadn't looked at it since the day Jeremiah gave it to her. She knew perfectly well that it was Thomas Henry who stared back at her from the frame, and yet it wasn't somehow. She had never known the fierce-looking soldier who looked into the camera with such determination and who held a revolver in each hand. She had known the gentle, brown-eyed boy who waited for the train every summer, who gave her candy and honeycombs and a cedar pencil. Had that Thomas Henry been long gone by the time he died on the battlefield? *It's what war is;* Jeremiah had told her that.

She took the daguerreotype out of the box after all and tried to see his face in the dimness of the cabin. She wanted to find some remnant of *her* Thomas Henry in his features.

But it wasn't there.

"Goodbye, Tommy," she whispered as she put the daguerreotype back into the box and closed the lid. *My whole life is in here,* she thought.

She reached for her shawl, then stepped quietly out onto the front porch. Already she could feel autumn in the chill of the morning air. Halbert had said she wouldn't last another winter here, but for whatever reason, that thought didn't frighten her as it might have yesterday.

I love you with all my heart….

She pushed Jeremiah's words aside and looked up at the early-morning sky. Thomas Henry had loved this place, and unfortunately, Halbert, in his own covetous way, did, too.

She stepped off the porch and walked to the big shade tree, pausing just long enough to give the swing a push and send it high into the air. Then she moved into the open and took a deep breath, savoring the dewy freshness of the early morn. It was still quiet, but any moment now the birds would begin to sing. She had always looked forward to that very instant when the world suddenly awoke.

This is the day which the Lord hath made,
We will rejoice and be glad in it…

I can do that, she thought. Despite her misery, she could still appreciate God's handiwork.

The mule brayed in the barn, apparently alert to the fact that someone was about. It kicked the stall hard several times as a less-than-subtle reminder that it hadn't yet been fed. She would do that, and she would milk the cow, and she would do her best to stop thinking about Jeremiah.

There was something lying on the bench under the tree and she walked over to see. It was a brown paper parcel of some kind. She picked it up, immediately knowing what was in it. Peppermint sticks. He was still doing what he could for his fellow orphans.

She put the candy into her pocket and looked around, hoping for some sign that he might still be here, but there was nothing. She could guess why he'd left the candy out here instead of putting it on the porch. He must have thought that either she or Rorie would shoot him.

"I did the right thing, Lord," she whispered. "Didn't I? I was right to send him away. If I wasn't, then I need your help. Please. *Please!*"

She looked around sharply at a noise that came from

the barn, one that didn't sound as if it were made by a hungry mule. For the briefest of moments she thought it was Jeremiah, but it wasn't. She didn't recognize the man walking in her direction or the one who came out of the barn behind him.

She looked toward the cabin porch, trying to determine if she could make it to the front door before they caught her. There was no doubt in her mind that that was their intent.

She suddenly picked up the skirt of her too-long work dress and ran for the cabin as hard as she could. She made it inside. She even got the door closed before the two men burst in behind her.

Both girls were awake and screaming. Rorie managed to grab her revolver out from under her pillow and fire, but her aim was high. One of the men took the revolver away from her before she could get off another shot. The man closest to Sayer grabbed her by the arm and dragged her outside onto the porch, and the girls screamed louder.

"Don't hurt them!" she cried, trying to fight him off enough to see what was happening behind her. "Please!"

"All you have to do is tell us where he is."

He pulled her off the porch and into the yard; the other man was bringing Rorie out. The girls ran past him and straight to Sayer, grabbing her around the waist.

"Where is he!" the man holding her yelled, his hand raised as if to strike her, and the girls, if they insisted on being in the way.

Sayer didn't dare say she didn't understand what he was asking.

"He's not here," she said evenly, holding on to the girls tightly. She realized that there were more men in the yard now, all of them on horseback. She had no trouble identifying three of them—Halbert Garth and his two henchmen. The other man was a stranger to her. He was clearly not a bounty hunter. He had pomaded hair, and he was smoking a cigar, the kind Halbert had liked to flaunt at the beginning of the war when he still had a supply. This man was dressed far too fine for such a base profession as bounty hunting.

"Hand those women over to Halbert's men and search the cabin," he said, tossing the cigar carelessly aside. Sayer didn't miss seeing how much one of Halbert's men craved it, discarded in the dirt or not, but he made no attempt to retrieve it.

The men dismounted and walked in her direction.

"No," Halbert said. "One of yourn and one of mine go looking. I ain't letting you claim I didn't have no hand in collecting the bounty."

The man who had Rorie in his grip was forcing her to walk over the rough ground faster than she was able. He suddenly gave her a hard shove and went inside the cabin to search with one of Halbert's men. Rorie went sprawling onto her knees. She cried out in pain, and the tears began to stream down her face. Sayer tried to go to her, but she couldn't get free from the man who still held her. She watched as Rorie got slowly— painfully—to her feet, her chin thrust out in defiance despite her tears.

A loud crash came from inside the cabin.

"He's not here!" Sayer cried, trying to jerk free again.

"Then where is he?" the well-dressed man asked mildly.

"I don't know. He left—"

"Let her go," he said, and he pointed to Amity. "Maybe *she* knows, then."

The man apparently understood what his employer wanted him to do. He suddenly grabbed Amity and held her high over his head. Amity screamed in terror.

"Stop! Stop!" Sayer cried, trying to hit him with her fists. He pushed her away with his foot and she fell on the ground.

"I'll ask you one more time," the well-dressed man said.

"I told you! I don't know! Halbert!" Sayer cried, scrambling to her feet again. She turned to Thomas Henry's uncle. "Amity is your kin. If there is anyone left in the Garth family who cares about you, it's Amity. She remembers you in her prayers—don't let him hurt her! Please!"

For the briefest of moments, she actually thought he might intervene, but the moment passed. One of the men came out of the cabin carrying the remaining box of Royal Doulton china. He threw it into the yard, causing it to bounce once, then tip over on its side, the shattered pieces spilling out on the ground. But there wasn't enough breakage to suit him. He dumped what was left of the china out and ground the remaining pieces under his boot.

Amity was crying hard now. Beatrice came running and hid her face against Sayer's shoulder.

"Halbert—!" Sayer cried, trying again. "Make him stop! Don't let him hurt her!"

"Don't go wasting your breath, Sayer," Rorie said. She pointed her finger in Halbert's direction. "Even I never thought you'd sink this low, Halbert Garth. It's a good thing for you your brother and Thomas Henry are in their graves."

"Where is he, old woman!" Halbert yelled. "We mean to find him!"

"If I knowed, I wouldn't tell you," Rorie said, never taking her eyes off him.

Amity gave another long piercing scream as the man holding her swung her around and tucked her under his arm, her head dangling toward the ground. "You got a well?" he asked. "Maybe you'd like to see her go down it headfir—"

The man abruptly stopped talking at the same moment Sayer heard the report from the musket. His left knee buckled, spurting blood, and he collapsed on the ground, dropping Amity hard on the way down. She scrambled up, and ran to Sayer, screaming again. Sayer had no idea where the shot had come from, and neither did Halbert and the others. Another shot came. This time the man who had thrown the box of china fell, his wound midthigh. The remaining men looked around in panic, and in the chaos that followed, Sayer began pulling the girls away toward the woods.

But the well-dressed man suddenly spurred his horse forward and cut off Sayer's escape. He jumped to the ground and grabbed her around the neck, pressing the barrel of his revolver hard against her right temple.

"Go," she whispered to the panicked girls. "Go to Rorie. Now! Go!"

They both ran in Rorie's direction.

"You see this?" he yelled loudly, holding Sayer so tightly she could barely breathe. He kept moving both of them around, trying to find something in the woods that would tell him where the man with the musket was hiding. "She's dead where she stands if you don't surrender now!"

Sayer was off balance, and it was all she could do to stay on her feet. She couldn't see Rorie and the girls now—she could only see straight ahead into the dark depths of the woods, apparently where the man holding her had decided the two shots had come from. Halbert moved into her line of vision. He was looking past her, where she thought Beatrice and Amity must be. Were they all right? She couldn't turn her head enough to tell.

"'Trust in the Lord with all thine heart...'" she whispered, and the man laughed.

"She's praying!" the well-dressed man yelled. "What do you think of that! *She* knows I mean it!"

There was a long moment of silence. Sayer could hear nothing but the girls crying and the groans of the two wounded men on the ground.

"'...and lean not unto thine own understanding...be not afraid of sudden fear, neither of the desolation of the wicked, when it cometh...'"

"Shut up!" he hissed against her ear.

"I believe—your desolation is—at hand, sir," Sayer struggled to say as his grip on her tightened. He pressed the gun harder against her temple. "Halbert Garth will look out—for himself, no matter—what."

"Call Murphy in," the man said. "Call him in *now!*"

"No," Sayer said.

"Call him in!"

"No!"

"I want your word you won't hurt her!" Jeremiah yelled from somewhere off to the left. "Not Sayer, and not the girls, or Mrs. Conley."

The man kept trying to locate where the voice was coming from and dragging Sayer with him.

"Don't, Jeremiah!" she cried.

"Shut up!" Vance said. "You have my word!"

"I don't want *your* word, Vance! I want Halbert's. Halbert, you have the most to lose here. Willard's been of a mind to hang you for some time, I believe. It would be better for you if you didn't give him a reason. I want you to swear that you won't let any harm come to any of them!"

"All right!" Halbert said after a moment. He looked in Farrell Vance's direction, whether in defiance or collusion, she couldn't tell. "I swear!"

Sayer could see Jeremiah now. He was coming through the trees, and he was holding a musket over his head. She thought his limp was less pronounced, but it was still there.

It was all Rorie could do to keep Beatrice and Amity from running to him.

"Well, well, if it ain't Jack Murphy," Halbert said. "Good to see you again, *Jack*. Wish I would have known who you was the other day when I was up here. It would have saved me a lot of aggravation—and I would have been rich a lot sooner."

"Sorry about that, Halbert," Jeremiah said. "You can forget about being rich, though. Whatever Farrell Vance said he'd give you to bring him up here, he's not going to do it, are you, Farrell? He's too much in the habit of getting things on the cheap and lining his own pockets with somebody else's money. I doubt if any of you gets paid."

Sayer kept looking at Jeremiah. She didn't understand why Halbert was calling him "Jack," but she understood the look Jeremiah gave her.

Trust me…

"Get him," Vance said to his men. "Tie him up. Bring me a rope."

"You going to hang me right here, Farrell? No trip to the magistrate in Jefferson? No due process?" Jeremiah asked, and Sayer thought his nonchalant tone was driving the man deeper and deeper into a rage. She could feel him trembling with it.

"Do I at least get to know what I'm being hanged *for?*"

"Halbert," Sayer said, twisting in Farrell Vance's grasp to see where he was. "Don't let him kill him! Please!"

"You all that worried about your step-husband, Sayer?" Halbert said. "The way I hear it, he was a busy man before he ever got here. The story I could tell you right now."

Sayer could feel Vance react to Halbert's remark. Apparently whatever Halbert thought he knew hadn't come from the man who held a gun to her head.

"I already know the story, Halbert. I'm more worried you'll have the blood of an innocent man on your hands," she said, and he laughed.

"Well, that's right nice of you, Sayer, but I don't reckon I need you to save me."

"Do you need me to get off this land?"

"Sayer!" Jeremiah called just as one of Halbert's men reached him. The man grabbed the musket out of Jeremiah's hands, then struck him hard with the butt end. Sayer cried out as he kicked Jeremiah forward so that he was lying facedown on the ground. He tied Jeremiah's hands behind his back, then dragged him the rest of the way into the yard. She could only watch as Jeremiah struggled again and again to get up.

"Halbert!" Sayer cried. "This man has no authority here. Make him stop if you want your birthright!"

"Be quiet!" Farrell Vance said, tightening his hold around her neck again.

"What are you talking about, Sayer?" Halbert asked in spite of Vance's command.

But Sayer couldn't answer him. She couldn't breathe; her knees suddenly buckled and she slipped from Farrell Vance's grasp. She sat hunched over on the ground at his feet, struggling to breathe.

Vance tried to make her stand up again.

"Leave her be!" Halbert said sharply, his revolver pointed at Vance's head. Vance took a step backward.

"If you think you can bring that gun of yourn up faster than I can pull this here trigger, go ahead," Halbert said. "Jim! Get that gun of his!"

The man called Jim, the one who had wanted the half-smoked cigar, ran up behind Vance with his gun drawn and jerked the revolver out of his hand.

"Go on," Halbert said to Sayer. "I'm listening." But Sayer was trying to see Jeremiah. He had stopped trying to get up. She got to her knees and would have made a run to get to him if Halbert hadn't grabbed her back.

"You leave him be," Halbert said. "I want to hear what your offer is."

"Don't let him kill Jeremiah," she said, causing Vance to make a noise of disgust.

"He is *mine*," Vance cried.

"Halbert," Sayer said urgently, looking into his eyes for some small sign of his humanity. "Let him go free—unharmed. If you do, I'll take the girls and leave here. There'll be no blood on your hands. You can say whatever you want to say to explain our absence, and I won't be here to interfere with anything you do. You'll be free to offer whatever legal claims you want to about Thomas Henry's land—"

"It's *my* land!"

"Not if I don't get out of the way," Sayer said. "You've been too open about trying to take it. If anything happens to me, you won't get anything. Listen to me. Please."

She looked over her shoulder once, trying to see Jeremiah before she began to plead for his life in earnest.

Jeremiah had to work hard to get upright. His head was still pounding from the blow from the musket butt, and he was having difficulty keeping his vision focused. He didn't think Sayer was hurt, but her being dragged around by the likes of Farrell Vance and his men was nearly more than he could bear. Even looking at her from this distance, he could tell she was determined—he had seen that look of determination before. He could only hear a word now and then, and he had no idea what she was doing. Whatever it was, she had apparently managed to get Vance at a disadvantage—something for which she would pay if the tables turned again.

Out of the corner of his eye, he caught a glimpse of Rorie. She'd left the girls sitting on the ground, alone and afraid near where the broken china was scattered about, and she was coming in his direction. The girls were clinging to each other for comfort and crying still.

Rorie hobbled over to the second man Jeremiah had wounded as if she had no idea she was putting her very life in danger by doing so, completely ignoring the numerous commands for her to stay where she was.

"I'm an old widder woman," she said without stopping. "And I ain't armed. I'm going to see how bad these two men is hurt—do something for them if I can—if one of you don't put a hole in me first. It's my Christian duty. Not that any of you would know anything about that."

"Rorie," he said under his breath, alarmed by her defiance and expecting one of Vance's men to oblige her at any second. But they didn't, and he breathed a sigh of relief. Rorie said a few words to the nearest wounded man, looked at the place where Jeremiah had shot him, and then hobbled in Jeremiah's direction, stopping by the younger of the two men, who was still writhing on the ground.

"If you're wanting to bleed to death, then don't let me look at it," Rorie said to him. Surprisingly, she struggled with her painful knees and with gravity until she managed to sit down on the ground beside him. Clearly it was a painful maneuver; she had to rest for a moment before she continued.

"Well, get your hands out of the way," she said to the

wounded man—who was not much more than a boy, Jeremiah suddenly realized. He glanced in Sayer's direction. She was still talking to Halbert.

"Rorie, what is she doing?" he asked as loudly as he dared.

Rorie stuck her finger in the blood-soaked hole the minié ball had made in the young man's trousers and ripped the fabric apart, making him cry out as the effort it took to make the tear heightened his pain.

"I reckon she's trying to save your life," she said, concentrating on what she was doing. "Whatever it is, you need to stay out of it."

"Rorie—"

"You're a sight worse off than your friend over there," Rorie said loudly to the wounded young man, clearly trying to hide the fact that she and Jeremiah were having a conversation.

"He ain't no friend of mine," the young man snapped.

"You two just ride around together hurting women and young-uns and doing murder if somebody tells you to, is that it? I don't know about you, but I'm twice glad your mama ain't here to see this."

"You don't know nothing about my mama, old woman."

"Don't be telling me what I know and don't know, boy. I knowed her for a long time, and you got her eyes. I ain't never seen nobody else in this world with eyes like hers except you and your brother and your sister. I know what she was accused of. I know they locked her up. I know what happened to her three young-uns because of it. And I know it was all because of a lying, black-hearted man just like that one standing over yonder, the one you think is going to pay you for doing all this. Your mama, she was innocent. Did you know that? No. You never bothered to find out, did you? You was too busy wasting your life when you could have been giving her some joy in this world."

He didn't say anything. He was very pale now and seemed to be having trouble keeping his eyes open.

"Weren't nobody to ask," he said after a moment.

"Could have asked *me*," Rorie said. She tore the bottom of his trouser leg off and stuffed it hard against the still-seeping hole above his knee. "The minie ball didn't go all the way through—I can feel it just under the skin. You keep that knee still. The more you bend it, the more it'll bleed. If me holding the blood in don't make it stop, you'll be needing to get that hole packed with spiderwebs lest you bleed to death," she said matter-of-factly.

"He did this!" he cried, glaring at Jeremiah.

"Well, I reckon if he'd wanted you dead, you'd be dead, so you might want to think on that. And while you're at it, if I was you, I'd think about finding a better class of good-for-nothings to run with. When they go, they ain't taking you with them. I reckon you know that."

Jeremiah saw the panic in the young man's eyes.

"You got to find a way to get your hands loose," she added mildly, and the young man seemed not to realize that the remark wasn't meant for him.

But Jeremiah couldn't get his hands free. The man who had tied him apparently had had a great deal of practice, and if Jeremiah dared to look as if he was trying to slip his bonds, he'd likely meet the business end of the musket this time.

He looked in Sayer's direction. Farrell Vance had taken a few steps to the left, and Jeremiah could no longer see her. He could hear her talking still, and he took what comfort he could from that. All the while, his mind raced.

Find something you can do and do it!

There were two wounded men, both of them still armed. And two not wounded—and armed. Farrell Vance no longer had his revolver—and Halbert was apparently in charge of whatever they now planned to do.

And Sayer was right in the middle of it.

Jeremiah shifted his position. No one was looking in his direction. He began to work at the knots in the rope binding his hands.

"Where's your brother and sister?" he heard Rorie ask the man he had wounded.

"My brother's dead in the war. My sister—she died when she weren't but ten."

"I reckon it's up to you then," Rorie said.

"What is?"

She didn't answer him; she moved until she was sitting closer to him—and to the revolver he had stuck in his belt. The man didn't know what Rorie was capable of—and he was too far gone to comprehend what she was likely planning.

"That was a bad thing you did, scaring that young-un over there like you did," Rorie said, her voice almost soothing. "And she never done nobody in this whole wide world any harm, especially not you. The sad thing is I reckon you done plenty worse than what I just seen. Ain't you?"

"Yes," he said, his voice trembling.

"If you don't die, then I reckon you got a hard row to hoe—that is, if you're wanting to make it up to your mama for all that suffering she went through—and I ain't just talking about her getting locked up. Her suffering come from knowing you might have turned out better if she hadn't been. Ain't nothing worse for a mother than that, thinking all the time she could have helped her child have a better life if she'd just had the chance."

"I can't make it up to her."

"If you was to do your best to be a good man instead of what you are now, then it—"

"She's dead!"

"Her body's dead, boy. She ain't. People don't get a lot of chances to fix the trouble and heartache they cause, but just maybe, you can—Jeremiah!" Rorie cried out in alarm.

But Jeremiah didn't need Rorie's warning. He had seen Farrell Vance suddenly whirl around and begin striding in his direction. Vance drew a pistol from inside his coat, something small—a four-shot pepperbox.

Jeremiah struggled to get his hands free, but the rope still wouldn't budge. He gave up and tried to get up, despite pain in his injured knee. He had no intention of dying under Farrell Vance's feet.

Vance was almost on him and he was taking aim. He heard Sayer cry out and the sound of the gunshot almost simultaneously, just as he rolled sharply away. He expected to feel the impact of the bullet, but it was Farrell Vance who lay sprawled on the ground.

The wounded young man Rorie had been so earnestly advising fell over into her arms, his revolver still in her hand.

Chapter Twelve

Sayer began to run. She couldn't tell if Jeremiah was hurt or not. She had seen him falling to the side as the gun was fired, and her heart was pounding with fear.

The girls intercepted her before she could reach him. She hugged them tightly for a moment, then pulled them aside. They kept trying to look at the place where both Jeremiah and Farrell Vance lay.

"Be brave for me a little longer," she said in a rush, making them look at her instead. "Sit right here. I have to help Jeremiah. Stay here. Stay safe."

"That mean man is crying, Sayer. Why is he crying?" Amity asked, trying to see around her.

"I think he's sorry," Sayer said. "And he's afraid. Rorie will take care of him. Sit down now. Be quick."

"Is that other man dead?" Beatrice asked. "Dead like Thomas Henry?"

"Sit down," Sayer said instead of answering. "Stay here."

They reluctantly did as she asked, and Sayer ran the rest of the distance to where Jeremiah lay on the ground.

She stepped past Farrell Vance, still not understanding what had happened.

"Jeremiah! Jeremiah— Oh!" she cried, kneeling down beside him. She could see his chest rising and falling, and she helped him to sit up. "Are you hurt?" she said urgently, looking for wounds.

"No," he said. "Vance—is he—?"

"I don't know. He's not moving," she said, trying to loosen the rope that bound Jeremiah's hands.

"Get the pepperbox away," he said.

The pistol was lying just a few inches from Farrell Vance's outstretched hand. Sayer quickly moved to retrieve it. She carried it back to Jeremiah and laid it beside him on the ground.

"I can't get the rope loose," she said, struggling again with the knot.

"Wait. Move around here," Jeremiah said. "Let me see you."

She moved to where she could see his face, and he suddenly leaned toward her, his forehead resting against hers for a moment.

"Thank God," he whispered. "Thank God!"

"Yes," she agreed, reaching up to press her hand against his cheek.

She moved so she could work on the rope again. Little by little the knot began to loosen. So far Halbert hadn't tried to keep her from freeing him, and she suddenly realized why. He was no longer here. He must have taken off through the trees in the confusion.

"What happened?" Jeremiah asked. "Why did Halbert turn on Vance? I don't understand. This can't be what he intended. His only means of getting rich is lying dead on the ground."

"I asked Halbert to let you go. I said if he did, you would take me—and the girls—away from here," Sayer said quietly. She kept pulling at the rope, without really registering what she was doing now. She stopped and gave a quiet sigh.

"And what does he get, Sayer?" Jeremiah asked, turning so he could see her face.

"He gets me out of the way so he can lay claim to the Garth land—"

"Sayer, you can't do that. This land is all that's left—"

"It's done. I've given Halbert my word that I'd go."

"And he'll hold you to it. You know he will."

"Yes."

"Why would you do such a thing!"

"It was the only way I could keep you alive," she said simply.

"I can't let you lose everything you have, Sayer. Not on my account."

Sayer was looking into his eyes when he said it, and she realized that perhaps he meant Thomas Henry's death, as well, whether it had happened as a result of a collective effort by the Union army or it was something he had done personally.

But she would never know the whole truth about that and neither would he. All she knew were the things Jeremiah had done since he'd come here. Perhaps his arrival had been of his own volition—and born of necessity— and perhaps not. It wasn't difficult for her to believe that there had been a reason for everything that had happened to them both, a reason that was still unfolding.

"What should I call you?" she suddenly asked.

"Call me?"

"Jeremiah? Jack? I have something to say to you and I want to know which name to use."

"Jeremiah," he said. "Jack is my orphan name, my army name."

"And what Elrissa called you," she said quietly.

"Yes. It's the name from my other life. Except for Father Bartholomew, it's what everyone called me before I came here."

She nodded, then looked at him steadily for a long moment before she continued. "Lost souls are important to me—but yours isn't lost, " she said when she was ready. "I know that with all my heart. Preacher Tomlin could see it, and so can I. I love you, Jeremiah Murphy— I— It's—"

"Sayer—" he said when she began to flounder. "I don't deserve your love. I've brought you nothing but trouble and it's not over." He looked toward where Farrell Vance lay.

"Halbert said there were no legal warrants issued for you. The bounty hunters in the jail at the crossroads told him—"

"I don't think he can rely on anything they said."

"He didn't. He wanted to make sure the law wasn't involved—because it might get in the way of his getting his cut. He went down to the railhead and sent a telegram to the authorities in Lexington. There was nothing."

"Nothing," Jeremiah repeated. "And he was still going to help them hang me."

"Halbert is a greedy man. His greed is the reason you're alive," Sayer said. "He would never have listened to me otherwise. I—"

She stopped, realizing suddenly how close to disaster they had come. She suddenly threw her arms around him and rested her head on his shoulder, completely overwhelmed by an onslaught of conflicting emotions—joy and sorrow, relief and worry, and the strongest one of all—love. Yes, she had loved Thomas Henry. She had loved him for most of her life and always would, but she loved Jeremiah, as well, and she needed to tell him what was in her heart.

"Sayer…"

She lifted her head and looked into his eyes again. "I thank God for bringing you into our lives. I don't believe our paths would have ever crossed otherwise. Not ever. I want you to know that I wouldn't be losing anything if I left here—as long as I was with you. I would have what truly matters to me—you, and Beatrice and Amity. I don't need or want anything else. I can go from here gladly because I believe we would have God's blessing. With His help we can start a new life wherever you say—unless you don't want to marry me," she added because of the troubled look still on his face.

"I…presumed too much," she said after a long moment.

"I'm not the man you think I am," he said. "I've lived through the worst things human beings can do to each other, and I shouldn't have. Far better men than me died. I don't know why I survived and they didn't. I'm not…fit…"

"Don't," she said. "I've seen the kind of man you are every day—even when I didn't want to, even when I found out you were Thomas Henry's enemy. I know your heart is broken and you don't sleep and your hands shake because of the things you've seen—" she touched his cheek to make him look at her "—and done. But the war didn't take everything from you. I know you're good and fine. Your kindness is—"

"No," he said. "I'm not any of those things. When I came here, it had nothing to do with kindness."

"But you stayed. You didn't leave us when we needed you. I…love you," she said again with a small shrug. "Even if you don't want to marry me. Even if you leave this very day and I never see your face again. I don't know why or how it happened. I just know it did."

"Sayer, don't—"

"I know you love me," she interrupted. "I *know* it."

"Yes. I love you—"

"Enough to marry me?"

"Yes. But I…"

"What? Tell me."

"I thought you and I could never be. I can't believe we could actually do this—that you would want to do this."

"Will you marry me or not, Jeremiah Murphy?"

"I would marry you right now if we could find Preacher Tomlin." He gave her a weary version of one of his "almost" smiles. "That is…if you ever untie me."

Sayer laughed softly. "I'd have to hear a firm yes to my bold marriage proposal first."

"Yes," he said every bit as firmly as she required. "There is nothing I want more than to be your husband."

She rested her head on his shoulder again because she was very close to tears. He would have died for her today. She knew that.

"Sayer! Sayer!"

Amity and Beatrice were calling her, and she held out her hand to them. They both came running.

"Help me untie Jeremiah so he can get married," she said to them.

"Who are you marrying, Jeremiah?" Amity asked, wide-eyed.

"Well, Miss Amity, I thought I'd marry your Sayer," he said just as Sayer got the knot undone and his hands free. "What do you think of that?"

Amity and Beatrice looked at each other with their mouths agape. He stood and helped Sayer to her feet, then collected all three of them into his embrace.

"We'd like for you to marry Sayer, Jeremiah," Beatrice said, leaning back to look at him. "Wouldn't we, Amity?"

"Yes," Amity assured him. "Jeremiah, can you teach us how to plow?"

He laughed. "I'll put that on my list," he assured her. "We'll teach Sayer, too."

Sayer smiled and looked into his eyes. She could see the love there, and he knew that she did.

"With all my heart," he whispered.

Epilogue

Sayer had thought they would be leaving the mountains and the Garth land, but God was still at work in their lives. There had been a codicil to Thomas Henry's will, one he'd filed shortly before he was killed. In it, he granted Sayer the right to live on the land for as long as she chose, with no stipulation that the privilege was to be rescinded if she remarried. He had hoped, in that event, that she would stay on so that Amity and Beatrice could grow up on the family land. In an effort to thwart Halbert Garth, he granted complete ownership of the property to Sayer's uncle, John Preston, to be held in trust for Beatrice and Amity until they were of age. And there was nothing Halbert could do about it. In a fit of rage, he had burned the cabin down and had been arrested for it.

She and Jeremiah had chosen not to rebuild on the same site. All that was salvaged was Sayer's keepsake box. Everything else, they left where it fell. With the help of Preacher Tomlin and the church congregation, a new cabin had been raised some distance away. It was waiting for them now. Waiting, as Jeremiah was wait-ing, for the two of them to begin their new life together.

Jeremiah had wanted their marriage ceremony to be held on the great outcropping of rock where Mr. Garth Senior and he himself had gone to talk to God—but only if she could reassure him that it wouldn't be too sad for her. She had no doubt that it was a place of worship and communion and perhaps had been long before the Garths came. As such, sadness was only a small part of what it encompassed. It was a place of humble awe and gratitude, as well, and joy and love—all the things she was feeling this day. Her heart was overflowing with it.

Sayer kept thinking what a long road she and Jere-miah had traveled to reach this point in their lives. She could see him now. He looked so handsome standing there next to Preacher Tomlin. She was reminded of the day he'd managed to shave despite Amity's "help," and she'd made him blush by pronouncing him "dashing." She had loved him even then.

She made her way to him, with Amity and Beatrice at her side. Amity gave him a little wave as they ap-proached, and he couldn't keep from smiling in return. Sayer paused from time to time to speak to a member of the congregation or to accept an embrace here, a kiss on the cheek there. How different it all was from the last time she'd been in this place.

She looked for Rorie and spotted her not far from where Jeremiah and Preacher Tomlin stood. She was resplendent in her best Sunday dress and bonnet—and the walking stick with the face Jeremiah had cut for her. Sayer had been worried that Rorie wouldn't get here in time for the wedding. She had gone to Jefferson to testify at the trial of the young man who had shot Farrell Vance, and she had come back happy, despite the fact that he was being sent to prison, not for the shooting, but for the other things he'd done in Vance's hire. She had offered him, probably for the first time in his life, a place to go and the prospect of a real home if he wanted it—on her farm. And she had told him bluntly, as only Rorie could, exactly what she would expect of him when he got out, including the part about settling down, finding himself a good wife and creating the kind of loving family he had never had. Knowing Rorie and the part she had played in making this wedding possible, Sayer was convinced that she could bring it all about.

Jeremiah was walking out to meet them now. He held out his arm, and Sayer took it, returning his smile as she did so.

"Are you sure about this?" he asked her as they all walked to where Preacher Tomlin waited.

"I am," she said firmly. "And you?"

"Very sure."

"Beloved of God," Preacher Tomlin began in his booming voice. "Grace unto you and Peace. We gather here now in this beautiful place to unite Sayer and Jeremiah in Holy Matrimony…"

"Don't forget me and Beatrice," Amity said, causing a ripple of laughter among the congregation.

"And to create a good and loving family for our Beatrice and Amity," he added. "Where they shall grow up—before Him—as a tender plant—is that all right?" he whispered to Amity, and she nodded.

"Excellent," he said. "Now. I charge you, Sayer, and you, Jeremiah, to remember as you stand before God that love and loyalty will avail as the foundation of your life together. Jeremiah Murphy, wilt thou take Sayer Preston Garth to be thy wedded wife? Wilt thou love her, comfort her, honor and keep her…"

Jeremiah said his vows in a strong and steady voice, and so did she. Neither of them stumbled as they committed themselves to each other before God and before the people who had come to wish them well. She couldn't help but think how much he would have liked to have had his orphan family here today.

"I love you, Sayer," Jeremiah whispered to her when the ceremony ended.

He kissed her gently on the lips—with much approval from the wedding guests.

"And I love you," Sayer whispered. "Always."

They stood together, receiving congratulations—and all the newlywed teasing that went with it—until they had spoken to each person and everyone began walking down the slope to the new cabin for refreshments and music.

"Before we go," Jeremiah said when Sayer would have followed, "I have something I want you to read." He reached into his coat pocket and brought out a letter. "It's from Father Bartholomew. He gave this to me when I went on the run. He told me not to read it until I was content."

"Content? I don't think I understand."

"Neither did I. But I do know I'm far beyond content today, Mrs. Murphy."

She smiled.

"Read it," he said, and she took the letter, hesitating a moment before she unfolded it.

Dear Jeremiah, she read.

You came back from this terrible war a discouraged and changed man, but you were not lost. I knew that when you brought catfish to our kitchen, and I was even more certain when you told me about the Ancient Mariner. I knew that God was trying to give you the comfort you so desperately needed in the only way you would allow.

If you are reading this now, then I will trust that my condition has been met, and you are content, perhaps even happy in your life. I pray that this is so.

Here is the thing that I hope you have learned. Adversity can have more than one purpose. It's not always simply a lesson we need for the betterment of our souls, though that is often the outcome, regardless. Sometimes adversity is not intended just for us alone, but it is a means to move us to a place where there is someone else in need. Through adversity, we become God's instrument for a greater good, and in the process, we ourselves are made better. It is my hope that you can see this now in your own life and that you will always be mindful of God's hand whenever challenges arise.

Be assured that we here will always keep you in our prayers. God's blessings be upon you and those you love.

Your friend in Christ,

Father Bartholomew

Sayer looked up at him, deeply moved by what Father Bartholomew had written. "Do you want to go back? To Lexington?"

"No," he said.

"It would be safe for you to go, wouldn't it—now that Farrell Vance is dead?"

"I…have another charge to keep—from yet another soldier. Little Ike. We always called him that whenever we wanted to tease him. I wouldn't have gotten away from Farrell Vance's men if it hadn't been for him. I owe him…everything. He told me I had to go and live my life for the ones of us who had died in the war—live for all the orphans we had to bury on the battlefield. I'm going to do that," he said. "Here. With you." He suddenly smiled. "Ike would love you. They all would."

He put the letter back into his pocket. He was quiet now, his eyes on the mountains. The wind ruffled his hair.

Jeremiah, she thought. *My husband.* She thanked God every day for this good man.

"What is it?" she asked after a moment because he was clearly lost in thought.

"I was thinking about coming here—this is where I told God I loved you."

"You did?"

"I did," he assured her. "I put a lot of heart into it, too—just in case He missed my sincerity."

She laughed softly.

"And I was thinking about you—and Mrs. Tomlin," he said, putting his arm around her.

"Mrs. Tomlin?"

"The song she sang at Thomas Henry's memorial service. I finally understand what the words mean. I've been in a dark place for a long time, Sayer, but I can... *feel* the joy she was singing about now—because of you—because of *us*—and Beatrice and Amity." He looked down at her. "Do you understand what I'm trying to say?"

She turned so that she could see his face. "Yes," she said—because it was true for her, as well. She had come out of her own dark time, and she understood exactly what he meant.

Bright morning stars are rising. Day is breaking in my soul.

* * * * *

REQUEST YOUR FREE BOOKS!

2 FREE INSPIRATIONAL NOVELS
PLUS 2
FREE
MYSTERY GIFTS

Love Inspired.
HISTORICAL
INSPIRATIONAL HISTORICAL ROMANCE

YES! Please send me 2 FREE Love Inspired® Historical novels and my 2 FREE mystery gifts (gifts are worth about $10). After receiving them, if I don't wish to receive any more books, I can return the shipping statement marked "cancel". If I don't cancel, I will receive 4 brand-new novels every month and be billed just $4.49 per book in the U.S. or $4.99 per book in Canada. That's a saving of at least 22% off the cover price. It's quite a bargain! Shipping and handling is just 50¢ per book in the U.S. and 75¢ per book in Canada.* I understand that accepting the 2 free books and gifts places me under no obligation to buy anything. I can always return a shipment and cancel at any time. Even if I never buy another book, the two free books and gifts are mine to keep forever.

102/302 IDN FEHF

Name	(PLEASE PRINT)

Address	Apt. #

City	State/Prov.	Zip/Postal Code

Signature (if under 18, a parent or guardian must sign)

Mail to the **Reader Service:**
IN U.S.A.: P.O. Box 1867, Buffalo, NY 14240-1867
IN CANADA: P.O. Box 609, Fort Erie, Ontario L2A 5X3

Not valid for current subscribers to Love Inspired Historical books.

Want to try two free books from another series?
Call 1-800-873-8635 or visit www.ReaderService.com.

* Terms and prices subject to change without notice. Prices do not include applicable taxes. Sales tax applicable in N.Y. Canadian residents will be charged applicable taxes. Offer not valid in Quebec. This offer is limited to one order per household. All orders subject to credit approval. Credit or debit balances in a customer's account(s) may be offset by any other outstanding balance owed by or to the customer. Please allow 4 to 6 weeks for delivery. Offer available while quantities last.

Your Privacy—The Reader Service is committed to protecting your privacy. Our Privacy Policy is available online at www.ReaderService.com or upon request from the Reader Service.

We make a portion of our mailing list available to reputable third parties that offer products we believe may interest you. If you prefer that we not exchange your name with third parties, or if you wish to clarify or modify your communication preferences, please visit us at www.ReaderService.com/consumerchoice or write to us at Reader Service Preference Service, P.O. Box 9062, Buffalo, NY 14269. Include your complete name and address.

LIHI1B

Love Inspired HISTORICAL

celebrating 15 YEARS

Discover a second chance at love with author

ABBY GAINES

Widower Dominic Granville needs to find a wife and fast. With five growing children, they are in need of a motherly figure, one who can introduce them to London society. Governess Serena Somerton intends to find one for him. Yet none of his prospective brides can meet Serena's increasingly high standards. Soon one fact becomes clear to Dominic—his imperfect governess could be his ideal wife.

The
PARSON'S
Daughters

*The Governess
and Mr. Granville*

Available September wherever books are sold.

When three bachelors arrive on Regina Nash's doorstep, her entire world is turned upside down.

Read on for a sneak peek of HANDPICKED HUSBAND by Winnie Griggs.

Available September 2012 from Love Inspired® Historical.

Grandfather was trying to play matchmaker!

Regina's thoughts raced, skittering in several directions at once.

How *could* he? This was a disaster. It was too manipulative even for a schemer like her grandfather.

Didn't he know that if she'd *wanted* a husband, she could have landed one a long time ago? Didn't he trust her to raise her nephew, Jack, properly on her own?

Reggie forced herself to relax her grip on her grandfather's letter, commanded her racing pulse to slow.

She continued reading. A paragraph snagged her attention. Grandfather was *bribing* them to court her! They would each get a nice little prize for their part in this farce.

How could Grandfather humiliate her this way?

She barely had time to absorb that when she got her next little jolt. Adam Barr was *not* one of her suitors after all. Instead, he'd come as her grandfather's agent.

Grandfather had tasked Adam with escorting her "beaus" to Texas, making sure everyone understood the rules of the game and then seeing that the rules were followed.

It was also his job to carry Jack back to Philadelphia if she balked at the judge's terms. Her grandfather would then pick out a suitable boarding school for the boy— robbing her of even the opportunity to share a home with him in Philadelphia.

Reggie cast a quick glance Adam's way, and swallowed hard. She had no doubt he would carry out his orders right down to the letter.

No! That would *not* happen. Even if it meant she had to face a forced wedding, she wouldn't let Jack be taken from her.

Will Regina find a way to outsmart her grandfather or will she fall in love with one of the bachelors?

Don't miss HANDPICKED HUSBAND by Winnie Griggs.

Available September 2012
wherever Love Inspired® Historical books are sold!

SHLIHEXP0912